Recall:
Face the Past or Forget the Future

KEITH C. MEYER

TO SEEING THINGS THROUGH TO COMPLETION, AND DOING SO ON YOUR OWN TERMS.

CHAPTER 1

How is this happening? It'd been so long, and for years he'd deliberately chosen not to remember. But now, a flood of details storming back into his mind in an incredibly intimate wave. And her, looking even more beautiful than he had been able to remember. The love of his life, though he hadn't known it back in this moment, twenty-one long years ago. If he'd had any idea, he was convinced he wouldn't have given up so goddamn easily.

They head into the cafe, their favorite cafe, the same one in which they'd shared so many wonderful moments over that summer. The hostess recognizes them almost immediately; she casually guides them back to their favorite area of the restaurant, near the giant oil painting of the Castle Saventum. Seeing that painting again, the site of it sends shockwaves down his spine. He couldn't believe he was back here again. It seemed completely real to him.

She orders them both a Belgian ale, and a bowl of the "eels in green sauce" dish he had been so reluctant to try the night they met. 'Paling in'tgroen' was its Belgian name, the words she had taught him that first night. He couldn't believe how much she had taught him in their three short months together.

He revels in their conversation, soaking in every word they share as if it was the first time he'd ever heard it. They finish their third round of drinks, and decide to head across the street to their favorite piano lounge. He was so happy he had stumbled upon that spot, only a week or so after they had met, and was able to start bringing her there: finally, he could be the one to expose her to something new and fun. He'd hoped the discovery would make him seem thoughtful and cultured, at a time when he was desperately trying to impress her in any way he could. Now they were holding hands as they entered through the dark wooden staircase, both of them completely at ease in each other's company.

The soothing melody of piano keys, playing softly in the room nearby. The romantic lighting, the fireplaces infusing the room with just the right amount of cozy warmth to counteract the summer night's unusual chill. The other couples around them, speaking lovingly to each other in languages he could not understand, but anyone could interpret. God how he missed this foreign land, a place he had many times told himself he would return to over the years, if only he could banish to the back of his mind the inevitable heartbreak that had occurred so many years ago.

She orders a bottle of burgundy, speaking the vintage's name in perfect French. He usually doesn't drink wine, but is always happy to be sharing a bottle with her. They sip from their glasses and reminisce over experiences they've shared together this magical summer. Laughter with friends, the incomparable sightseeing, the ability to do almost anything at the drop of a hat. The affection for each other they'd initially been afraid to let show, but both grew to covet.

He knew even back then he needed to cherish these moments to the fullest of his abilities, as his time as an exchange student was quickly nearing its end. Now was not the time for such painful realities however, and he turns his attention back to that perfect setting, and her perfect existence in it. Her face was even more beautiful in that glowing candlelight. He could barely make out the soft freckles on her nose, next to those stark hazel eyes. As the wine runs its course, she smiles with more frequency, a slightly crooked smile that endears her to him even more. 'How perfect is this night?', he allows himself to ask for now the second time in his life. If only he never had to deal with what was to come in just a few short days. If only he could live in this moment forever…..

Chapter 2

Kyle walked into The Commons Restaurant in the Mission District of downtown San Francisco, where an attractive brunette in a low-cut black dress greeted him as he entered. She showed him over to the lounge area, where Kyle quickly spotted Travis sitting up at the bar. Kyle walked over and gave Travis a friendly fist bump, and took a seat at the barstool next to him. The bar was not especially packed, though Kyle hadn't expected it to be, given that he'd cut out of work a couple hours early and they'd arrived before the tech crowd usually started filtering in.

"Cheers buddy," Travis said, as he slid one of two freshly ordered craft beer pints over to Kyle. Kyle took a surprisingly long drink from his glass, downing about a third of it in one swig.

"Thanks man. Good choice, don't think I've had this one before."

"Yeah it's pretty good isn't it? High alcohol content too, it'll get you there quickly," Travis replied.

Kyle took another sip from the glass, more conscious this time of his drinking pace. "So how's the new gig? Think you can make it work there for at least a couple months?"

"Seems alright so far. Don't think the workload will be too killer, which I'm obviously a big fan of," Travis snickered. "Only met with my boss for a couple of minutes today. Seems like a fuckin' uber-nerd, but a nice enough fella. I'll tell ya, there's some fine ass in that place too. I'd probably give half of the administrative assistants a shot at the title." *It was good to see Travis had his priorities in order,* Kyle thought to himself.

"Well you better give this one a decent chance. Rent in this part of the country ain't cheap, and your days of freeloading on my couch are through!" Kyle exclaimed jokingly. Several months prior, when Travis had first moved to the Bay Area, Kyle had let him stay at his apartment while he got on his feet. Unsurprisingly, it had taken Travis weeks to even bother to start looking for employment, and almost another two months to finally land a job. Kyle knew Travis still harbored a bit of a grudge for making him move out of his place, but it really was for the sake of the friendship that they keep at least a little bit of mileage between each other.

"Yeah asshole, that's why I'm subletting a spare bedroom in fuckin' Hayward instead of waking up to the San Fran skyline every morning like you are," Travis snapped back. "You're lucky my roommate travels a lot and I can actually bring chicks back there. Otherwise I'd be a lot more pissed off at you."

"Well what can I say, you've got to work hard to make it to the big time like me!" Kyle said sarcastically. "I'm sure Hayward isn't that bad though. It's got to beat the hell out of being back home in Arizona."

Travis laughed. "You're not wrong there. I'll cheers to that." The two tapped glasses and downed their beers, with Travis immediately ordering up another round. They then spent the next twenty minutes or so catching up on what was going on in each other's families. Kyle was usually hesitant to dig too deep into Travis' family life, which was riddled with a variety of landmines. Travis had cut off ties with his father years ago, and was always on and off speaking terms with his mother. She'd separated from his father about ten years prior, before Kyle and Travis had met, and she'd been living with another man for the past couple years. Kyle had accompanied Travis to visit his parents once or twice when they were both still living in Arizona. He did not recall the visits as being overly encouraging, to say the least. Travis' father had been half in-the-bag when he and Travis dropped by his trailer park one weekday morning. The conversation quickly veered into dangerous territory whenever the topic became something other than sports. Travis' mother at least appeared to have put her alcohol addiction in the past, though her gruff attitude and shortness towards Travis didn't make it seem like she was much appreciating the dry life. After seeing first-hand how Travis' parents treated him, despite Travis' efforts towards amicability, Kyle had always tried to keep stashed in the back of his mind that his friend's shortcomings were maybe not completely his own fault.

Kyle and Travis had put down about five beers each by the time the bourgeois of San Francisco started funneling in from their nearby places of employment. In Kyle's humble opinion, most of these people fell into two different categories: There were the younger, yuppier types who were typically in their late 20's or early 30's, around Kyle's age. They prided themselves on their Type-A personalities, or their valiant attempts at feigning them, and their conversations often seemed to be little more than recitation contests, where participants would take an unreasonably rigid stance on a topic and compete to see who could throw out the most quasi-relevant buzzwords the quickest. These types tended to hold jobs in the Financial and Biotech sectors. They also spent more on their wardrobe and hairstyles than most of the country spends on their mortgage.

The other group consisted of the older, more hipstery crowd. Typically in their late 30's to mid-40's, this group chose to eschew the materialistic fashions of the younger crowd. Though in many cases, they could still justify paying hundreds of dollars for hoodie jackets and sandals, as long as purportedly free-trade materials were used. They often held jobs with high-tech companies and startups, and were certainly pulling in money on par with the Type-A crowd, though they'd much prefer to spend it on a vintage record player or an imported espresso machine than a gas-guzzling sports car. Kyle found it intriguing to watch these two very different sections of the population interact within the same setting. One was all double Jack 'n' Cokes and top-shelf tequila shots: the other was hand-crafted cocktails served with a sprig of organic mint in a copper mug. Though Kyle found it impossible to identify himself with either group, after a few beers his frustration usually died down and turned to amusement. This was certainly a very different world from the one where he'd originated.

Travis looked around, feeling much the same sentiment that Kyle was experiencing. "You better not ever become like these sellouts, man. I know you're a good-looking guy with a high-paying job and a badass apartment and everything, but if I see you start to walk and talk like these jackasses, I'm putting poison in your wheatgrass avocado smoothie."

"Oh you flatter me so Mr. Trayborn," Kyle replied. "Unfortunately, these jackasses you speak of pretty much represent the pinnacle of our generation. Wealthy enough to do what they want when they want. Most of them are in great shape physically. Probably have enough money coming down the line in inheritance that they can fuck up a couple times and pay off the legal system to avoid their much-needed stint in drug rehab."

"Ha, that's the Kyle Drake I love to hear! Bitingly sarcastic but still somehow poignant. Though you have known me for like six years at this point, so I can say with certainty that you've learned from the best."

Travis leaned into the bar to catch the female bartender's attention. "Hey sweetheart, just thought you should know that you're currently serving the only two gentlemen in this whole damn bar who refuse to conform to a crappy generational stereotype. True pioneers we are. Sometimes the only team you can pick is no team at all!"

"Oh is that right?" the cute bartender replied as she handed them their next round of beers. "Well that just sounds too good to be true! But if you are telling the truth, you'll have to tell me how you do it, because it's hard to come by guys like that in San Francisco."

"I would never lie to a pretty girl like you! You see my esteemed colleague here Mr. Drake and I are not from around these parts. We come from the mean streets of suburban Arizona, where a man is legally required to develop his own identity and earn his sense of self-worth. It's truly a fascinating place, you should let me take you around there some time."

The bartender smirked. "Well you do make it sound pretty irresistible, so maybe someday down the line that could be arranged. But for now, I actually have to close you guys out. Ending my shift early tonight so I can go home and study for my mid-term tomorrow. If you guys come around here again you should ask for me. I'm usually working the bar and I always enjoy shooting the shit with a couple of intellectuals like yourselves. Name is Lindsey."

"Well Lindsey, luckily for you we do come here often, and luckily for you I never forget a pretty face," Travis emoted in a throwback chivalrous 1950's style.

Kyle took the check from Lindsey, receiving a noticeably friendly smile as she again said goodbye to them.

"What the fuck?" Travis griped at Kyle. "You didn't even say anything as she's giving you the 'come hither' stare?"

"Probably too young for both of us anyway. At least she didn't run away crying like most girls you drunkenly talk to," Kyle said.

"Ha ha, very funny. Well hey, I'm kind of done with this place for tonight. It's still pretty early though, I say we head back to my house and get our relax on," Travis suggested.

"I dunno man, that's like an hour away and we both have to get up early tomorrow for work."

"Dude it's fine, you're in your 30's, not your 70's. You can handle it. Plus you haven't even seen my place yet. And since you didn't get me a housewarming gift, I think a simple request for your company for one night isn't too much to ask."

"Hmmm...well alright I guess. I just need to be back home at a halfway decent hour. Is your drunk ass planning to drive us all the way back there?"

"No worries. Sun hasn't even fully set yet and I'm a champion at this," Travis replied.

Kyle and Travis arrived at Travis' house without incident, and Travis immediately went to his liquor cabinet to mix two rum and cokes. Kyle took a quick look around the house, and felt it was actually a pretty good setup for Travis. A little bit older of a building, but plenty of space, and Travis basically had a separate wing of the house so he wouldn't have a chance to irritate his housemate too much.

Travis took a seat on the living room couch and turned on the TV, turning the channel to a Giants baseball game. Kyle and Travis each drank casually from their glasses as they watched the remaining innings of the game. As the game drew to a close, Travis walked into his bedroom, and returned to the living room holding a large glass pipe. He reached into his pocket, pulling out a small baggy filled with pot, and packed the pipe with expert precision.

"You're crazy!" Kyle exclaimed. "Tomorrow is your second day at work and you're gonna go in hungover AND stoned?"

"Yeah exactly, it's my second day tomorrow. They're not gonna have me do shit. This is Grade A stuff too. Here, you take a hit. You gotta live life man!"

Kyle hadn't smoked pot in quite a while, and when he did he tried to contain it to an occasional weekend. However, in his current state of inebriation and with Travis pressuring him, it was too tough for him to say no. He had a pretty quiet morning at work tomorrow anyway, Kyle told himself......

Kyle awoke in a panic, laying on the couch, unsure of where he was until his burning throat reminded him of the previous night's festivities. "Craaappp," Kyle grumbled. It was 7:14 AM. Kyle was almost always in the office a little before 8:00 AM, though sometimes he could get lucky and go undetected for the first hour or two of the morning. He would have to take the train straight there, which would take about 90 minutes from Hayward, but first he needed to get his hands on a pair of clothes that didn't reek of Travis' illicit hobby. Kyle walked into Travis' bedroom and saw him slowly getting dressed for work.

"Goddamnit Travis, I told you this was going to happen! I'm going to be so fucking late now. Why did you have to make me smoke when I said it was a bad idea?"

"Whoa there buddy, calm down it's going to be okay. You told me last night you don't even have any meetings until the afternoon. Actually you probably don't remember it, but you told me a lot of stuff last night that was pretty fucking hilarious. You're lucky I'm a good friend and I don't blab. Here, I figured you'd need some clothes to get you through the day. These are a little big on me so they should fit you well enough to get the job done."

Kyle quickly sized up the clothes on himself, deciding they would do, and threw them on in a hurry. He then started towards the door, checking his phone for the nearest train station he could take into Santa Clara.

Travis called out after him from his bedroom. "Bye dude, thanks again for hanging out last night. Sorry we overslept but we'll both be fine, trust me."

"Yeah yeah. Gotta go, I'll call you this weekend or something." Kyle called back gruffly. He quickly descended the stairs down to the sidewalk, and ran the five blocks to the train station in time to catch the 7:28 headed south.

Sitting on the train, panting in his seat and surrounded by well-dressed professionals responsibly headed into the office, Kyle was afforded plenty of time to assess his moronic decision to join Travis in his pointless weekday debauchery session.

CHAPTER 3

"Hey Kyle, don't know if you remembered but we have those visitors from Santa Barbara coming in today," chirped Kyle's boss, Stan, in much too cheerful a manner for a Kyle to handle at the current moment. "They're here for the annual conference over at Assembly Hall, but are planning to drop by for a quick tour this afternoon. You still think you could show them around the place? Thanks a bunch!"

Kyle had a vague memory of being briefed on the visit during one of the teams review meetings a few weeks back, but the thought honestly hadn't crossed his mind until Stan had just reminded him.

"I'm in budgetary meetings all day with the board or else I'd tour them myself. We'll probably be tied up there through Friday if you need to find me for any reason. Though with the way you've been working lately, I doubt you'll run into any issues," Stan finished as he exited the office.

You sure picked the wrong day to throw me that compliment, Kyle thought, as he sipped from his fourth cup of coffee for the morning, still feeling the aftereffects of his late-night slumber party at Travis' place.

Stan really was a nice guy and a decent boss, and Kyle knew he shouldn't let things like Stan's occasional cluelessness or misplaced enthusiasm irritate him. He was lucky to have someone who managed with the hands-off style of Stan. In fact, he'd always been lucky in that regard, even dating back to his graduate degree work in Arizona. He wondered if half of the time his supervisors had any idea how indifferent he usually felt towards the success of his projects. Sure, there were occasional days when Kyle felt inspired by the work was doing. He'd always had a knack for efficient problem solving, and was usually superior to his colleagues at quickly identifying what information was relevant and what was extraneous. He was often amazed at how sidetracked many of his colleagues could get when trying to perform simple tasks that could, God forbid, actually add value to the institution. Perhaps that was the reason Kyle had been able to achieve management status at all of his employers in a relatively short amount of time. For what he lacked in "Gung Ho", he made up for in being able to present practical information to the right people at the right time.

Around an hour after Kyle returned from lunch, the lab secretary Nicole brought in the group of five visitors from the UC Santa Barbara clinic. Kyle had given a couple of these "ooh, ahh" tours over the past few months, and had become pretty good at going on autopilot. That talent would come in handy today, given that Kyle was definitely feeling less than 100%. And at least he'd be wearing a lab coat, so the awkwardness of Travis' ill-fitting clothes could be minimized.

"Thanks Nicki. Hello everyone, my name is Kyle Drake, and welcome to the Keane Institute for Learning and Memory, or as some of us call it: *KIL Me*". That joke never failed with the scientist crowd, and it was accompanied by the requisite laughter in this case as well. As Kyle was introduced to each member of the group, he was not surprised to find that all identified themselves as either scientists or lab technicians. They would be primarily interested in the technical details of the experiments the lab was conducting, so Kyle planned to tailor his tour accordingly.

"Here at Keane, we've essentially been commissioned by the National Institute of Health to study the limits of long-term vivid memory recall. More specifically, the ability of the average person to display a photographic recollection of certain events of their past. This is referred to scientifically as 'eidetic memory'."

"Yes Kyle, I should tell you that before we left Santa Barbara we were briefed on the research your lab is doing here, and we all found it very exciting!" said Saya, one of the scientists in the group. "Now I've heard there have been a fair amount of claims of photographic memory in the past, even by some rather famous people, but none have been firmly substantiated to this point?"

"Didn't Tesla claim to have an eidetic memory, Mr. Drake? I think Teddy Roosevelt might have claimed that as well," replied Marcus, one of the younger technicians.

"Please, call me Kyle. And yes, there have been claims, although unverified, that Roosevelt could recite entire sections of the newspaper after reading just once. There have actually been many cases of similar abilities demonstrated since Roosevelt's time, but almost all of them can be attributed to pattern recognition much more so than an expanded capacity for memory. This type of patterned memorization also tends to dissipate quickly, in a matter of hours, rather than being retained as long-term memory for many years."

Kyle could see this information was fascinating for his audience, so he decided to continue addressing the more popular claims of photographic memory a bit further. "And Tesla's genius in many areas no doubt contributed to his reputation for memory retention. Tesla was known for possessing a skill called 'picture thinking', in which he was able to visualize a physical idea from all angles, assemble and disassemble the item into complex layers, and store the schematics in his mind as a sort of blueprint. While no doubt a remarkable skill, this doesn't qualify as true eidetic memory, as no prior events from his life are being recalled."

"I suppose the same thing goes for Luria's work in Russia in the early 20th century?" Marcus asked. "I remember reading his 'The Mind of a Mnemonist' during school. I think I remember a chapter about a patient who could listen to a speech and recite it word-for-word days later. Something to do with using colors to memorize?"

"Very good! You've got a pretty good memory there yourself my friend!" Kyle joked, capitalizing on the chance to inject some more office-friendly humor into the tour. "Luria's work is very popular around this lab, for obvious reasons. The phenomena you're referring to is called 'synesthesia', and it can manifest itself in several different ways. But the basic principle is that when one of the five human senses is stimulated to create a memory, an attempt is made by the brain to associate the other senses to create an even stronger memory. For instance, some people have reportedly been able to memorize very long sequences of numbers by associating colors, tastes and scents with the numbers. This principle isn't far off from how we envision true eidetic memory recall would work. All of the senses would call upon their individual imprint for a particular memory, and would work in unison to present a vivid sensory experience for the person who had lived through the memory."

"But if so many of these stories of photographic memory are proven scientifically invalid, what approach is the institute taking in attempting to validate the potential to enable this ability?" questioned Saya.

"I thought you'd never ask," Kyle joked. "Follow me this way, and I'll show you what we've been working on lately." Kyle led the team through the office mezzanine down to the main laboratory area. This room had always struck Kyle as a higher-tech version of a dentist's office, if you swapped the sharp instruments of torture for fMRIs, EEGs and flat screen monitors. In the lab currently were two of Kyle's direct reports. One was sitting in the assessment chair, hooked up to a series of electrodes and sensors. The other was diligently monitoring an EEG output screen that was displaying the neural oscillations of the "patient". Kyle had half-hoped this room was going to be empty: he knew his chances of getting away with the express version of the tour were now slim to none.

"Okay guys, welcome to our lair! You picked a good day to come up for a visit, looks we have a confirmatory experiment being conducted as we speak. Normally I'd be able to take you into the room, but we don't want to disturb Michael and Ryan, our technicians." Michael, standing by the EEG monitor, gave a brief acknowledgement wave and went back to his notations. Ryan was sitting in the chair with his eyes closed, attempting to lay as motionless as possible.

"As you may or may not know, memory is primarily divided into three types: sensory memory, short-term memory, and long-term memory. Sensory memory is just that: messages being sent to your brain from your five senses. With so many messages being sent from your sensory experience at a given time, only a select few progress through the brain's filtering mechanisms into short-term memory."

"Now short-term memory is actually much shorter-term than most people think. The classic definition is that humans can only hold about seven distinct items in short-term memory for about 20 to 30 seconds at a time, before the memory is either washed away or committed to long-term memory. This is actually the main reason why phone numbers are sectioned the way they are, with a set of three digits paired with a set of four digits, like 555-1234. You can obviously dial a phone as fast as you'd like, and the phone makes no distinction between the first and second sets of digits. But by parsing the string of numbers, this makes it easier for the numbers to stay in short-term memory, and eventually be committed to long-term memory."

Kyle gave the group a moment to digest the information before continuing.

"Most scientists believe long-term memories are controlled by parts of the brain known as the hippocampus and the frontal cortex. These brain areas analyze both sensory and short-term memory, and determine if the information is worth committing to long-term memory."

"Do scientists know how these memories are stored from a physiological standpoint?" inquired Saya.

"Actually, within the last few years there's been some substantial discovery on this topic. Both short-term and long-term memory are now believed to be enabled by protein synthesis that allows the storage of information in neurons. These proteins are referred to as 'prion-like', and are related to the types of prions that have been in the news in recent years as the suspected cause of Mad Cow Disease and Parkinson's," Kyle informed them.

The group appeared to remain enthralled by the information they'd been given so far, and Kyle could already tell he'd be receiving very positive feedback from the tour, which he wasn't really sure if he wanted or not. If he wasn't careful, he might get stuck becoming the de facto tour guide for the whole facility.

Kyle continued: "The more a short-term memory is rehearsed by a person, the more the synapses in the brain are fired, which causes the chemical release of magnesium. This release of magnesium actually enables the attachment of calcium to the neuron, which in turn strengthens the memory much like it would a bone, and retains the memory long-term."

"Fascinating! I'm guessing the breakdown of this calcium is probably related to the decline in memory as a person ages?" asked Marcus.

"It's complicated...but yes that is one of the factors," responded Kyle. "As time goes on, the original protein and calcium deposits can breakdown. To prevent this, the brain undergoes a process called 'long-term potentiation' which attempts to strengthen the synapse signals to strengthen the proteins. However as a person ages, the ability to release acetylcholine, one of the most critical neurotransmitters in the brain, generally declines and limits the ability of these synapses to send signals. The net result is a steady decline in long-term memory recall as a person ages."

"So what exactly are these lab tests studying for?" chimed in Thuong, the other lab technician in the group.

"We actually have a couple different studies running concurrently. One is focused on trying to determine the critical mass of neuronal calcium deposits needed to retain a memory. The other study, and my primary focus as of late, has been on figuring out how to sustain a particular pattern of synapse signals for an extended period of time. The end result being the enabling of a photographic recall of a particular event. Where we're running up against a wall is figuring out how to lock in a particular pattern, which would correspond to a particular memory. Our hypothesis is that if we could lock in on this pattern, the increased frequency of targeted signals being sent would rapidly strengthen the neuronal pattern, to the level where a person could vividly recall details of that particular memory, potentially even as far back as early childhood."

Wow, the group seemed to simultaneously exclaim. Kyle was on a roll. But unfortunately, he didn't have a whole lot more definitive information he could give to them at this point.

"Now I don't want to get you all too excited, because we've got a ways to go yet before we have people remembering what kind of cake they had for their 3rd birthday. But I feel we're definitely taking the right approach, and the results will get progressively better as we continue forward."

"Amazing stuff I must say!" declared Saya. "I think we need to start heading over to the conference now, but thank you so much for taking the time to show us around. I can't wait to get back to Santa Barbara and tell the guys there about the exciting stuff you have going on up here. We're definitely going to have to step up our game if we want to keep pace!"

Each member of the group thanked Kyle for his wonderful tour, and they exchanged final pleasantries, insisting that Kyle visit their facility if he was ever in the Santa Barbara area.

As the door to the lobby finally closed, Kyle breathed a quick sigh of relief. He was feeling pretty worn out, especially after talking almost non-stop for the past 45 minutes. He decided to head over to the break room to grab a soda. Some caffeine would help him get through these last few hours.

As Kyle cracked open his drink, into the break room walked Frank Bernstein, another employee of the Keane Institute who was working on a separate but similar project to Kyle's. Frank was an electrical engineer, and a seemingly very skilled one from what Kyle had seen from him so far. In fact, Frank was one of the few people Kyle didn't actively try to avoid when he saw that they were about to cross paths. Frank was a tall, heavier-set guy, standing a couple of inches taller than Kyle, and was probably four or five years older. He'd been with the lab since its inception, and was considered one of the go-to guys whenever technical questions relating to equipment arose. In Kyle's opinion, Frank probably didn't get the credit he deserved for his work over the years at the institute. If he were Frank, he'd be pretty pissed off that people like Kyle were able to transfer in at a higher level than him. From the talks he'd had with Frank though, it seemed like he could care less about climbing the corporate ladder. Managing other people wasn't exactly one of his proclivities.

"You do anything fun last weekend?" Frank asked Kyle. Usually Kyle gave a pretty canned, vanilla answer when asked this question by one of his coworkers. Frank didn't seem to get worked up about anything though, and was not much of a gossip, so Kyle felt comfortable opening up a little bit more around him. Kyle suspected that Frank probably viewed him as the "cool guy" in the office, and perhaps even wanted to hang out with him outside of work, but must have just been too afraid to ever really ask.

"Hit downtown San Fran pretty hard with one of my buddies on Saturday. I felt the need to behave like I was still in college for no apparent reason," Kyle responded.

"Oh man, I bet you did. You still don't look like your normal GQ self even today. Must have been a good one."

"Yeah it was okay. How about you, did you get into anything fun?" asked Kyle.

"Nothing special. Worked on that video game I'm designing all Friday night and Saturday. Actually came in here for a little bit on Sunday to run some batch file testing on my project without anybody bothering me."

"You're a more dedicated man than I," Kyle responded. "How are things going on your project here anyway?"

"Pretty good, pretty good. We're actually ahead on most of our milestones, which you hardly ever see in such R&D-heavy work. We've got another ten months still before we have to re-up on our grant funding. You know how academic funding goes though, once the cork's been popped it usually takes a while for them to notice they might want to control the pouring. There's a lot of 'keeping up with the Joneses' going on with the Basel Institut around here right now, which I'm sure you've noticed."

"Yeah I have," Kyle agreed. "I've heard their names mentioned more in the past month than I think I have the whole rest of the time I've worked here. I've always found it kind of sad we can't just play nice and get along. I bet we'd have a ton to learn from each other."

"No doubt B.I. and Keane would have a lot to share, mein freund. But the higher-up's at this university have been duking it out with the evil empire in Switzerland since long before you and I have been around to suggest otherwise. We must both be paranoid that one of us is going to win the space race of unlocking the mind's potential, and collect the accompanying accolades and financial windfall therein. Getting there first is what matters most to the financial guys, I suppose. Anyway that's not even my domain, I'm just a lowly worker bee. How did it go for you today with the Santa Barbarians?"

"Piece of cake. We had a beta test going on when they came through, so I actually had something interesting to show them."

"Yeah, I've been meaning to mention to you, I saw your lab guys setting up for that test this morning. You know, I could probably rig up a better interface to cross-reference your measurement readouts if you wanted? Might save you some duplication of work on the backend."

"Oh…thanks man I appreciate that. I may even take you up on that some time down the road. Right now we're so focused on figuring out how to generate the data we need, I haven't even thought that much about how we're going to use it."

"Well just so you know, offer is on the table," Frank reiterated.

Kyle thanked Frank, and returned back to his desk to figure out what else he had to get done before he could take off for the day. He had a good hour's worth of email to catch up on, and then he was hoping to get out of the office before the budget meeting let out. He knew the office would be abuzz with gossip on which departments at the university were getting funding priority and which weren't. Kyle could care less about that type of thing. Just a little while longer and he could go home, relax, catch up on sleep, and get his week back on track.

CHAPTER 4

"Damn this place is packed!" Kyle proclaimed as he and Travis entered the new Polk Street Distillery at 10:30 PM on Friday night. Kyle had once again ended the work week with the best intentions of taking it easy over the weekend, and feeling refreshed for once come Monday morning. He'd even been invited to go on a day hike on Saturday morning with some new friends he'd recently met. But somehow, as he had so many times before, Travis was able to convince Kyle that he needed to get his ass out of his apartment so they could go out on the town together.

"Back bar, less crowded," Travis pointed out, as the two made their way through the crowd and over to the ultra-modern cocktail lounge near the back of the building. Taking a quick scan of the exclusively top shelf liquor selection, Travis accepted the fact that his go-to order of well rum and coke might not fly at this establishment. "Two Old Fashioned's, Woodford bourbon, Angostura bitters, and one sugar cube please," Travis requested.

"Power order right there," Kyle observed. "Careful though, I've seen you drunk on whiskey before and a pretty site it is not."

"You've got nothing to worry about my friend. Tonight I plan to be a perfect and upstanding gentleman, who will offer one extremely lucky lady a chance at the experience of a lifetime. And by that, I mean I'll probably try to drunkenly grope her in your spare bedroom while she's vomiting into a trash can."

Kyle laughed. "Jesus, have you resigned yourself to that fate already? You know, it is a viable option to try and have a real conversation with a girl. Who knows, she might even not find your chauvinistic sense of humor completely repulsive!"

"Hey funny man, why don't you quit nursing that drink and let's get this party started. Two more Old Fashioned's please," Travis directed at the bartender. They grabbed their drinks and slid down to the corner of the bar, looking out on the massive crowd which was continuing to form near the dance floor.

"Look at this place, man! Look at where we are right now. Did you ever think a couple of average Joe's like us from Nowhere, Arizona would be able to make it here? Half the motherfuckers in here have trust funds from their rich ass parents, who probably have buildings at Stanford named after them. And here we are, mixing it up with them, and at least feigning the appearance that we might be equals."

Kyle could tell the liquor was already starting to hit Travis. He often liked to wax poetic like this whenever he was starting to feel a good buzz. Nevertheless, Kyle appreciated the sentiment, and was glad to hear Travis was grateful in his own way. "Beautifully stated. It is pretty awesome, I must admit."

"For a while there, I was beginning to think I'd probably never get away from that barren wasteland we grew up in. I mean Arizona has some pluses, don't get me wrong, but 30 years is a long time to spend there. And my hometown was even shittier than yours was," Travis said. "Not to get all weird on you bud, but I just want to thank you for being the smart one in the group, and working as hard as you did to pave your way out. I'm fuckin' glad we met at Arizona State all those years ago, and I'm glad I can ride your coattails for a while out here until I can hopefully figure my own thing out."

"It's all good my friend. Here's to keeping the good times rolling," Kyle proposed, toasting his glass.

"Salud!" Travis accepted.

The next few hours at the Polk Street Distillery were spent in typical fashion. Travis was never shy about approaching a group of unsuspecting strangers and thinking of inventive ways to strike up a conversation. On this particular night, he started things off by complimenting a pair of cute sisters on their decision to drink Manhattans, then proceeded to mock them for choosing bourbon instead of rye whiskey. After initially being put off, they warmed to the attention and extended an invitation to join them at their table. After about half an hour of banter focused around their involvement in opening a theater for indie films, the girls excused themselves to use the restroom. Travis decided it was too early to "put down roots" just yet, and suggested they checkout the DJ area instead of waiting around.

Several hours and numerous rum and cokes later, the night was picking up. Kyle got separated from Travis and met a male PhD student at the bar named Ahmad, who was very into San Francisco's professional sports teams. His buddy Raymond had flown in from out of town, and the two had gone to the Thursday night 49ers game the night before, and were now out exploring the nightlife. The three of them talked about their favorite football teams while highlights from the Thursday night game played on the giant flat screen. After taking turns buying rounds of Patron Silver shots, Ahmad and Kyle made a friendly exchange of numbers, and Kyle went looking for Travis.

Travis had made his way to the dance floor, and was dancing with three girls who appeared to be enjoying his routine. He was sporting his patented "perma-grin", which meant he had no doubt been hitting the booze pretty hard for the previous hour. Kyle himself was starting to feel pretty loose and uninhibited, so he briefly joined the dance circle and pulled off a semi-decent corkscrew move that was usually his go-to in those situations. He then started chatting with one of the girls, Mallory, whom he guessed was probably about eight years younger than himself. She seemed nice enough, but the combination of the alcohol kicking in and the pounding music made a legit back-and-forth challenging. As Kyle began to lose conversational momentum, he grabbed Travis and suggested they get another drink from the bar. Travis was elated by this idea, even more so since Kyle would undoubtedly be picking up the tab.

A while later Kyle had gone to the restroom while Travis waited for him, hungrily eyeing the line outside the door to the women's room. Travis was maybe halfway through his umpteenth drink of the night when his impatience began to manifest itself. It was already too late when Kyle overheard Travis trying to orchestrate a romantic interlude with two of the girls in the line. Clearly they were on the verge of overstaying their welcome.

Kyle was about ready to suggest they cut their losses, grab a couple slices of pizza and call it a night, when he felt a light tap on his shoulder.

"Kyle, hey! You're still here! I was wondering where you guys ran off to?!?" exclaimed Tara, one of the Manhattan-drinking sisters they had met at the beginning of the night. Judging by the glazed look in her eyes, she had been keeping pace with Kyle on drinks. She placed her hand on Kyle's chest and whispered: "I'm glad you didn't leave already. I thought you might want to know that you're the nicest guy I've met in this bar all night. My sister is being a pain in the ass tonight, do you want to get out of here with me?"

Tara's sister, seeming to be much less inebriated, did not appear amused by Travis' slurring advances. Kyle decided it was probably time to say goodbye to the sober sister and head back to his apartment. With a half-conscious Travis in tote, the three of them exited the bar, jumped in a cab and rode back to Kyle's apartment on the east side of San Francisco.

Kyle awoke the next morning with a splitting headache, and a strange girl lying next to him in his bed. After a brief moment of shock, he was able to piece together enough of the night to remember leaving the bar. Kyle chuckled to himself. *What a night*, he thought. *Aren't you a little too old to be binge drinking and picking up drunken floozies from the bar?*

Kyle attempted a congenial conversation with Tara when she awoke minutes later, but it was clear she was not feeling great and was only interested in going home and crawling back into bed. Kyle walked her to the front door of his building, where he programmed her number in his phone at her request, and exchanged an awkward goodbye hug. When Kyle returned to his apartment, Travis was in the kitchen, vigorously downing water straight out of the Brita pitcher.

"Kyle Drake, you bad bad man! You see the great things that can happen when you let loose with your best buddy Travis?"

"Ha, yeah man, you uhh, really worked your magic last night. Maybe next time you can start a fight with a bouncer just to bring the full cliché to completion."

"Hey, if it wasn't for me you wouldn't have even been out there, so quit your bitching and let's get some pancakes at that place across the street."

"If it wasn't for you I wouldn't have a heavy metal band playing a sold-out concert in my head right now. I'm going back to sleep. Lock the door when you head out."

"Hey man it's only Saturday, we're doing it all over again toni---". With that Kyle slammed his bedroom door shut, face-planted onto his pillow, and acknowledged that at that moment he felt every one of his 32 years of age.

CHAPTER 5

Jamie had committed a week ago to meeting with her friend for happy hour in Tiburon, across the bay from downtown San Francisco. Her boyfriend Manny had insisted she make her best effort to follow through and not back out again.

"Jamie, it's important that you try to get out there more and socialize with other people. I mean it's kind of crazy to me that you've been friends with Casey for almost two years, and I don't think you guys have ever done anything outside of Fremont together!" Manny exclaimed. "I mean it seems like she's always inviting you to go do fun things with her and her friends, but there's always some kind of excuse coming from you."

"That's not true, I do make an effort. I've just had a hard week. It's not a huge deal, I'll snap out of it like I always do."

It was true that Jamie felt guilty for not being more involved in her social circle. She was pretty lucky to have applied for that apartment and ended up with Casey as her neighbor when she first moved to Fremont. It was perfect timing for someone like Casey, someone completely devoid of pessimism, to enter her life. And she was so socially connected. Those first few months of hanging out with Casey and her friends, experiencing her new town and being able to finally spread her wings a bit, were such a release for Jamie. For the first time in years it seemed like she might have a chance to live a normal, fulfilling life. But things had somehow taken a wrong turn. She'd barely said ten words to Casey the past few months. She often tried to lay blame on her unpredictable schedule at the hospital, sometimes requiring night and weekend shifts. Manny, however, was not so easily fooled. Over the course of the time they had been dating, he'd seen a gradual shift in her mood. She had become more reclusive, more unsure of herself. These expressions were usually heightened whenever Manny attempted to play therapist and ask Jamie what was bothering her. In any case, Manny felt a quick visit up to the big city might be exactly what Jamie needed to get out of this haze and get her head back in the right place. Jamie knew Manny was right about this, and eventually, she relented.

As Jamie pulled her car up to the valet at the Shores Beach Club, she started to feel that maybe this could be the first step in gaining back some normalcy in her life. The restaurant itself looked like a beautiful beach resort, with an opulent décor and luxurious window treatments, which adorned the floor-to-ceiling windows of the giant patio overlooking the San Francisco skyline. Luxury yachts and sparkling sailboats lined the harbor adjacent to the beach. Jamie was escorted outside to an oblong white metal table with an ornate floral design. She was the first of the group to arrive, and used that opportunity to grab a seat in the middle of the table where she would be able to interact with the most people. Normally, Jamie might become anxious in a situation like this, the first to arrive and being left alone to worry about which direction the night might head. So far she was remaining composed, and was actually starting to feel excited to see her friends, some of whom she had not seen in almost a year. She sipped patiently from her water glass, and stared out into the nearby San Francisco Bay. At that moment, she felt appreciation for what she had accomplished over these past few years. She had come a long way from the sadness she'd left in Eureka. Through hard work and perseverance, she had put herself through nursing school, and had been able to land a job that afforded her the chance to start a new life in an exciting city. Jamie knew she needed to settle on a life path that would provide her the stability and peace of mind she so desperately desired; at this moment, she was actually feeling that it might not be too late.

Twenty minutes after she'd arrived, Jamie saw a group of familiar faces walking through the dining area and out to the patio. "Hey Jamie, so great to see you! You look great, how long has it been?" asked Caroline, one of the girls Jamie had always been most fond of when Casey brought her around. She had a very slight southern drawl, and looked like she could have been Miss Teen South Carolina in a past life. She was accompanied by Justine and Mary, both of whom Jamie had met many times before, and a slew of about 12 other young professional women. Jamie had never understood why it usually seemed to be her receiving the compliments on her appearance, when all of these other girls were so pretty and had such outgoing personalities. Casey took a seat next to Jamie, giving her a quick hug and whispering: "Thanks for coming." The waiter popped a few bottles of blanc de noirs champagne, and the women went off talking about how their days at work had gone. Jamie made a conscious effort to remember names around the table, and at least a few details on everyone as far as where they lived and worked. She was never really a big drinker, so she made sure to only take small sips from her champagne flute, and to not try to keep up with the girls who were refilling their glasses seemingly by the minute.

"So Justine here finally locked down that Adonis of a man of hers and got engaged three weeks ago, for those of you who hadn't noticed that rock on her left hand," started Mary. "And it happened after they somehow scored dinner reservations to The French Laundry in Napa. How romantic is that?" A round of oooh's and ahhh's swept over table, causing Justine to blush and playfully punch Mary in the arm. It was oddly comforting for Jamie to see someone else at the table feeling uncomfortable for a few seconds.

"If I was in Justine's shoes, and Matt had gotten down on one knee after treating me to a seven-course meal at French Laundry, I think I would have torn his clothes off and consummated the engagement right there under the table!" Mary exclaimed, sending the table into an uproarious laughter. Jamie laughed along, feeling a bit out of the loop but enjoying the story nonetheless.

Caroline turned to Jamie, putting a friendly hand on her leg. "For Justine's bachelorette party, we're trying to get a big group together for a girl's weekend out in Lake Tahoe in a couple months. You should come with us, it'll be so much fun!"

"Oh, wow! I've never been to Lake Tahoe before, it's supposed to be a beautiful place. Thanks so much for the invite, I'll have to check and see but I should be able to get the time off of work. I can let Casey know either way," Jamie responded. She was genuinely flattered to be invited, given her absenteeism in recent months. She hadn't exactly been much of a destination traveler so far in her life either. She'd never been out of the country, and other than a few trips to Seattle during her childhood to visit extended family, she couldn't really think of another trip she'd taken to a real city outside of Northwest California. She should have been ecstatic at the prospect of attending her first bachelorette party with a group of likeable girls at a place as beautiful as Lake Tahoe. So what was wrong? Why did she feel like there was very little chance of her realistically going on that trip?

The waitstaff was now bringing over to the table a stunning array of hor d'oeuvres. Jamie barely recognized anything that was presented, but as the serving trays were passed around she obligingly added a few items to her plate. She wasn't even sure which utensil to use to eat most of this stuff, so she patiently waited until she could observe the other girls and make sure she was at least in the ballpark of proper etiquette. The group also ordered several bottles of a sauvignon blanc that one of the girls had recently discovered on a trip to Sonoma County. Jamie took a sip from her glass, thinking the wine tasted the same as most of the other white wines she'd had in the past. Sitting there listening to these girls rattle off names of wineries they'd visited and varietals they enjoyed, Jamie's could sense her feelings of inadequacy beginning to rise to the surface. She'd tried so hard to prepare herself, and she had started off the night so well. But she knew what might be coming, and Jamie couldn't believe this was happening to her again.

"So Jamie, how do you like working at Fremont Memorial? And remind me, your boyfriend's name is Manny right?" asked Emily, who had switched seats with Caroline several minutes earlier.

"The job has been good. I'm a nurse in pediatrics. It's nice being around kids most of the day, and my coworkers are all pretty friendly."

"And what about Manny? How did you two meet?"

"I met him at a coffee stand outside the hospital. He's a rep for a medical device company, and was at Fremont Memorial for a meeting with a physician's group. He stopped me and asked me for directions, so I walked him over to his building. We got to talking, and by the end of the walk, I guess he worked up the courage to ask me out on a date." That was about all the level of detail Jamie could muster at the moment.

"Well he sounds like a very nice guy! Are there any marriage plans on the horizon?" Emily asked.

Jamie was now having a hard time focusing on what was going on around her. She was beginning to feel lightheaded, and her pulse began to spike. Her vision started to blur, and she could feel her hands sweating. She felt an increasing desire to flee the table, but knew doing so was out of the question: she couldn't make a scene like that in front of everyone. She had no choice but to try and force herself to relax and breathe, and hope no one else could tell what was going on with her. In the midst of this panic attack, she remembered that Emily had just asked her something about marriage, and she did her best to answer with something short and generic.

"No...err, yes, we've talked about getting married. Neither of us are in a rush to do it right now though."

She could see in her face that Emily was trying to be friendly and show an interest in Jamie's life, but Jamie simply wasn't able to reciprocate that effort at the moment. She could only feel herself continuing to withdraw from her surroundings, and she felt as if there was nothing she could do to stop it.

"Hey everyone, before I forget, I've got some extra tickets to the San Francisco Ballet Opening Night Gala next Saturday. Casey, you said you could come right?" asked Mary.

"Absolutely! I went last year and it was one of my favorite things I did all year!" replied Casey. "Oooh Jamie, you should come with me and we can ride into town together!"

With that statement, all eyes were now agonizingly upon Jamie. What she knew deep down to be nothing more than an innocent invite to a friendly gathering, now felt to her like a terrorist interrogation. She tried to reply...say anything, a whisper, even a scream...but couldn't utter a word. Her thoughts were frozen, paralyzed. The eyes that were now focused on her were showing expressions of confusion, as Jamie noticed she was now in motion, moving quickly away from the table.

"Jamie, where are you going? Are you okay?" Casey asked with concern.

Jamie was now moving faster, her arms and legs functioning unconsciously. She felt herself bump into a table, then ascend a few feet into the air. As Jamie gathered her balance, she stared ahead at the beautiful downtown skyline, seeming so serene in the descending sunset. In her periphery she could see people moving towards her, but that image quickly faded away as she continued forward towards her unknown destination.

"Oh my God Jamie, don't jump!!!" was the last thing Jamie heard, as she plunged into the icy waters of the San Francisco Bay.

CHAPTER 6

"Kyle, this is my main man Gregor. Known him since I was eight years old."

"Nice to meet you Gregor," Kyle said as he extended a hand towards Frank's childhood friend. Gregor offered a somewhat limp, rather unimpressive handshake. He wore a bright orange polo shirt that, despite probably being an XXL, was still clearly a few sizes too small for him. What hair remained on his head was pushed back into a rather unkempt quasi-ponytail. Through working in a university setting and being in close proximity to Silicon Valley, Kyle had seen plenty of these types of guys before. Usually nice enough dudes, but undoubtedly on the nerdier end of the spectrum.

"Likewise," Gregor responded. "Glad you two could meet up for lunch. I've had a hard time getting Frank out into society the past couple months. Things must be really killer at your guys' lab right now, or maybe it's just that video game he's been working on interminably."

"Ha, well maybe I'm just intimidated by you and your unparalleled intellect! You see Gregor here is a bit of a brainiac. Got hired on by an antivirus software company across town by telling them their product was full of holes and he could hack into their server with ease. When they told him they didn't believe him, he hacked them three times! They had no choice but to bring him on board!" Frank exclaimed.

"Well it didn't exactly go like that...but let's just say that I made them an offer they literally couldn't refuse," Gregor gloated, unable to contain a jolly grin from spreading across his face. Kyle had often noticed that many of the more socially awkward people he encountered had a tendency to "humble brag" about their accomplishments when they were around him. Kyle didn't especially mind: he guessed it was because he probably came off to these types as being a more socially accepted and plugged-in person than they were. It was probably their weird way of trying to bring themselves up to his level.

"Must have been a hell of an offer. I know damn well you're already making crazy money at that place and you haven't even worked there for a year! So do you even have to physically go into an office there, or is it one of those progressive think-tanks where everyone makes six figures for sitting around brainstorming on a giant whiteboard while playing with bouncy balls and remote-control helicopters?" Frank joked.

"Sometimes my physical presence is required, and sometimes my virtual presence does the job just fine," Gregor playfully retorted. The table went ahead with ordering their lunch, with Kyle noticing he was the only one of the three whose meal stood a chance at clocking in under 1,000 calories. Healthy living didn't seem to be at the forefront of either of these guys' agendas. As they ate their meal, Kyle looked around the restaurant and took note of the interactions at the other tables. Being a pretty upscale lunch joint in Silicon Valley, Kyle found himself wondering which companies these other patrons worked for. In the middle of the restaurant was a long table, primarily occupied by a group of boisterous and very well-dressed men, who appeared to be employed in a profession that was not averse to ordering a few cocktails with lunch. *Maybe they're lawyers*, Kyle thought, or more specifically given the current location, *corporate attorneys*. Kyle guessed each of their suits cost well over $1,000, and each sported black patent leather dress shoes that appeared to be in mint condition. Kyle himself had purchased a designer suit for

$1,800 when he first moved out to the Bay Area to begin his new job; he figured that since he was in a management position that paid pretty well, he needed to be prepared to look the part in a pinch. In actuality, he had worn the suit only once to a friend of a friend's wedding, and it had sat hanging in his closet ever since.

Kyle certainly had an appreciation for the business casual atmosphere of his work environment, and most of the Bay Area in general. He did however often wonder what it would be like to have one of those careers where your image mattered almost as much as your competency. Kyle could imagine it being an exciting way to live your life in your 20's, constantly striving to put your best face forward and trying to convince people into buying what you're trying to sell. In a way it was much like playing the singles game in a big city, trying to outwit your competition to land the hottest girl. Knowing himself though, after a few years of living in that lifestyle, he would undoubtedly burn out and start to fall behind the curve. He knew he didn't have it in him to live like that for the long haul.

After devouring his half-pound kobe beef BBQ cheeseburger with duck fat fries in what seemed like less than five minutes, Gregor asked Kyle how he was enjoying living in Northern California so far.

"It's not bad, not bad at all. I moved out here a little over a year ago, mainly for the job, and to check out a different part of the country than where I'm from in Arizona. Didn't really know anyone out here when I came, but it's been pretty easy to meet people and make friends. I was lucky enough to land an apartment downtown, so there're plenty of people around who are near my age at least. San Francisco's a cool town, not hard to find something entertaining to do here."

"You see Gregor, Kyle here's a bit of a playboy. Always telling me about his crazy weekends and how many chicks' phone numbers he gets," Frank joked. "Good looks, good paycheck, out-of-towner appeal...man I can only imagine what you're doing out there when you're not stuck in our office."

Frank and Gregor smiled and looked at Kyle, seemingly waiting for a witty response. Normally Kyle would stick to the policy he made long ago of trying to appear as much of a straight arrow around coworkers as possible, to compensate for his occasional tendency to come into work struggling from the night before. But in this case he knew he was in good company, so he decided to give these poor guys something to fantasize about.

"Actually...you fellas want to hear a good one?" Kyle inquired.

"Oh man...is the wild child about to open up? Hell yeah we want to hear a good one!" Frank exclaimed.

"Okay then, so check this out...about six months ago, I'm sitting at home watching a basketball game on TV. I had actually just gotten out of the shower, and I'd dried off but didn't get dressed yet because I'd rushed back into my living room to check the score of the game. So I have a towel around my waist, but that's it. I check the score, and the game is tied with only a few minutes left in the second half. So I decide to run over to the fridge, crack a beer, and take a seat on the couch to catch the end of the game live. A few minutes go by, and I hear this knock on my door. I figure it's some solicitor or something so I ignore it, and a few seconds later there's the knocking again. For some reason, and maybe it's because I don't want the knocking to keep distracting me from the game, I decide to answer the door to tell the person knocking to piss off. So I open up the door, and standing there before me I shit you not are two 10 out of 10, knockout girls who are already dressed up to go out. Meanwhile, I'm just standing there in the doorway in a goddamn bath towel, completely caught off my guard."

Frank and Gregor stared at Kyle in amazement, giving him their complete attention as he continued.

"So one of the girls asks me if I know how to get up to the 30th floor of the building? My building is 30 stories tall, with the 30th floor being the Penthouse level, and I live on the 29th floor which is as high as you can get without having a special key. As it so happens, months back I'd managed to get my hands on a key to the Penthouse level that I'd borrowed from the landlord and forgot to give back. I'd mainly just used it a couple of times to go out on the roof and drink a few beers during sunset. So anyway here I am, standing there trying not to make this situation any more awkward than it already is, and I decide to go ahead and help the girls out. I say to them 'Oh yeah, you need a special key for that floor, are you guys meeting someone who lives up there?'"

"They tell me that one of their fathers owns a Penthouse in the building, and they're visiting from out of town and staying at his place for the weekend. He apparently forgot to arrange for them to get a key, so they had gone around knocking on doors on my floor and I was the first to answer. Lucky me."

"Lucky you is right, are you fucking kidding me!" Frank shouted excitedly. A group of older women in a nearby booth shot Frank a dirty look, and he gave them a sheepish smile in apology.

Kyle continued: "So I grab the key, which is in a cabinet by the door, and I walk them up the stairs to the 30th floor entrance. Mind you, I'm still in nothing but a bath towel and a pair of flip flops that I had sitting in my living room. So I swipe them into the door to the 30th, and one of the girls turns back and says to me: 'Thank you so much for helping us out, we would have been stuck here forever without you! And, umm...thank you for giving us something good to look at during the trip.' At first I had no idea what the hell they were talking about...until I remembered that they were walking behind me up the stairs...and I was in a towel...and the stairs are open-sided..."

"Oh man, you gave them a free peep show! Hope it was a warm evening that day sir!" Gregor exclaimed.

"Ha, well I figured I'd probably never see them again, so what the hell, it's not the end of the world. So after that happened I went back to my apartment and got dressed, and I met my friend Travis at a bar down the street for a drink. We hung out there for a few hours, and then Travis decides he wants to check out a new nightclub that just opened up next door. I didn't really feel like it at the time, but we were already really close to my place so I had no valid excuse to head home early. So we go to the club, pay the stupid cover charge and head up to the bar to get some drinks. Well sure enough, who's standing there at the bar right next to me?"

"No!" Frank said, mouth agape.

"You guessed it...the two girls from earlier that night. At first I wasn't sure if they'd recognized me fully-dressed and without my hair all messed up, but they saw me pretty much right away and came right over to me. I must say they did seem pretty excited to see me again, for whatever reason. So they ask Travis and I if we want to do shots with them. Travis immediately says yes, and next thing I know we have like ten of those flaming rum shots lined up in front of us. So the bartender does his thing and lights up the shots, the girls blow them out, and we down them all pretty quickly. Now the girls want to dance, so we go out and tear up the dance floor for another hour or so until the lights come on and last call gets announced. So then the girls say they want to hang out back at my apartment and have one more drink, and we all start walking back there together. When we get inside, one of the girls says she's going to run upstairs to grab some more comfortable clothes for them to change into. So we mix some drinks in my apartment, and Travis and I talk for a bit with the cute blonde girl who stays behind. About 20 minutes go by and the other girl is still not back yet, at which point Travis, who's been holding in a massive piss ever since we did the shots, decides to run to the bathroom quickly before the other girl gets back. But the second he closes the bathroom door...the blonde girl jumps off her chair, grabs me by the collar, and literally drags me into my bedroom. Up to that point, I'd thought I might have had a decent chance of getting with her, but in no way was I expecting that! A gentleman never tells details...but you can use your imagination about what happened next."

"Bravo my friend...BRAVO!" Frank declared, literally standing to give Kyle an ovation. "Oh I hate you SO much now...but I must say, bravo..."

"I think I'm officially submitting my petition to live the rest of my life vicariously through you, if you don't mind."

Kyle laughed. "Ha...do what you gotta do I guess. I swear my life isn't normally anywhere near that exciting, but yes, I will admit that was a pretty fortunate experience."

"Well I don't know how I'm going to concentrate for shit the rest of today after hearing that story. But I suppose we should end this lunch on a high note and head on back," Frank said.

"Yeah I should get back soon too actually. Great meeting you Kyle, thanks for sharing that awesome story with us. From now on I'm going to think twice about not answering my door when opportunity might literally be knocking," Gregor said with a smile, this time affording Kyle a halfway decent handshake.

Kyle and Frank walked to the parking lot across the street where Frank's car was parked, and Kyle hopped into the passenger's seat. As they drove away, Kyle noticed that he was in an unusually upbeat mood for some reason. Maybe it was from reliving the story he'd just told to Frank and Gregor. Overall he did have to admit to himself, he'd had a better time at that lunch than he'd expected to have. Kyle thought about the way Frank and Gregor interacted with each other, playfully ribbing on each other's accomplishments and shortcomings. It was in a way like a geekier version of himself and Travis. But it also seemed like a more stable, balanced friendship than what he and Travis had. It seemed like those two would be friends for life, and part of Kyle wished he had that stability in more of his relationships. Sure, it might be boring at times, but it was also a lot less dramatic and exhausting. There were probably worse things in life to have than predictability.

CHAPTER 7

Jamie wasn't surprised in the slightest that she was currently being scolded by her therapist.

"You really should be coming in here to see me more than once a month. I think we both know that's not going to be enough to get to the root of what's causing you to do these things," said Dr. Chavis, Jamie's off-and-on therapist for about the past six months. When Jamie's anxiety attacks has started to escalate a few months back, Manny had encouraged her to seek help. They'd found Dr. Chavis on a website listing independent mental health providers in the area. Jamie probably could have gotten coverage through her health plan with the hospital, if she wanted go through with filing an official claim. But she was very reluctant to step this far out of her comfort zone, and this more casual arrangement with Dr. Chavis was the only thing keeping her attending therapy sessions at all.

In reality she had very little to complain about in terms of Dr. Chavis' treatment. She was actually surprised at how well she felt her sessions had gone. In her first session, she'd given Dr. Chavis a high-level summary of her life story, and he'd finished the session by asking her a series of personality profile questions. She'd found it interesting at the time to learn about the different personality types, and to get a deeper understanding of where she fit in and which decisions people like her were most inclined to make.

She had felt encouraged after those first few meetings, and had told Manny as much.

"I'm glad you convinced me to finally go through with this. I never realized how refreshing it would feel just to be able to talk to someone who isn't already familiar with your life's story. I like the way Dr. Chavis handles our sessions too. He doesn't make me feel judged. He seems to really listen to what I'm saying. And he doesn't throw too much at you all at once," Jamie had told Manny after completing her third session. Manny was ecstatic that Jamie was showing positive results so quickly. He was growing increasingly concerned the more Jamie tried to put up walls between herself and the outside world. Manny himself was an outgoing person, and enjoyed meeting and interacting with new people as often as possible. As much as he loved Jamie, and as much as he was willing to sacrifice to be with her, it was critical to him that they find what was driving her socially avoidant behavior before it became too much for them to handle.

Now, six months since that promising first session, Jamie again felt the overwhelming guilt and confusion she had felt so many times before. *Why did I fall off the wagon again? What do I have to do to fix this problem? Is it even fixable?*

"As you know, I spoke with Manny briefly yesterday," Dr. Chavis stated. "He did his best to fill me in on the incident you had at the restaurant in Tiburon. I'm sure you're feeling terrible right now, and as always I'm not here to condemn or pass judgement. I'd just like to hear where you think things went wrong, and let's see if we can understand the thought process you were going through that night."

Jamie stared at the floor, trying to organize her thoughts in a way that would make sense. Tears of frustration began to well in her eyes. She called upon her years of experience to push them back down within herself.

"I'm just feeling really frustrated lately, because I feel like whatever my problem is, it keeps compounding and getting worse. I mean last week was like an out of body experience for me. I didn't feel like I was there in that moment with those girls at that restaurant. I could feel myself detaching, and I always end up doing that, and it's just getting so fucking frustrating!" Jamie yelled. She was quite surprised to hear herself curse out loud like that; being raised in a Catholic family, that was basically forbidden growing up. She'd picked it up a little in college, but still didn't make it a regular habit.

"The thing is, I had tried so hard to get myself ready for that night. I mean it's crazy to hear myself even talk like this, saying that I had to psych myself up for what was supposed to be a nice relaxing evening with friends in a beautiful part of town. But I did, I tried to prepare myself mentally to be social and outgoing and come off as a likeable, normal person. And it was working at first! But then in comes that cloud of darkness to ruin everything..."

"These girls are so nice too. They're exactly the type of people I feel like I need in my life. It makes me so sad that I scared them like that. I mean I jumped off the patio into the fucking bay! Oh God it's so embarrassing...I can't even think about it anymore."

"I understand your frustration Jamie, and I appreciate you sharing so honestly with me," Dr. Chavis said. "It's interesting to me that you seem to be so aware of the potential consequences of your actions, both after you commit them and often even before you do. This suggests to me that there is unfortunately an element of self-sabotage involved here. I'd say more so than a traditional anxiety disorder or something along those lines. Subconsciously, it's like you want to keep yourself from moving forward and getting on with your life for some reason."

"But why would that be though? I'm miserable with the way my life is going now. I have so little to look forward to, and so many things to be fearful of. I'd give anything to be like any one of those girls from the restaurant and lead a normal, happy life. I feel like that's almost impossible for me at this point though...like it's already too late."

"Trust me Jamie...it's never too late," Dr. Chavis replied.

"I've seen patients far further down a path of self-destruction than you, who were able to turn their lives around and get back on track. I wish I had a magic quick-fix for you that would enable you to do so as well. But the key here really is to find and address what is bothering you head on, to acknowledge and accept how it has affected your life thus far, and to make a conscious decision to put it in the past and move forward. There are no short-cuts for that. Unfortunately your issue seems fairly deep-seated, and has been tougher to diagnose than most. It's going to take some more work on both of our parts to get to the bottom of it."

"I hear what you're saying...and I agree. I just don't know what else I can tell you. I mean we've covered my childhood in pretty thorough detail already. Could have been better, could have been worse. My parents separating when I was still pretty young could have affected me, I guess. It was hard dealing with that at the time, but I feel like I got over it quickly and was able to accept my new situation in life. My father still continued to support the family as best as he could, which was good enough for the four of us to get by. As I told you, I have fallen out of touch with him in recent years, but back then we were still able to see each other fairly often and have a good time together. The man my mother remarried is a good man, and living with them while I saved up money for school really wasn't so bad. I actually feel like my brother and sister had it tougher than I did growing up, and they both are doing great with their lives. Overall I'd say I'm pretty okay with how things ended up for us, and I'm very grateful I was at least able to get through school and get on a solid career path."

"So you're still enjoying what you do, even in the midst of all of these challenges?" Dr. Chavis asked.

"Yes I am, maybe even more so because it's given me a safe-haven from what else is going on in my life. Thank God my issues haven't spilled into my work at the hospital. I've somehow been able to block it out, and just focus on what I have to do that day to provide the best patient care I can. I'm thankful for being able to help people for a living."

"That's excellent that your work provides that positive outlet for you. Now we just need to figure out how to translate that into a healthier lifestyle outside of the job. If we could for a second, could you tell me again about what your life was like after your parents split, before your mother remarried?" Dr. Chavis asked.

"Okay...," Jamie responded. "Like I said, my father moved out while my mother, older brother, younger sister and I stayed in the house. He still supported us with what money he could, but we all had to pitch in to make things work. My mother started picking up more hours at the restaurant where she worked. My brother got a job with a local construction company. And when my little sister didn't need babysitting, I worked a few hours at an ice cream shop in the neighborhood. This kept us all pretty busy, and unfortunately my grades did begin to slip a bit when I added these after-school responsibilities. Then about a year after my dad moved out is when I first met Mr. Harris."

"Yes, you've mentioned in the past that he was a very influential person in your life. Tell me a little bit more about your relationship," Dr. Chavis said.

"Well I met Mr. Harris one day walking home from working at the ice cream shop. He joked with me about how fast my ice cream was melting and getting all over my hands. I thought he was a funny old man, so I followed him around his yard as he did his gardening. He had a beautiful yard full of flowers, which he said had been a passion of his wife who had passed away the year prior. He kept the flowers alive and well maintained in her memory. I thought it was really sad and sweet, so I decided to try to come over and help him with his yard work as often as I could so it would make his wife up in heaven happy."

"It was actually a lot of fun hanging out with Mr. Harris.

He taught me a lot about many different things. He was a retired businessman, and mainly kept to himself now that he was older. He read a lot though, and he seemed to know a lot about a wide variety of topics. My mother took quickly to me and Mr. Harris spending time together after school, since he began tutoring me on some subjects that I was struggling with. He also would come over to our house from time to time when something broke and help out with some simple repairs. My mother would usually try to get him to stay for dinner, but he always felt bad for imposing, so she'd at least send him home with enough food to provide a few good home-cooked meals."

Dr. Chavis nodded, observing Jamie's body language as she continued to speak about her childhood.

"For a couple of years I would go over to his house at least a few times a week when I didn't have to babysit. I really felt like he was having a positive influence on me. My grades started to turn around, and I started to feel more confident in my ability to succeed academically and in other areas. I don't know, I just really liked his approach to life. It was a positive outlook, but it didn't come off to me as preachy. He found happiness in the simple things in life, and never seemed to get stressed out about anything, even when his health started to take a turn for the worse. I just really saw him as someone to look up to."

Dr. Chavis finished recording some notes, straightening his glasses. "So this should take you right about to the point where you and your family moved away from your hometown, somewhat suddenly if I recall correctly?"

"Yes we did...and that was pretty hard for me. I was barely through my first year of high school, and I didn't want to start over at a new place. But mostly, it was hard for me to say goodbye to Mr. Harris. He had recently been diagnosed with Stage 1 lymphoma, and even though he promised that he felt fine and wasn't going to let it get him down, I still felt terrible leaving him all alone like that. I knew I would miss him too, and I didn't feel like I was able to properly thank him for all he had done for me. I asked my mother if we could have a going away party and invite him to do something nice for him, but for some reason she seemed fine with just blowing him off and getting out of town as quickly as we could. So the day we left town, I went over to his house to say goodbye, but no one answered. It's sad that our friendship ended that way. I often wonder what ever happened to him."

"So how did the move end up for you and your family?" asked Dr. Chavis.

"It ended up working out okay. My mother told us she wanted to move to a bigger town for better career opportunities. She ended up getting a pretty good job in an attorney's office, which is actually where she met the man she would eventually remarry. I found a new school that I liked, and ended up finishing high school with decent grades. After that I took a couple years to work in a doctor's office so I could get some exposure to the medical field. From there I was able to save up enough money to attend nursing school...and that's basically everything really."

"I see. Well thank you for sharing, I know it's tough for you to go down Memory Lane yet again. Although it does seem that there are certainly plenty of good memories mixed in there with any bad ones. Our time today's almost up, but here's what I'm thinking: I'd like you to start coming in to see me twice a month for the next few months. And normally I would request more time, but I actually have something else in mind for you that I think would help you. There's a group therapy session focused on self-management that is held weekly over in San Marcos. I know the guy there Darren who runs it. He's very effective at getting people to explore what's really bothering them, and to talk it out in a social setting. I think that aspect of being around other people and listening to them open up would be really beneficial for you. Here's the info," Dr.Chavis said, as he handed Jamie a card. "I'd suggest you go as often as you can, and then we can discuss what you think about it in our sessions. That sound okay?"

"That sounds fine with me. I'm willing to try almost anything at this point," Jamie said earnestly. "Thanks again Dr. Chavis for all your help. I apologize I haven't been seeing you regularly like I should, but I promise I'll get better at making a consistent effort."

As Jamie exited the office and made her way back to her car, she was feeling slightly more optimistic about her situation. At the very least, there were people out there who cared about her and wanted to see her get better. If she could just figure out what event in her life could be triggering these episodes, and get a handle on how to deal with it properly, she believed she could at least have a fighting chance at one day finding happiness.

CHAPTER 8

Kyle had vowed to call his parents the week before, and last Wednesday, he had even set aside time to make the call. He'd planned to do it from work at the end of the day, when things were slow enough that he could still get some email done while zoning out his parents on the other end of the line. For some reason or another it had completely slipped his mind, and he'd managed to forget about it for another week and a half until his younger brother had sent him a text message that Sunday: *Mom and Dad would still really like to catch up with you and see how you're doing. Please give us a call today if you have time.*

Kyle immediately felt remorse over blowing off his family yet again. It used to be that he'd at least remember he was supposed to call them, but end up postponing it in favor of doing something more exciting. Now he was starting to forget that he should even be making the effort in the first place.

Kyle did love his family in his own way, but it had become almost unbearable for him to listen to the boring hometown gossip his mom would spout out, or the generic words of wisdom his dad would try to impart upon him. It'd been a long time since he was a teenager, but they still often talked to him like he was one. Kyle knew it was hard for them to watch him grow up and leave town, especially with what happened to Ben, his older brother. Now that his younger brother Andrew was finally getting his act together and looking at going off to college, he knew that sooner rather than later he needed to start making more of an effort to be an attentive family member.

At around 3:15 PM on a lazy Sunday afternoon, Kyle finally picked up the phone to call home. After only two rings, his mother quickly answered. "Kyle is that you?" she asked.

"Yep it is, hi Mom!" Kyle replied, trying to sound as enthusiastic as possible.

"Kyle how are you doing? Guys get in here, Kyle's on the phone!" Kyle could hear shuffling in the background as his brother and father entered the room, most likely the kitchen.

"Kyle I'm going to have Andrew put you on speakerphone so we can all talk at once. Andrew can you help me out honey?" Kyle's mother asked.

Kyle heard a click, and could now hear his father in the background yelling. "Hey son, how is the land of fruits and nuts treating you?"

"Ha, very funny Dad," Kyle replied. He'd heard that line from his father many times since his move. He was all too familiar with his father's repertoire of jokes, consisting only of about ten lines his father insisted on recycling nearly every time they spoke.

"What have you been up to out there? How are things at the university? Any ladies in your life?" his mother inquired all at once.

"Oh you know, I feel like I'm still just kind of getting acclimated to the way things work out here. It takes a while to get used to everything, and it's a whole different world out here. But it's been exciting, and I'm having a good time. The job is going well. Nothing too interesting to report but things are moving along fine, and there's plenty of job stability working up in this area." Kyle knew he was already running out of things to say to his parents.

"That's good to hear! Andrew is thinking about starting college sometime next year, aren't you Andrew? Maybe he can be a brilliant scientist just like his big brother!" Kyle's mother gushed.

"Actually he wants to go into civil engineering. Be a city planner just like his old man," Kyle's father rebutted.

"So what else is going on in your life? I've heard there's so much to do in San Francisco, you must be seeing so many neat things!" Kyle's mother said excitedly.

Kyle kept his answer pretty generic as usual. "Yeah it's great, there's definitely a lot to see and do. Work is keeping me pretty busy, but I try to get out and checkout the parks and museums and stuff when I can. We don't have the constant sunshine you guys have over there in Arizona though, so I'm indoors a good amount just sitting around watching TV in my free time. The Giants had a pretty good year so I've been watching a lot of baseball games. Dad are you still following Arizona?"

"Yeah I watched most of their games this season. That damn new manager they have is screwing up the team royally though, can't find a starting pitcher to save his life. It was a rough season to watch," Kyle's father said bitterly.

"Yep I hear you on that. Well I'm sure they'll get it turned around next season. How's the rest of the family doing? Haven't caught up with any of them in a while." Kyle was already getting antsy with the phone call, but knew he should try to hold out as long as he could. He knew that asking about the extended family would put his mom on a rant for at least a good ten minutes, during which he could watch sports highlights on TV in the background.

Kyle listened passively as his mother continued to fill him in on all the drama going on in the family. He heard her mention something about one of his cousins signing up recently for the Army Reserve. Also something else about his aunt moving down to Tucson to take a teaching job there. Kyle mostly just muttered "Yeah" and "Oh wow" every few sentences while his mom continued to ramble. He could almost imagine his dad and brother trying to sneak out of the room while the endless discourse continued.

Kyle decided he needed to try to get off the phone before

his parents had a chance to ask him about the holidays. He knew he was overdue for a visit, but he just didn't feel up to dealing with holiday travel this year. Actually, Kyle had been hoping to visit Oregon with some friends at the end of the year to checkout Portland. But before he could wind down the conversation, right on cue his mom popped the question. "Kyle, are you going to be able to make it back home for Christmas?"

Caught a bit off guard, Kyle scrambled to come up with an excuse that would at least allow him to postpone the official announcement. "Not sure yet. I mean I'd like to get back and see you guys, but December is going to be a pretty busy month at the lab, and I'm not sure if I'll be able to get that much time off. I'll definitely keep you guys posted though."

Kyle heard the silence on the other end of the line. He could tell his parents were disappointed. But his mom soon regained her upbeat demeanor. "Well we'd love to see you if you can make it, but we understand if you can't. We don't want to take up your entire day today, so we'll let you go here in a minute unless you had anything else you wanted to fill us in on?"

"Nope, I think that's about everything. It was really great catching up with you guys. I'll try not to wait so long next time between calls," Kyle said, still feeling bad about basically blowing them off for the holidays.

"It's no problem, we understand you're busy. Do try to call though again before Thanksgiving if you can." Kyle's mother asked.

"Definitely, I will do that. Okay well I love you guys, say hi to everyone else for me and I'll talk to you soon," Kyle finished. He then heard his brother take the phone off speaker and whisper to him "Hold on a sec" while his parents left the room. His brother had pulled this trick a few times previously, since it was sometimes tough for him to get Kyle on the phone otherwise.

"Hey bro, they're out in the living room now," Kyle's brother Andrew said quietly. "Brutal huh? Can't blame you for not calling more often, I wouldn't spend my time doing that either if I lived in San Francisco. I can barely stand living here anymore. Almost got enough money saved up to move in with my buddy Jason near campus. Can't happen soon enough!"

"Yeah man, I'd probably be going crazy too if I was still shacked up there. I do feel bad about not calling or visiting you guys more often though. I'll try to work on that. Well anyway good for you for hopefully getting out soon. You'll have a lot of fun going off to college, and I'm sure you're gonna do great in whatever you end up doing."

"Thanks Kyle, I appreciate that. I'm also hoping to save enough money for a road trip up to see you someday before I start school. That is of course, if I'm invited?"

"Of course you are lil bro, anytime! Would love to show you around the town up here," Kyle replied.

"Thanks man. Hey, I wanted to make sure you don't forget: October 13th is the 15th anniversary of when Ben died, and Mom is planning a special memorial service at the church this year. She's been working on it for a long time, and I think it would be really important to her if you can make sure to call on that day and send her some love."

"OF COURSE I'm going to remember to call on the 13th," Kyle snipped, almost defensively. He quickly collected himself. "I mean, yeah I'll definitely make sure I do. Thanks for giving me the heads up."

Kyle hung up the phone with his brother, and took a moment to reflect on where his life had taken him in the past couple years. Kyle had certainly worked hard to get to where he was, but at that moment he wasn't feeling like he really deserved much of what he had. In his mind, there was no doubt that his brother Ben, when he was alive, was ten times the son and older brother that Kyle was. Ben wouldn't even let traveling around the world get in the way of making sure the family felt loved and appreciated.

His family had been through a lot with Ben's passing at such a young age. Kyle wished he had in him that magic spark that Ben had. He wished he did a better job of being more considerate of other people. He'd give almost anything to know how Ben did it, how he maintained that balance. He'd give almost anything to have his older brother back.

CHAPTER 9

"Dude, we should be doing this every night! Where the hell have you been?" snarked Travis, as he took a seat next to Kyle on the BART train destined for San Jose. Kyle knew this particular guilt trip from Travis was probably coming, and at the moment he didn't feel much like dignifying it with an acknowledgement.

"I mean what's the point of us moving to a place like this if we're not going to take advantage of it? I came 1,800 miles across the country just to keep your ass company. Least you could do is pretend to be grateful, and let me show you how we should live it up in this town!"

After nearly seven years as friends, Kyle was well aware of Travis' penchant for using sarcastic accusations as a motivational tactic. In fact it used to work quite well, back when Kyle and Travis were tackling the bar scene in Tempe. In truth, Kyle did feel a little bad about not spending more time with Travis in recent weeks. But with Travis' recent brush with the law and Kyle's surprisingly mounting workload, he knew his reasons were plenty valid. Besides, even if Kyle went out partying with Travis every day of the week, chances were he still wouldn't be satisfied.

"Well I don't know what kind of 'Save the World' hippie crap you've been working on in that lab of yours, but while you're out frolicking in academia, I've been getting my ass reamed by my new boss for six weeks straight," remarked Travis. "And right now they just have me processing the already completed insurance policies, which I'm fairly confident a gerbil with dementia could handle. Whoa is fuckin' me if I ever make it up to agent and have to sell actual policies for that shithead…"

"You really should be thankful just to have a job man. Especially if you have to start cutting out early for those counseling sessions the court is making you do. I'm just saying, you're getting too old to go back to hustling for a living."

"Shit man, sometimes I wonder…," Travis said pensively. "I guess I really don't know what to think. I mean, I'm grateful and everything to still sort of have some of my youth left. I'm not the creepy old guy out at the bar just yet. But imagine how awesome it would be to have the memories of someone who's really lived life, ya know? Even if it meant you had to be an old man, and you were closer to death."

"What do you mean…like a famous musician from back in the day or something?" Kyle asked, confused by Travis' line of questioning but somewhat intrigued.

"Yeah. Like say you could trade places right now with…I don't know…Tom Petty. He's probably twice our age, but the dude's been famous for like 30 years. Would you be willing to give up those years of your life, in exchange for the memories he has? I mean think of all the packed concerts he's played, all the girls who worship him, all the insane partying he's done in far away countries we'll never get a chance to travel to in our lives. Would you trade 30 years of a par-for-the-course life to have those experiences in your head? I don't know man…sometimes I think I would."

"No way, not me," Kyle replied. "In fact, I'd be willing to bet you Tom Petty would seriously consider making that trade with you. All the money and fame in the world can't make up for time you can never have back."

"You're crazy! Petty wouldn't make that trade in a millions years!" Travis exclaimed. "Actually, I guess maybe he's a bad example for this. Since I think he's only in his 60's still, and he probably still gets laid way more often than I do."

Kyle laughed. "You may finally have a valid point there my friend."

As the train pulled up to the stop for San Jose State University, Travis received a call on his phone. "Yeah we're on our way. Probably about five blocks out. Yeah we'll stop and get some booze to bring over. Alright see you soon man," Travis finished as he hung up.

"I still can't believe you're dragging me to on-campus party. You do realize we're both 32 years old, and I happen to work at the public university two towns over?" Kyle asked, shaking his head.

"I can't believe you're complaining about this! We get to party on campus again like the old days! And it's gonna be mostly grad students here anyway, so we're not THAT much older. You'll probably love it, a house full of lifetime academics just like yourself. What, did you have something else better planned for this fine Friday evening?" Travis inquired.

Truth is Kyle hadn't had much going on outside of work for a while now. He had started to feel guilty about the level of partying and carousing he'd been engaging in with Travis, and had wanted to take a break for a little bit. He'd made efforts to refocus himself at work, and made some solid strides in ensuring he'd be positively reviewed by Stan at the end of the year. He'd also joined a gym near his apartment and had been working out more often than he had in years, which was helping him clear his mind and get to sleep more easily. All in all it had been a good couple of weeks in the right direction for Kyle. But man had it been boring.

"I'm not complaining bud. Actually, I'm glad we're doing this. I could go for blowing off some steam," Kyle said.

"Happy to hear it! Let's swing by this liquor store real quick and get some beer for the party." Kyle and Travis stocked up and made the remaining three block walk to the house party. They entered the house and made their way to the kitchen, where Travis saw his friend Moby, who was currently living at the house.

"Hey Moby, what's up brotha? Hey this is my buddy Kyle, came down from San Fran to get crazy with us tonight."

"How goes it Kyle? Well mi casa es su casa, so help yourself to anything we've got. Drinking games in the living room, bonfire and barbecue out back if you wanna check it out," Moby informed them.

Kyle and Travis made their way to the backyard which was packed with people, most of whom were either drinking and playing bean bag toss, huddled near the grill eating burgers, or just hanging out and talking heatedly about various topics. Kyle and Travis each cracked a beer and decided to head over to the grill area.

"Way to work those burgers man, you've got some serious skills!" Travis directed at the long-haired gentleman currently manning the grill.

"Thanks dude, yeah I share this house with Moby so I'm always out here cooking on this thing. My name's Mario. You guys up for chugging one to celebrate the start of the weekend?"

"In!" Travis responded, as the three of them quickly pounded their beers, with Travis immediately opening them fresh replacements.

"What are you going to school here for?" Travis inquired, as Mario deftly removed a stack of perfectly cooked burgers, and replaced the grill space with a package of bratwursts.

"Culinary school. Just kidding, I'm studying web development and database administration. How about you guys, you taking classes here?"

"No...we've actually got a couple of years on you I think. Both finished up grad school a few years back," Travis fibbed. "I'm in finance and Kyle is in scientific research."

"Well awesome, welcome to the party. Feel free to grab a burger and mingle around," offered Mario.

Travis and Kyle each took a plate and found a seat in the circle of lawn chairs nearby. Sitting there as the sun was setting with a case of cold beer, good food in hand, and surrounded by interesting and attractive people, they were both starting to feel pretty good about their decision to attend the party. Kyle gave Travis a pat on the back as he stood up to grab another set of beers from the cooler. With both of them about four deep at this point, they decided to walk over to the bean bag toss setup, where a game was just finishing up.

"Great game guys. Hey, you two want in next?" the guy standing behind the boards directed at Travis and Kyle.

"As long as I can play this game with a beer in my hand, I'm in!" chimed Travis. With Kyle as his teammate, they decided to play a best-of-three series against the other two guys. They split the first two games, and Travis and Kyle took the other team to within two points of winning the third game before eventually being defeated. Kyle decided to stay and play another round, while Travis went inside the house to check out the drinking games with Moby and his friends.

After about another hour of playing the game with moderate success, and with several more beers down the hatch, Kyle made his way over to a group of people in the backyard who were sitting in a circle of chairs around a fire, passing around a metal pipe packed with weed and discussing what appeared to be the upcoming political election in California. Kyle had never really considered himself politically minded, though lately he'd been reading more than he usually did about global affairs, and felt that he had a decent set of core opinions. He found a cluster of empty chairs near the circle and took a seat, listening to the passionate debate while enjoying his beer and watching the fire slowly burn.

"I for one believe you need to earn what you get in life. I wasn't raised by wealthy parents who made millions just buying property at the right time, and then that paid for everything we ever needed in life," said one of the guys in the circle, who appeared to be one of the few who was neither drinking nor partaking in the pot smoking. "I worked my ass off during undergrad here, so that I could get a scholarship to go to grad school and set myself up for a solid career."

"Is that all that's really important to you though? Setting yourself up to have a prestigious title on your business card and earn an impressive salary? That just..that comes off as pretty self-involved to me. Do you really think that that way of living is going to give you a fulfilling life?" countered one of the girls sitting across from Kyle in the pot circle, slurring her last few words as she finished.

"Yeah, it's that selfish 'me-first' attitude that got this country into economic trouble in the first place," added another guy who had just joined the conversation a few minutes earlier. "Everybody was exploiting every cutthroat tactic they had to try and make as much money and climb as high on the corporate ladder as they could. Then when the world realized that it wasn't sustainable, everything collapsed."

"You're crazy, that's not what screwed up the economy at all!" said the sober guy. "The real problem is the incredible levels of debt that the developed nations of the world have accumulated. That debt has mainly come from government spending run amok on socialist welfare programs. I mean, just look at the state of California if you want a shining example. If more people would stop expecting handouts and start taking accountability for their own lives, we could reign in that spending and get control over our mounting debt."

"This is America though...everyone here deserves a fair shot! When people are being denied basic human rights like health care...education, mainly because the prices have been driven up so high by greedy millionaires...something is seriously wrong with the way our country operates!" the drunk girl rebutted.

By now Kyle was following the conversation with a high level of interest. Everyone involved was making pretty solid points, he thought, and he was having a tough time choosing a side. A few of the others in the group chimed in with their thoughts, and were for the most part backing either the sober guy or the drunk girl. Kyle realized he hadn't been involved with an in-depth conversation like this in a very long time. Most of his weekly interactions consisted of boring small talk with his coworkers. It was stimulating to hear these people defend something so passionately, something that really did fundamentally mean something in the world.

Kyle grabbed for another beer from his cooler, feeling only a couple more left inside. He had to admit he was feeling pretty buzzed at the moment. In the back corner of the yard there was a small group still playing the bean bag game under the outdoor lighting. Most of the people who were by the grill earlier had gone inside. Kyle was now wondering where Travis was, and when he took out his phone to send him a text, he heard a deep voice asking him a question.

"Hey quiet guy in the back, want to get in on this conversation? What are your thoughts?" asked a rather muscular gentleman Kyle had seen hanging out with Mario by the grill earlier.

"Umm...I don't really know," Kyle responded. He was caught off guard, and was having a tough time collecting his thoughts on the spot like this. The multitude of beers he had put down that night weren't making it any easier either. "I guess I'd say that you're all making good points. People in this country should at least have the bare necessities, to give them a chance at achieving a decent quality of life. But you do have to show you're willing to work for it. I think a lot of people are starting to think they're owed something just for being born in this country, and that's not the case," Kyle was able to muster.

"But what about the disadvantaged, how are they supposed to work their way up to a higher status if they aren't starting on a level playing field? The rich get richer and the poor get poorer. That's fucked up," the muscular guy responded.

"I just think that's an overly simplistic way of looking at it," Kyle replied. "I mean you can't deny this country got to where it is today by welcoming those who were willing to take big risks for the chance at a big payout. And now the rest of the world probably looks up to us as a model of how they should be taking risks to improve their governments and infrastructures. We've taken on a responsibility to be leaders in the world, and demonstrate how even a country of our size and diversity can adapt and improve itself. All this bickering between extremists is getting people nowhere, and it's embarrassing for our country. I think about what it must be like to be born into a third world country...and then when I see that the leading country of the free world is riddled with this much inertia and dishonesty, how does my third world country ever stand a chance?" Kyle was nearly blown away by the rant he'd just put together. Save for maybe athletics, he hadn't strung together that many strong opinions about a topic in a long time. The muscular guy he had been speaking to, he noticed, seemed rather agitated by losing a point in the argument.

Kyle shrugged it off and opened another beer, and began talking to the couple sitting next to him, both of whom offered their support of the points Kyle had made on his little speech. The couple was from the San Diego area originally, and were both in dental school at the university.

They asked Kyle about his move out to San Francisco, and about his job at the lab, which Kyle noticed was much easier for him to converse upon when he was inebriated. The couple mentioned they were both starting to get into sailing in the Bay during their free time, and Kyle informed them that he was looking to pick up another hobby he could do outdoors. The couple invited him to come out on the boat the next time they planned to sail, and Kyle exchanged phone numbers with Alan, the boyfriend, so they could coordinate.

Kyle noticed he was now on his last beer, and decided it would probably be a good time to find Travis and decide what they wanted to do for the remainder of the night. Just as he was about to stand, the muscular guy from the earlier debate approached Kyle, readily apparent that he was not in a good mood.

"You know, you're wrong about everything you said earlier. Without people like us challenging the system, our country would just keep going down the same path of self-destruction it's been on for years. What you said was bullshit!"

"Okay, whatever man...it's not that big of a deal. I just said what I thought at the time, but if I thought about it a little longer, I'd probably end up agreeing more with your side," Kyle said, attempting to defuse the situation.

"Oh, so we're trying to have a serious debate here, and you're just faking it the whole time? What's the matter with you? And what exactly do you mean by 'your side'? What am I some pussy liberal to you?" the guy responded angrily. Kyle could sense his own temper starting to rise, and he had no intention of ending the night with a black eye, so he slowly began to rise out of his chair in an attempt to walk away and keep the situation from escalating.

"That's what I thought," the guy said as Kyle continued walking past him. "Not enough balls to stand up for what you believe in."

Kyle knew that he should just let that comment go, let it roll off his back. He knew it...but then he thought about how much it would eat at him later if he did. The following week, when he was bored at work and he had time to think back to that moment. He knew he'd be pissed at himself that he just took the insult and did nothing about it. Kyle was aware it was the wrong decision...but he decided that he had to take the bait.

"Hey fuck you asshole. This isn't the debate team, we're all just sitting here trying to chill out and have a good time, and your panties are all in a bunch about some stupid comment I made 20 minutes ago. Get a fucking life."

In the blink of an eye, the guy stormed after Kyle and stepped right up to his face. Kyle was shocked at how instantaneously the guy was on him, and feeling that the guy was about to throw a punch, Kyle pushed him in the chest as hard as he could, knocking him to the ground. The guy quickly shot up and ran back at Kyle, grabbing him forcefully by the arm and trying to sling him to the ground. Kyle stumbled but was able to stay on his feet, as the guy came after him again. This time he connected a punch to Kyle's midsection. Kyle responded by kicking him in the leg, hard enough to back him up a few feet. Kyle could now hear yelling from the crowd that was forming in the back yard, as those who were inside the house were now running out to see what was happening.

The guy came swinging at Kyle again, and Kyle sidestepped just in time to dodge the punch and land a solid one of his own to the back of the head. Quickly swinging around, the guy landed a hard punch to Kyle's ribcage. Kyle felt pain shoot through the left side of his body, but he shook it off and kept approaching. As they were about to engage again, a group of guys jumped in between them, demanding that they break up the fight. The guy Kyle had fought was still screaming and swinging wildly as his friends attempted to subdue him. Kyle saw Travis running towards him, grabbing him by the shoulder. "Dude what the fuck did you do?? Let's get the hell out of here!!"

Travis led Kyle through the side yard gate out towards the street. They jogged quickly a few blocks away from the house, before either of them spoke.

"What the hell happened back there? How did that fight start?" Travis asked.

"That asshole got all pissed off about some harmless thing I said and started throwing punches at me! I didn't even do anything!" Kyle said, exasperated.

"What do you mean you didn't do anything? You must have done something to piss him off that much," Travis replied.

Kyle looked down at his shirt, which was ripped from the right sleeve down to about halfway through his torso. He checked for blood but didn't see anything visible at the moment.

"Well I guess I did talk back to him a little. Actually I think I called him a 'fucking asshole' right before he attacked me," Kyle told Travis, a smile starting to creep in on his face.

"Ha are you serious! Dude, you're my hero!" Travis declared. "That was so crazy. I'm inside just chilling and smoking weed with Moby and all the sudden I hear everybody outside yelling like someone's on fire, and I look out the window and I see you trading punches with some jacked motherfucker. Craziest shit I've seen in a long time. You okay?"

"Yeah I think I'm fine. Chest and stomach are a little banged up, he got me pretty good but I don't see blood anywhere. I'll probably have a wicked bruise for a few days," Kyle said. "I feel terrible that I got into a fight at your buddy's house. He was so nice to invite us over and now he's probably gonna hate us both."

"Oh dude, don't worry about him. It's totally cool. I heard a bunch of people say that that guy you fought is a huge dick and nobody likes him. They'll probably be glad somebody put him in his place," Travis replied.

"Okay good...that makes me feel a little better. Let's jump on this train and head back to my place, you can crash there if you want. I think I'm gonna need another drink after all that excitement," Kyle said.

"Sounds like a plan to me. Kyle Drake: Ultimate Fighting Champion. Who would have ever known..."

CHAPTER 10

As Travis pulled into the parking lot of the San Marcos Counseling Center, an unexpected pang of guilt stung him sharply. Luckily for Travis, over the years he'd become skilled at converting these moments of introspection into self-satisfying cynicism and contempt for his environment. *What kind of arbitrary bullshit was this anyway? Court-mandated group therapy? For selling a little bit of weed to a consenting, full-grown adult man?* Jesus his luck had been rotten lately.

He'd been through this therapy crap before, after he was expelled from his first high school, and during one of his mother's rare moments of feigning interest in his life. Over the course of the eight or so sessions he'd had with Dr. Landry, all he'd really taken away from it was that his lot in life sucked, and only a biblical combination of struggle and faith would provide him with an inkling of a chance to escape his destiny as a born loser. Oh, and also that therapists are wannabe intellectuals who've never had the balls to take their own advice.

Dreading what he now had to endure for the next two hours, Travis slowly walked up the stairs to the main entrance of the building. *I'm sure this group leader will be a real fuckin' gem*, he thought to himself as he scribbled his name on the sign-in sheet and took a spot in the circle of seats closest to the exit. He watched as the rest of the group started to shuffle in. Two of the older women who were now sitting in the circle across from him were old-school prostitutes, Travis was convinced, judging from their amply exposed and sun-damaged cleavage, and their 80's-style teased perms. The man sitting next to them was a clean-cut, relatively well-dressed guy who appeared to be very nervous, and was a couple years younger than Travis if he had to guess. *Wonder what he's in here for, probably computer fraud or some shit*, Travis thought. To Travis' right, two attractive girls had just taken a seat. One was short and very cute with olive skin, and looked like she was at least partially Hispanic. The other one was a blonde who, upon further examination by Travis, happened to have a pretty smoking body, and dressed like she knew how to have a good time. Maybe these sessions wouldn't be so painful after all.

A tall, lightly-bearded man who was chiseled in that lean, vegan sort of way took a seat at the head of the group, carrying a small set of books. *This must be the guy*, Travis thought. He did actually look a lot more normal than Travis would have guessed. Not the type of guy he would expect would be willing to waste his life providing public service to groups of rejects such as this. Travis surmised that he must have had a nasty drug habit back in the day, probably as a roadie for Warrant or something lame.

The group leader began: "Hello everybody, thank you for all for coming to our session today. My name is Darren Clark, and I'll be facilitating these group meetings over the next few weeks. I really do appreciate your openness and cooperation during these sessions. I know some of you are not here voluntarily, but rather as part of a diversion program. Just let me tell you that I've been at this for a long time, including sitting where you're all sitting right now, and I have absolutely no intention of wasting anybody's time here."

The group then began the typical "tell me a little bit about yourself" introductions, though fortunately starting the opposite direction from where Travis was seated. *Good*, he thought, *now I can zone out and fantasize about that naughty little blonde and what brought her in here today. Hopefully it was something good like daddy issues or drug addiction, and now she wants to replace those needs with something a little bit more "nourishing".*

The group continued slowly around the circle with the check-ins. Travis paid enough attention to learn that one of the two presumed "working gals" was into shooting up heroin with her daughter, and had been given a wakeup call recently after her daughter narrowly survived an overdose. Another guy in the group had gotten drunk at his job as a forklift operator, and had errantly dropped a load of landscaping rocks that almost crushed a nearby customer. A young black guy named Harold recounted to the group a story about how he had lost his academic scholarship to a university in Oakland due to falling back in with his childhood friends, who were now gang members, and who he had worked so hard to separate himself from. *A veritable who's who of sob stories and misplaced intentions*, Travis thought. As Travis realized his turn was approaching quickly, he decided to compose himself and frame what he wanted to say, so he could hopefully get this over with as quickly as possible.

"Thank you Harold, I'm sure I speak for the group when I say I appreciate your candidness in revealing so much about your past," finished Darren. Pointing a gentle hand at Travis, he politely asked "Would you like to give us your story at this time?"

Travis slowly arose, quietly cleared his throat, and began: "Hello everyone, Travis here. I've only lived in California for about four months now, but I've already managed to get myself into trouble with the state." *Tough crowd*, Travis thought. He expected a little bit of a laugh there, but so far all eyes were on him intently. He decided to continue on before he had the chance to get nervous. "I'm specifically here today because I was recently busted for selling drugs outside of a Giants game. I wish I could say that this was my first time dealing, but I'd be lying. I've just never really been caught before. Instead of pursuing sentencing the court recommended I attend these meetings. I'm admittedly a little skeptical about therapy and shrinks and stuff like that, but part of me is happy I have this opportunity. I've never really had it easy in life, and I've had to do some rough things to get by. I don't want to bore you with my family history, but let's just say my parents weren't exactly Clair and Cliff Huxtable. I grew up in a poor area of suburban Phoenix, Arizona, and was barely able to make it through high-school there. After working some odd jobs and doing some 'extracurriculars' on the side to make money, I finally made enough to move out of that town. I decided to set up near the university, and over the next few years I was lucky enough to meet some solid, dependable people who were able to help keep me on track a bit. At least for a while. After a few more dustups in Arizona, I decided to follow my buddy Kyle out to the Bay Area and see if I could get a fresh start. And I'm working on it, I really am. But judging by the fact that I'm here, I obviously still have some work to do. I guess that's about it, thanks everyone for listening."

An empathetic applause arose from the group, and Travis couldn't help but feel somewhat proud of himself. That silver tongue of his had worked its magic again. What he had told the group was actually pretty true, technically. But he knew that a lot of people out there, and certainly some in this room, had had it much worse than him growing up, and he could give two shits about sympathy from a group of strangers. That spiel he had just given would buy him a lot of slack-off time in the sessions to come. So mission accomplished, he figured.

After the final two group members had finished their check-ins, Darren suggested they all take a 15 minute break. Some of the group went outside to grab a smoke. Travis headed over to the coffee counter, and started filling a styrofoam cup when he heard a gentle voice say "Travis, right? That was very touching what you said in group earlier." Travis turned and saw it was the cute girl he had noticed at the beginning of the meeting. She continued: "I don't know if you remember my introduction, but I've been going through some tough times recently as well, and I wouldn't have be able get through it without having a great support group of friends to lean on when I needed to. I hope you can find that out here in your new home too."

Travis honestly had zero recollection of the girl's introduction, let alone her name, and would have just started rattling off Hispanic girl names if not for the "Jamie" nametag on her left breast.

"Oh, well thank you very much Jamie. I do remember your story, and believe it or not it actually inspired me to dig a little deeper and share a little bit more about myself than I had originally intended." This statement received a warm smile from Jamie, and Travis knew he had to go in for the kill.

"Do you live around this area, or what part of town are you in?" Travis inquired.

"Oh, I'm across town over in Fremont. I live in an apartment with my boyfriend Manny. Grew up upstate in Chico, but have lived down here for about five years now."

"Very cool, very cool. I'm over in Hayward, not too far away. I'm working at an insurance agency over there. I actually just got a promotion to Senior Agent, so I guess things are going pretty well for me at work at least. How about yourself, what do you do?"

"I'm a registered nurse at Fremont Memorial. Pediatric unit. It's nice there. I love helping the kids and seeing how strong they can be in facing some of the debilitating conditions and challenges they have to face."

"That sounds great. I love kids too actually!" Travis fibbed rather egregiously. "Hey it sounds like they're about to call us back into the session. I don't mean to be too forward, but would it be okay if we hung out sometime outside of group? I don't know a ton of people around here yet, and you seem like someone who could be a positive influence on me. You think I could maybe have your number?"

"Sure! Just so you know I normally work a lot of weekends, but outside of that I'm usually pretty free to hang out and do something whenever you think you'd be available."

"Sounds great, thanks!" Travis replied. He entered Jamie's number into his phone, and they both returned to their seats within the group circle. Travis then spent the remaining 45 minutes of the session thinking about several things, not one of which had anything to do with his road to recovery.

Chapter 11

So far it had been a typical, monotonous work week for Kyle. Earlier in the week, he'd been given some generic instructions from his boss Stan to "conduct a quick proving experiment on the impact of sensor placement on brainwave measurement intensity", which was a complete waste of time given they'd already run an almost identical study months ago. The request must have originated from some half-assed postulation thrown out by one of the many pretentious tenured professors at the university. Probably delivered sometime last weekend by one of the lab heads over plates of prosciutto-wrapped Arctic Char and bottles of $200 vintage French wine, purchased with their inflated university salaries. Kyle would see these "shot in the dark" theories handed down every so often, and it pissed him off that he had to kowtow to these clueless idiots. It was hard enough for him to fight the suffocating inertia of academia and find fulfillment in his work: running pet projects for the nameless, faceless bourgeois of the UC System was truly the last thing he needed.

Kyle was a few hours into laying out the experiment when he received a call at his desk from Ryan, one of the lab technicians he managed. "Kyle, you've got to check this out! Come quick! I think we just discovered something!" Kyle had heard similar elation before from his lab techs, and while he considered it a positive that they showed such enthusiasm for their project, most of the time these calls resulted in some marginally significant fix, like a software patch or an improved calibration cycle. Kyle was sure this would end up being something of that realm, but he had just spent the past three hours at his desk typing up a bullshit protocol for Stan, so in this case he was happy to turn his attention to something else for a couple of minutes.

Kyle made the brief walk from his office area down to the laboratory. Through the looking glass he could see Ryan and Michael, along with Farida, a tech from another UC branch who was doing a nine month assignment in Santa Clara. They seemed very animated, and were talking excitedly around the assessment workstation. When Kyle entered the normally subdued room, the volume of the conversation startled him for a second. Maybe something really had happened?

"Great, Kyle's here, Ryan you show him what you just showed me," said Michael, the most senior of the three techs and usually the most reserved.

"Actually it was really Farida's discovery, maybe she would be best to give the explanation?" Ryan responded.

"I've been at this for many hours now, and I'm getting a little loopy, but I'll try to start from the beginning and see if we can make sense of it," Farida said, in a thick but easily understood Israeli accent. She sounded and looked exhausted. Kyle knew she had been working overnights the past few weeks so she wouldn't interrupt the primary experiments that were occurring during the day. Working on what though…he had to admit to himself he didn't really have the slightest clue. The day she arrived she'd brought with her an already planned out nine month itinerary, which they'd only quickly skimmed together during a birthday celebration in the break room.

Farida began: "So last month when you submitted your quarterly update, I went through it rather thoroughly to get myself up to speed on the work being done here. I was especially intrigued by a comment you made about isolating a synapse pattern to deposit the right amount of calcium to enable vivid recall. You gave several interesting ideas on how to theoretically go about doing this. One particular idea centered around increasing the electrical potential between synapse endpoints, which could in theory cause the electrical signal to repeat itself more rapidly and powerfully. I believe you called this the 'Voltage Case', since this is in effect how voltage works to generate electricity."

Kyle nodded, unsurprised by what Farida had said so far. He did indeed remember that particular theory he had given in last quarter's report. It had been a rough quarter as far as progress, and generating feasible ideas of what might take the project to the next level had proven very challenging for Kyle. The "Voltage Case" was one of the few ideas that Kyle didn't view as a total crock of shit, though he had very little idea of where to start as far as actually testing it out.

"This theory reminded me of some of the work I did years back as an electrical engineer, at a semiconductor factory in Tel Aviv," Farida continued. "There we worked with a process called 'recursion', in which a system calls upon its own function to achieve a desired result. This has widely known applications in Computer Science and software development, but also proved very useful for the microprocessor units I was working with. I spent the next couple weeks trying to think of an application for this principle in terms of enabling visual memory recollection in this eidetic memory project."

"I decided to start by trying out the neurotransmitter mapping model you guys already had in place. It proved very useful in identifying target synapse patterns that corresponded to distinct memory sets. After several successful modeling runs, I ran into basically the same issue you three have been encountering: how to isolate an individual synapse path, and how to hold that path over an extended period of time."

"Exactly," said Ryan. "This is when Farida connected with Michael and I on the 'calcium critical mass' study we've been running." This study was one of a handful Kyle was directly managing. It involved studying the ways the body deposited small amounts of calcium onto a particular synapse path the more a particular memory was rehearsed, converting what was being rehearsed into long-term memory, and essentially making the memory impossible to forget. "As you know, we've been trying to use the neuro-headset to stimulate magnesium release across an entire target synapse path. And as you also know, we've only been successful at triggering this release one time per session."

"Yeah, and instead of repeating the targeted synapse fire, other synapses in the hippocampus just randomly trigger," added Michael. "Like the example we always use here of when you're asked a question about your past, and you're searching throughout your mind for the correct answer? It's like we've been able to isolate the target path, but then everything goes haywire when we attempt any repetition."

Kyle was certainly familiar with these issues, though he didn't feel as up-to-date on the subject matter as he probably should be, given he was Project Manager.

"So I gotta ask: What's all the excitement about? You're not gonna tell me Farida already found a way to repeat the signal?" asked Kyle.

"Actually...that happens to be exactly what we ARE going to tell you," Ryan replied, unable to mask his excitement. Kyle was now feeling intrigued. After months of relative stagnancy, a breakthrough like this, even an incomplete one, would take a lot of pressure off his shoulders.

Farida walked over to the workstation console next to the assessment chair, with the rest of the team following her. On the computer screen was displayed a 3-D model of a brain scan. Farida manipulated the model to zoom into a quadrant of the hippocampus. "As per the testing protocol, I selected a memory from my past, and focused my thoughts on the beginning of that memory. I then ran the synapse mapping software to generate my synapse map. This is a scan of my synapse activity as of 3:08 AM this morning. "

"Wait wait...3 o'clock in the morning? You did this before anyone else was here?" Kyle asked, concerned with what he was hearing. "You know you shouldn't be self-experimenting, especially when no one else is around here to supervise, right?"

"I know...and I apologize. But after I was able to successfully program my idea into the modeling software...I just couldn't wait to try it out!" Farida declared. "So continuing on, if you look here you'll see a close-up of the target synapse path, highlighted in green." Kyle leaned into the workstation, as Farida pivoted the model to fit the entire target path on the screen. "The memory I chose in this case was of a time growing up in Israel when I accompanied my mother to the market. I was around 12 years old at that time, and on this particular occasion, I remember she had just bought me a new dress to wear out for the day. I have often tried to remember what this dress looked like; it was such a rare occasion that my family would make a purchase like this, but I'm afraid to say that over the years I've forgotten most of the details of the dress. This has always saddened me. I decided to start my memory path with the first thing I could remember from that day, which is leaving the house with my mother, and kissing my father goodbye as he stayed behind. The endpoint I had in mind for the memory is last thing from that day I remember, which is eating a piece of licorice on the walk back from the market to our house."

"Now comes the fun part," said Ryan eagerly. "Tell Kyle about how you used recurrence."

"Well back to the analogy I used earlier for recurrence, I decided to code an algorithm in the software that would not only locate the endpoints of the synapse pathway...but would recursively move these endpoints inwards towards each other. I theorized this might be able to solve our repetition problem. Since each intentional trigger signal we send would technically be on a 'new' synapse path given the changing endpoints, maybe we would be able to maintain the target path, and no longer encounter the signal loss and random synapse firing."

It was a brilliant, elegant idea. Kyle couldn't believe no one had thought of it earlier.

"After updating the software, I went ahead and ran a full test on myself. I know I should have waited until someone else was here...but just wait until you see this." Farida punched up a new window on the screen. As Kyle watched in amazement, the 3-D model showed a steady stream of green pixels jumping back and forth, in a web of slowly decreasing size. Unlike the models he had seen many times before, the green pixels did not begin jumping randomly around the screen after the first few seconds. They continued to follow the same steady pattern, with consistent shrinking occurring on all sides.

"Unbelievable!" Kyle exclaimed.

"If you want unbelievable, ask her about what she remembered in th---," Ryan blurted out, as Michael smacked him in the arm with his clipboard.

"Dumbass, it was her discovery, let her give the big reveal!" Michael yelled at Ryan.

Farida smiled, blushing a bit as she continued: "Well the first few seconds of the testing session proceeded as normal. Then all of the sudden, my mind was jarred into what I can only describe as a kind of parallel reality. I was still aware that I was sitting in the assessment chair, testing myself. But the present reality was being blurred out by the memory of the trip to the market with my mom. Everything was coming at me so fast, images and sounds and even emotions. They were incredibly lucid, and I had a hard time focusing on them. However, as the timer went off and the session ended, I was left with one image in my mind, the image I had sought out originally. I was leaning over to pet a little puppy...and on my left arm I saw a yellow and white sleeve, with horizontal stripes."

Stunned, Kyle's jaw dropped to the ground. "You've got to be kidding me."

"I couldn't believe it myself! Not at all! I was still tinkering with the model readouts a couple hours later, trying to make sense of what had just happened, and that's when Ryan and Michael arrived at the lab this morning."

"It took us a while to follow what Farida was trying to explain to us. To be honest it wasn't making a whole lot of sense, and some of it still doesn't. But when Farida mentioned the dress, that's when I got the idea to have her call her mother in Israel, and ask her about that dress so we could try to verify what she had seen." From Ryan's beaming expression, Kyle could almost tell what was coming next.

"Israel is ten hours ahead of California, so it was around 6:30 PM Israeli time when I made the call to my mother. When she answered the phone, I immediately asked her about that day, the day she bought me the new summer dress and let me wear it out to the market. My mother recalled almost instantly the dress I was referring to, again since we were not a wealthy family, and it was rare that I received any clothing that wasn't previously used. When I asked her if she remembered what the dress looked like, what color it was, she paused for a moment. Then she replied--"

"No way....."

"Bright yellow and white. With horizontal stripes."

CHAPTER 12

Only three days had passed since Farida's incredible discovery, and the team was already working diligently to set up a legitimate trial, this time ensuring they followed the proper protocols. What Farida had done, running an unauthorized experiment on herself without the mandated supervision and precautions in place, could unfortunately put the entire project at risk if they were not able to take a step back and properly cover their tracks. Removing the data from Farida's unauthorized attempt from the system would be relatively simple. In order to move forward in the direction they intended, the team needed to develop the proper test protocols that would document exactly what types of experiments they would be running, and how they would be operating them. Since Farida's method of recursion was a completely new model, this meant a ton of administrative work on properly loading the model into the system, and demonstrating its safety and potential efficacy. The team had been working double-time the past few days to get through this work as quickly as possible, but there was still plenty left ahead before they could get to the fun part: running another full experiment. Convincing them to come in on a Saturday had not been a difficult task.

It came as little surprise to Kyle that management at the lab had basically no idea that anything out of the ordinary could be happening right under their noses. Even though there was significantly more activity than usual going on inside the lab, the only sign of acknowledgement came from Stan the previous day, when he briefly approached Kyle after lunch to compliment the work ethic of his team.

"Still getting after it on a Friday afternoon, that's the dedication I like to see!" Stan had said. "It seems like on Fridays most of this university starts to wind down before it's even lunch time. Impressive to see your team still has their foot on the gas pedal. Excellent work!" Kyle couldn't help but laugh at Stan's continued cluelessness, though it was not lost on him that he himself had been completely out of the loop on his team's progress only days before.

Kyle had planned ahead and brought in breakfast for the team that Saturday morning from one of the most famous pastry shops in San Francisco. Though he saw that the three of them were already hard at work when he arrived at the office a little before 9:00 AM, he insisted they take a break and enjoy the array of danishes, croissants and donuts he had brought in to give them all a jolt of energy before they continued.

Huddled around a table outside the laboratory, the team members enjoyed their breakfasts in relative silence, each running through his or her mind the work that remained to be done for the day. Kyle took the initiative to break the silence.

"Thanks again for coming in here on a weekend. It's been a crazy week and I know there's still a lot left ahead of us, but you guys have been doing a fantastic job, and I really couldn't ask for a better team. I don't want anybody to get burned out or overwhelmed by what we have ahead, so if you need to take a break or head home for a couple of hours, I'm sure we'll all understand. Let's try to have some fun with all of this."

"Amen!" Michael echoed. "And thanks for the treats Kyle. I think I'm on my third donut already, giving me a nice little sugar rush!"

"Yes these are outstanding, where did you get these?" Farida asked, wiping the crumbs from her face as she debated going in for another helping.

"There's a fancy French bakery pretty close to my place

in San Fran. I know they've been featured on some foodie shows on TV and they're supposed to be known as one of the best in the country, so I figured they'd be pretty good."

"They're incredible! This jelly-filled pastry actually reminds me very much of a popular item in Israel I used to eat as a young girl called a 'sufganiyah'. Very similar and also quite delicious. Thank you again Kyle, this is just what I needed."

"Don't mention it, glad I could help out," Kyle said warmly. "So Farida, I feel bad we haven't had much time to chat in the time you've been with us. I know we've sort of been working different schedules, but that's really no excuse for my negligence. I really do apologize for that."

"Oh it's okay, you don't have to apologize. Really, everyone has been great to me since I've been here. I'm really enjoying the work so far," Farida replied.

Kyle was pleased to hear that Farida was not upset by his lack of engagement. "Still, I feel like I know very little about you. How long have you been in the States? And are you liking this part of California so far? What do you like to do here in your spare time?" Kyle asked.

"Well let's see...I've been in the States a little over five years now. After I fulfilled my military duty in Israel, I attended university in Tel Aviv. I then did some schooling in Massachusetts for a couple years, and was able to get a job with the University of California system upon graduating. I've been at UCLA for the past two and a half years prior to coming here. I really love California, so beautiful and so much variety, both the landscapes and the people. I never want to move back to the Northeast, or back home for that matter!" Farida offered with a laugh.

"No kidding. Well I'm in complete agreement, I've only been out here a little over a year and I never want to leave either!" Kyle added. "What about your family, do you miss them?"

"Of course, yes I do very much. My parents and my

brother are still back in Israel. My parents are getting older now but I still try to talk to them at least once a week. I'm finally getting them to learn how to video chat so I can at least see their faces when we talk. They are happy for me though, happy that I'm living my dream and I'm doing something I enjoy. My sister also now lives in the States near Boston with her husband. I try to visit her as often as I can, once or twice a year. I hope that one day we can all live in the same town again together. Who knows if it will happen, but for now things are good."

Ryan and Michael smiled at Farida's warm sentiment towards her family. They were both from Northern California, both of their hometowns a relatively short driving distance away from the campus. Kyle knew that Michael came from a very well-off family, and suspected Ryan probably did as well. They both appeared to be close with their families, based on what Kyle had observed over the past year. Kyle wondered if his team would be surprised to know how distant his relationship had grown with his own family back in Arizona.

The team finished with breakfast and headed back into the lab. With their assistance, Kyle had created a list of tasks for the day and divided them up to make sure there was as little duplication of effort as possible. Farida would be finishing up loading her recursive model into the system, hopefully by the end of the day. Ryan and Michael would be calibrating the neuro-headset and the monitoring equipment to match with the sequences of Farida's model. And Kyle would be generating the requirements for the validation plan.

After a surprisingly short amount of deliberation, the team reached the decision to use Ryan as the subject for their upcoming pilot test. Initially the team felt Farida should be the first test subject, since she already had a successful trial run under her belt. However, they ultimately decided it was more critical to have Farida at the operator's console to help direct the experiment. Ryan also had a decent amount of experience on the system, as he was usually the one in the chair whenever he and Michael would run calibration tests on the equipment. Now with a test subject in mind, Kyle focused his attention on completing the validation protocol according to the lab's regulatory requirements. It was pretty monotonous work for Kyle, but at this point in his career he had plenty of experience in pumping out documents like these, which needed to be able to be interpreted by a layman, but still pass the muster of an experienced auditor.

As the hours ticked by, the team continued working in silence, focusing in on executing their individual missions as mistake-free as possible. Ryan and Michael would occasionally break the silence by calling out adjustments to the EEG monitor settings. Kyle looked over to Farida, and could tell she was frustrated by the rigid procedures she had to follow to load her model within compliance, as opposed to the guess-and-check version she had gotten to work for her a couple days prior. It was tempting to try to create shortcuts for the team, but Kyle had heard too many horror stories in the past about researchers with brilliant ideas which never saw the light of day, usually because of sloppy documentation practices and non-compliance with appropriate standards. Kyle knew that a pilot run producing anything close to Farida's results would be a marked leap forward in progress for the project. But even if things went as well as they were hoping, the team would still need to follow up the experiment with many subsequent trials, in order to demonstrate the repeatability of the results, set boundaries around the allowable experimental duration, and determine several other key parameters. This would likely take months, and would need to be completed before the lab could really publicize their accomplishments to the outside world. It would be a while still before they could really get an idea of what kind of difference a breakthrough of this magnitude might make in the scientific community.

In any case, Kyle remained optimistic about the possibilities, and tried to stay focused on his duties as the manager and facilitator of the project. As he was attempting to put the finishing touches on one of the main clauses of the test protocol, he felt his phone vibrate in his pocket. He took the phone out, leaned back in his chair, and read to himself the text message that was displayed on the screen: *Hey bitch, missed you on Thursday, we had a killer time going out after the Giants game. Don't tell me you're being a lame ass tonight too?*

For a moment Kyle debated crafting a lengthy rebuttal to Travis' call out, before realizing that this was the first step that usually led him into giving in to Travis' heckling. *Wait a minute, what the hell am I doing? I'm 32 years old and I'm really going to go on the defensive about why I'm too busy at my career to go out and binge drink, blow lots of money, and wake up with terrible anxiety and a pounding headache? I don't think so.* Kyle quickly formulated an appropriate response to Travis: *Not going to happen tonight. Real world issues. Let you know when I get some free time.* He then turned off his phone, returned it to his pocket, and spent the next 40 minutes working on a new section of the protocol. When he finished he took a look at the clock, and realized that somehow almost eight hours had already passed since they'd gotten started that morning. Kyle figured they should try to call it a day soon, and decided to walk around to see how everyone else was doing.

"It's all good over here, boss," Michael informed Kyle. "We've got everything calibrated pretty much to the endpoints of Farida's neuron pathway model. Just ran a quick simulation and we didn't get any red flags. It's definitely not completely finished, but we can probably lock it up in the next day or two I would guess."

"Awesome. How's it going over there, Farida?" Kyle asked.

"Ugh...it's been an exhausting day but I've actually made more progress than I thought I would. Come take a quick look and I'll show you what I've done."

Ryan and Michael followed Kyle over to the workstation area where Farida was seated. She brought up the home screen of the brain synapse mapping software they were all familiar with.

"So I've added this shortcut key here at the bottom of the home screen titled 'Recursive Model' that will essentially get you where you need to go to get started on running the experiment. I've added in most of the verifications needed to advance to the experiment itself, including the calibration of the neuro-headset that Michael and Ryan are working on. I used the headset sensor placement 'Option B' during the successful trial I ran this week, so that's what I've coded into the software. Other than that, once you've got the headset in place and the calibration is complete, the software basically takes it from there. I've placed an archive folder on the desktop as well, so you can easily locate the data from each run and move it around as needed. Everything else should pretty much be programmed in at this point. I'd try to tell you for sure, but to be honest I'm starting to get a little cross-eyed from staring at this damn thing all day."

"No problem, it can definitely wait until Monday," Kyle said. "Well great job guys, seems like we're getting really close here. I'd expect we could probably schedule the pilot run for some time towards the end of next week. For now let's call it a day and all get some rest."

"Sounds good to me. This is getting exciting! This place is going to go nuts when we tell them what we've discovered. We'll be the talk of the town around campus, at least for a couple of weeks hopefully," Ryan said.

"I can't wait to see the look on management's faces when they see us pull off this magic trick. Kyle, your reaction to Farida's revelation was pretty great, but Stan's face when he sees what we can do now with this machine is gonna be fucking epic! I don't know if I can wait that long, are you sure we can't just demonstrate it on Monday?" Michael joked with the team.

"You're right…I actually can't wait to see Stan's reaction either," Kyle added. "We might have to get some defibrillators in here to resuscitate him."

"Shotgun not the mouth-to-mouth giver!" Michael yelled, barely able to get the words out through his laughter.

The team continued to laugh together for another minute or so, after which they were able to compose themselves and start packing their supplies. Kyle powered down the lab after they exited, and the team made their way up the stairs towards the main office area.

"I'm gonna grab a soda from the break room so I can keep my eyes open during the drive home. Drinks are on me if anybody else wants anything," Ryan offered.

"Big spender, can't turn that down," Michael answered, as the four of them followed Ryan on his detour.

Quietly seated around a table in the break room, Kyle decided to follow up on his pledge to show more of an interest in the work-life balances of his direct reports. "What do you guys all have on the agenda for the rest of this very short weekend? Anything fun planned?"

"Actually, Michael and I are going to try and meet up at that new high-speed go-kart track in Oakland tomorrow. It's supposed to be a nice day out, and I have a buddy who works there so we can pretty much ride for free all day long," Ryan said excitedly.

"So don't be surprised if one of us comes back in here on Monday in a full-body cast," Michael joked in his usual sarcastic manner.

"Well that sounds fun at least. It'll be good for you guys to get away from the computer screen and get outside for a day. Do be at least a little bit careful though. I'm kind of counting on you guys to help me finish off something important," Kyle joked. "Farida, how about you?"

"I'm going on a geocaching trip out near the mountains tomorrow with some friends from the university. I've really gotten into that since I've lived in California," Farida replied.

"Is that the thing where you use GPS to go on a treasure hunt, like where people hide items near a hiking trail and you have to try to find them?" Kyle asked.

"Yep, that's pretty much the gist of it. Some people take it really seriously, but I just kind of use it as a fun excuse to get outside and get some exercise. I usually bring along my book on bird identification and end up doing more bird-watching than treasure hunting, but it's still a good time. I'm definitely looking forward to it tomorrow even more than usual," Farida said with a smile.

"Well I'm very glad you're all getting a nice break from this place, if only for a quick day," Kyle said. "I'm probably just going to hang out and watch sports like I usually do on Sundays. Might try to walk around the town for a little while so I can enjoy some of this nice weather too. And hopefully we'll all come back somewhat refreshed for the home stretch next week."

When the team finished in the break room, Kyle wished them all a great rest of the weekend and gave each of them an appreciative handshake as they headed towards the parking lot. Kyle planned to drop off his notebooks at his desk, then get the hell out of there and grab some take-out food on his drive home. There was a big baseball game starting in a couple hours, and he hoped to have a nice relaxing evening watching it on his couch with a couple of craft beers. That was exactly what Kyle intended to do when he glanced over at the empty lab. That entire week he could feel something inside himself calling him...tempting him to try out the machine. *Very bad idea*, Kyle tried to convince himself. They had just spent a good amount of time trying to erase Farida's unauthorized experiment and prepare for a valid one. The last thing they needed was data from another run on their hands to deal with. Although, Kyle knew that Farida had fixed the system to where data could now be easily transferred to different folders, or even erased from the system if one was so inclined.

Kyle tried to keep walking towards his office, and made it another few steps, but stopped again. Something inside him wanted desperately to see what that machine was capable of...what his mind was capable of. Almost without thinking, he reentered the lab, booted the workstation for the neuro-headset, and watched as the system quickly booted up to the new home screen. For some reason he felt as if he was almost in a trance, not nearly as worried about the massive risk he was about to take as he felt he should be. He began to rapidly filter through the memories in his mind, trying to decide which one he wanted to try to recall. For this first go around, it had to be something relatively simple. A memory where he knew the basic context, but wasn't able to recall specific details. He thought for a few moments, and ultimately decided he would go with a road trip he remembered taking as a child with his father, uncle and cousin to see a monster truck rally in Colorado. Through the years he had always thought back fondly on that trip, but being only about ten years old at the time, he only remembered bits and pieces of it. Unsure if it was just nostalgia, Kyle recalled that this trip was one of the few times he remembered seeing his dad really let loose, one of the few times Kyle viewed his dad as a cool guy. It was funny to think about now, that one of his biggest bonding experiences with his father was watching monster trucks crush cars with a bunch of rednecks. But for whatever reason, this memory had stuck with him through the years.

Kyle decided he would focus specifically on the actual rally event itself, and see what level of specific detail he could recall. Farida had set the timer for the system at 30 minutes, which would be plenty of time for Kyle to see if this thing was for real or not. He put on the headset as he'd been shown, and placed the sensors to the correct configuration. He then did his best to follow the directions he'd been given on calibration. After a few minutes, the system displayed an icon indicating that the calibration was complete, and everything had checked out. Now all that was left to do was start the program, lie back and see what happened. *Last chance to stop this you idiot*, Kyle told himself. Taking in one deep breath to calm himself, Kyle pressed the start button on the monitor, laid back into the experimentation chair, and began breathing in and out softly and slowly.

Kyle visualized the outside of the stadium, the picture he'd had in his mind of it all these years. He remembered his father buying him a hot dog from a vendor outside the stadium, and tried to shift his focus there. He tried to remain focused on that moment, remember everything he could…..

I'm here! Oh my God oh my God it's working! Ok stay calm…stay calm. Focus, you can do this. It's…it's really nice outside! Wait a minute, I always thought it was winter when we took this trip? It couldn't be sunnier out, and it seems hot based on how everybody is dressed. I see the stadium, it looks a lot different than I remember it too. It's much bigger. Oh my God, there's my dad talking to my uncle, and they both look so tall! Now my dad is grabbing my hand, and we're all walking towards the stadium. I take a bite of the hot dog I'm holding, and then I give it to my cousin Danny to take a bite. I haven't seen Danny in probably 15 years. We're now walking up a long staircase into the stadium, and it's getting really loud. I can hear people shouting and engines roaring everywhere. I can tell I'm feeling really excited now. My dad and my uncle are getting a beer from the concession stand. I hardly ever remember seeing my father drink before I reached high school age. Now we're running up another set of stairs. My uncle finds our seats and we quickly rush over to them. This stadium is gigantic, and there are so many people here! Everyone is making noise and cheering. In the middle of the stadium I see a row of broken down cars. Then I hear a loud rumbling noise under my seat. I'm really getting excited now. My cousin and I are jumping

*up and down. Now a big door is opening, and out comes a huge
black monster truck with flames shooting out the top! We all start
cheering as loud as we can. The giant truck drives up to the
starting line of cars, and stops. Everything goes quiet for a second.
Then suddenly, the truck roars its engine, so loud I can barely hear
my dad shouting right next to me. This is so awesome. Now the
truck is speeding towards the line of cars. It hits the first few and
flies up in the air. It lands with a loud smack on top of the other
cars, and keeps demolishing them as it plows forward. I can see
metal and glass flying everywhere. My cousin and I are going
crazy. So is the crowd. We can barely contain our excitement. The
truck is still pushing forward, nearing the end of the line.....*

"Where did it go?!?" Kyle shouted out loud to himself,
echoing inside the lab. His heart was still pounding and his
palms were sweating as he looked over at the control
monitor. The timer read "00:00", indicating that the 30
minute session had expired. Kyle remained seated in the
experimentation chair, attempting to catch his breath. He
couldn't believe what had just happened to him. The
machine had worked, and it was 100 times better than he
could have ever imagined. He was able to recall so much
detail, so vividly.

"Un-fucking-believable," Kyle muttered to himself. As
much as he understood about the physiology of the human
brain at this point, he still couldn't grasp how this much
stored memory detail could possibly be locked inside of it,
just waiting for the proper catalyst to bring it forward.
Eventually Kyle began to regain his composure, and slowly
rose up from the chair, placing the headset back into its
cradle. Kyle walked over to the control monitor, and on the
screen was displayed a transparent 3-D model of a human
skull, with different areas of the brain highlighted in
multiple colors. The model was zoomed into the
hippocampus area of the brain and was currently displaying
a green highlighted section, with what looked similar to
green electrons moving back and forth within a complex

network of branches. The recursive model had worked, just as Farida had said it would.

On the workstation computer Kyle opened up the folder where Farida had told him the data would be stored. He was easily able to locate the file he had just generated, since it was the only file residing in the folder currently, and he performed a permanent delete on the file. This prevented the file from being held somewhere else on the server, where it could later be discovered. Kyle knew there were still ways for someone very computer-savvy, like Farida or Ryan, to potentially figure out that a new file had been generated. But that was only if someone had a suspicion to dig that deep for some reason, and Kyle viewed that as very unlikely. By the middle of next week, they'd all be so involved in running the pilot trial, no one would be bothering to look back at any of the system history.

Kyle gathered his supplies and powered down the lab once more. It was now 5:17 PM. Kyle hadn't eaten since the breakfast he had brought in that morning and was starving. He began walking towards his office, rolling through his mind the different food options he could get for dinner, when he heard a noise coming from the back office area. He stopped dead in his tracks, his heart pounding. *Was somebody else there?* No one else had been at the lab all day besides his team, and he had watched them all leave the building over an hour ago. He knew the cleaning crew came in on Thursday evenings, so it wouldn't be them. If someone who worked for the university was there, and had witnessed what Kyle had just done, he would be royally fucked. He stood in silence for another minute, trying to see if the noise would present itself again.

Hearing nothing, Kyle quickly walked to his office to drop off his belongings. He grabbed his car keys, locked up the door to the office and headed towards the exit. Stopping again for a moment, Kyle looked down into the long dark hallway. He swore to himself it felt like somebody else was there. Debating doing another lap around the office just to make sure, Kyle decided he was just being paranoid, and it was time for him to go home. He closed the door to the building, punched in the lock code, and headed out to his car to begin his shortened weekend, with a million different things simultaneously running through his mind.

CHAPTER 13

Travis scoured through the center console of his Monte Carlo, searching for a piece of gum to conceal his breath from that morning's festivities, which had primarily consisted of smoking two joints and eating a bag of pretzels while watching TV alone on his couch. He'd sprayed some cologne on himself before he'd left the house, though he wasn't sure how effective it would be given that he'd had the bottle in his possession for so long the label had completely worn off. Travis was actually a little nervous about seeing Jamie again. She hadn't been in either of the group therapy sessions the prior two weeks, so it'd been a while since Travis had last seen her. He'd decided after the last session to shoot her a text message and see how she was doing, and also to check if she wanted to meet up that Saturday for a cup of coffee. She responded quickly, saying that she had a few errands to run in the morning, but she did have the day off from work and could meet him around noon if that worked for him. Travis had suggested they meet in Palo Alto, since it was relatively close to where they both lived, and there were a lot of cool places to check out near Stanford University.

Travis found a parking spot right in front of the coffee shop where they were supposed to meet. As he was a couple minutes early he remained in the car, trying to think of a few topics they could talk about together. Travis didn't want the entire conversation to be focused around therapy and the struggles they both were going through. But at this early stage he knew very little about Jamie, and didn't know what else she was interested in. Travis wasn't overly concerned though. He was pretty good at adapting and thinking on his feet in one-on-one situations like this. That skill had paid off for him many times throughout his life.

Travis had discovered this coffee shop through a website that ranked businesses near Stanford, and upon first inspection he was pretty satisfied with his choice. The building was modern looking and trendy, and there were a couple of large plush leather couches and chairs located in a middle section of the shop, although currently they were all occupied. Travis went up to the counter and ordered a large Americano, then grabbed a two-person table near the back of the shop and took a seat. He waited about five minutes until he saw someone who looked like Jamie walk through the entrance. Jamie removed her sunglasses and glanced around the building until she finally spotted Travis towards the back. She gave him a friendly wave, then pointed towards the cashier to indicate she was going to place an order first.

As Jamie waited in line, Travis found himself examining her figure. She was wearing white denim shorts with a pink tank top. In this outfit she was showing a good amount of skin, and Travis was certainly a fan. Jamie definitely had a nice figure, with smooth olive skin and good curves. She wasn't overtly sexy by any means, but she was certainly quite cute, easily cute enough for Travis to be very interested in her already. Although she had mentioned her boyfriend when they first met in group therapy, Travis was never one to let that stop him, especially when it came to girls who were going through severe emotional issues, who Travis usually felt could be coerced into changing their minds more easily than most girls.

Jamie grabbed her coffee from the barista stand and joined Travis at the back of the coffee shop. "Hey Travis, how's it going?" she asked, giving Travis a friendly hug. "How cool is this place!"

"I'm doing good, thanks for asking. Yeah it's a pretty

cool place, I like this area a lot. How did running errands go for you this morning?" Travis asked.

"Oh ya know, great fun as always. Went to a home goods store to buy some new pots and dishes for our kitchen. Then I ran over to the pet store to get some food for our cat. Riveting stuff, I know," Jamie joked.

"Ha ha...yeah that sounds exhilarating. More action-packed than my weekend has been so far though. Last night I played basketball at the YMCA near my apartment for a couple hours, then ordered a pizza and went to sleep at like 10:00 PM. Haven't accomplished much this morning either," Travis admitted.

"Well I'm glad you asked me to come out here, I've never been to Palo Alto before but it's beautiful! My boyfriend Manny is out of town on business this week so I'm glad I'm not just sitting at home alone in that empty apartment right now. Thanks for getting me out of the house," Jamie offered cheerfully.

"Pleasure to be of service," Travis added. "So, how long have you guys been seeing each other?"

"It's been...about a year now. I moved in with him around four months ago. It's been good, I like where we live in Fremont better than where I was at before. How about you, do you have a girlfriend or anything right now?"

Travis tried to laugh suavely at this, but what came out of his mouth was more like an awkward throat clearing. "Nothing too serious right now...ya know, just kind of playing the field for the time being. Been pretty busy at work lately actually, I think I told you I recently got a promotion to Senior Agent," Travis fibbed again. "I've been lucky that they haven't found out about my little run-in with the San Francisco P.D. at the Giants game."

"Oh yeah...well I think you did tell me about the promotion, that's great, good for you!" Jamie said cheerfully. "So how is it working there, do you like it or not so much?"

"It's not a bad gig. Get paid pretty well, hours aren't too

killer, work is somewhat interesting. Overall I can't complain," Travis said matter-of-factly.

This led to a pause in the conversation, where neither of the two could think of a topic to bring up next. Travis was normally great at coming up with ideas on the fly, but at this moment he was striking out. Finally, Travis remembered something from their first conversation that he could ask Jamie about. "So I think you told me you grew up in Chico, right? I still haven't been north of San Francisco yet so I know very little about that part of the state. What did you think of the area?"

"Chico is...umm...okay. I mean it kind of gets a bad reputation in the bigger cities, but I really didn't think it was that rough or anything. Just like most other medium-sized cities in California, ya know? What about you, where are you from again? Oh Arizona right?" asked Jamie.

"Yep Arizona, that's right," Travis responded.

"And you moved out here because your best friend had moved here recently, right?"

"Yep you got it! Yeah his name is Kyle," Travis said. He was impressed Jamie remembered those details from their short talk several weeks ago. "Where I'm from is probably a lot like Chico actually. Smaller town about 15 miles outside of suburban Phoenix. Nothing too exciting going on there, that's for sure. Glad to be in a place like this that has so much more to offer for people our age."

"Me too, we're so fortunate to be able to live in such an amazing area of the country. I love it here. So anyway, Travis...how have you been doing lately?" After the lighthearted banter they'd been sharing so far, this blunt question caught Travis off-balance.

"Umm, fine...Better, I've been doing a lot better actually. The promotion has kinda helped keep me out of trouble. I've been hanging out with Kyle a lot lately too. He's a solid dude, definitely has his shit together more than I do. He's got a really good job in a scientific research lab over at UC

Santa Clara. I think they study human memory or something. Anyway, he's got a really cool place in the Russian Hill district of downtown, so I try to head over there as often as possible on weekends so we can check out some cool places in the city."

"That sounds great Travis! I'm glad to hear you're doing well and enjoying your time here. I unfortunately don't get downtown often enough, but I know there are tons of amazing things to see and do there. By the way, I'm sorry I missed group the past two weeks. I feel kind of bad about it. I ended up picking up a shift for a coworker and had to work a double both of those days. How do you think the sessions went?"

"I thought they went pretty good. You know Harold, the guy who lost his scholarship and dropped out of college?" Travis asked. Jamie nodded yes. "Well he just got accepted to an online university program that's in the field he wants to work in. So everybody was really happy for him. Then that led the conversation for the night towards second chances, and the leader Darren had a really funny story about a second chance that he got after he'd kicked drugs for the first time. I'd tell the story to you but I'm sure I'd butcher it. Anyway it was a pretty decent session."

Travis was desperately trying to come up with a way to ask Jamie about how she was doing with her issues, but he was having trouble working up the courage. Jamie was being genuinely kind to him, which was making it tough for him to play the mind games he usually favored when trying to impress a girl he was attracted to. Before long Jamie was finishing her cup of coffee and preparing to leave, and Travis was realizing he'd blown his opportunity for the day.

"So Travis, thanks again for inviting me over here to hang out with you. I feel like I'm usually too reserved to invite people to do stuff like this, so I'm really glad you took the initiative. It's nice for me to get out of my little circle and see a cool new part of town. And I also want you to know that I think you're a really easy person to talk to, if you don't mind me saying that," Jamie added.

"Of course not! Thanks for the compliment, I'm very glad you feel that way," Travis said, trying to mask his excitement.

"Well I think I'm gonna head home now. Need to feed the cat, she hasn't eaten in a while and is probably tearing our house apart as we speak. But let's try to do this again sometime soon. And I will definitely see you again next week at group therapy, I promise this time," Jamie said.

"Yeah, let's do this again sometime soon. I know of a bunch of cool places around town, so I'll find another good one for us."

"Sounds perfect! Maybe next time you can even invite your friend Kyle, and I can try to bring Manny so we can all meet each other," Jamie suggested. Travis smiled, trying not to grimace at the idea of the four of them awkwardly sitting around eating danishes and drinking lattes in some quiet coffee shop.

"Sure, it's worth a shot. Hey I'll walk with you outside." Jamie grabbed her jacket and the two of them made their way to the parking lot. Upon reaching her car, Jamie surprised Travis with another hug, this one noticeably more familiar than the first, as she again said goodbye and reminded him that he could call her anytime if he needed someone to talk to. Travis waved to Jamie again as she got in and drove away. There was now no denying for Travis that he was officially smitten, and he spent his entire drive home trying to plot out how he could possibly make Jamie Fontana his own.

CHAPTER 14

Although three days had already passed since the successful pilot run on Ryan, the vibe around the Keane Institute for Learning and Memory seemed largely unchanged. The team had completed their protocols on Monday of that week, and had scheduled the pilot run for Tuesday morning. Ryan decided that for his trial, he would recall a memory of his first trip to a waterpark as a child. Something simple, specific, and verifiable. He came into the office that morning admittedly a little overly excited for the upcoming experiment. In fact, the team had to delay the start of the run about an hour while they calmed him down and forced him to try to relax. As Ryan himself knew, if his mind was focusing on too many things at once, their system would have no way to properly lock in the endpoints of his target memory path.

Eventually Ryan was able to relax, and the team went forward with conducting the experiment. They had invited management and several other employees of the institute to view the pilot run. Unsurprisingly, it seemed the importance of what they were about to accomplish was mostly lost on their coworkers, which was not unusual in an environment where substantial new discovery could often take years to come to fruition. The team was altogether not upset by this, as they would rather have several confirmatory experiments under their belt before running their results up the flagpole, at which point they'd then be inviting in the requisite second-guessing and bureaucracy from the higher-ups at the university.

The experiment itself had been a resounding success.

Within the allotted 30 minute timeframe, Ryan was able to direct the beginning of his recall session to his only distinct memory from that day. In this case, it was standing in the shallow end of a wave pool with this father teaching him how to swim. From there, Ryan's mind was guided through the short sequence of events that followed. He saw himself and his sister climb a wooden staircase up to the top of a waterslide. He watched as his terrified sister, with the assistance of the slide operator, worked up the courage to let go of the crossbar and shoot down the slide. He could almost feel the cool tingle of the water himself as he entered the slide, and he felt the rush as he swung back and forth through the winding tube, finally crashing into the shallow pool of water at the bottom as his father and sister cheered him on.

Ryan had wanted to go for a longer session, but the team, led most vocally by Farida in this case, had determined more testing was needed before a subject could be exposed for a longer time period. The team was spending today combing through their extensive library of case studies and scientific research, gathering information in order to justify a potential extension to the allowed experimental duration. In addition, Farida was designing a simulation model to characterize the potential amount of calcium deposited on the neuron pathway if the experiment was extended beyond 30 minutes.

Kyle, as Project Manager, should have been leading the charge on making sure the team had their procedures in place for any proposed changes to the approved model. However, in the last few days he'd had a tough time letting go mentally of the experiment he'd run on himself the prior week. It had been such an intense experience, and for Kyle it was the most alive he'd felt in a long time. In only 30 short minutes, he was able to relive a rare bonding moment with his father, even if it was over something as frivolous as a monster truck rally. He was surprised at how easily Ryan and Farida seemed to be able to let go of their journeys back in time, and refocus themselves on the work that needed to be done for the project. He hoped he himself could do the same, and quickly, before temptation led him towards another serious error in judgement.

Kyle could tell his team was starting to go a little cross-eyed from cataloging research for the past two days straight, so he decided to order them all to take a long lunch break, and not return to the office for a couple of hours.

"Thank God," Michael responded. "These whitepapers are starting to read like hieroglyphics to me. I'm employed as an engineer at this university, not a goddamn research fellow. Give me spreadsheets and schematics all day, not 100 page essays on the difference between implicit and explicit memory."

"I hear you. I don't think this is what any of us would ideally be spending our time doing. But it's important we have as much justification as possible for our experimental plan, and then we can get back to the fun stuff as soon as possible," Kyle said.

"I guess having to do this crap is why they pay us the big bucks!" Ryan said jokingly. "Hopefully we just need to grind through this a little longer, and then maybe I can jump back into that chair and take it for another wild ride!"

"Yeah right numbnuts, next time it's my turn!" Michael snapped back. "Well...unless Kyle wants to do it I suppose. You and Farida have already had your shot."

"It's alright Michael, you can be the next to go," Kyle replied, still worried in the back of his mind that his secret solo run could be uncovered if he didn't put some distance between his experiments. "But that's still down the road a ways. For now, everyone get out of here and go get some fresh air."

"Don't have to tell me twice," Michael said, as he and Ryan gathered their belongings and left the lab. Kyle made the mistake of stopping by his office to check email before heading out. He saw an email from his boss Stan, inviting him and a guest to the annual Fall Gala at the university. *Yuck* and *Hell No* were the immediate thoughts to enter Kyle's mind, though he put the invitation message aside until he could think of a more valid excuse to decline. *Who would he have brought with him anyway? Travis?* He laughed for a brief moment as he thought about the look on everyone's faces when Travis walked in, in all likelihood stoned off his ass, completely underdressed, and beelining it straight for the open bar. Talk about two worlds colliding.

Kyle decided it would be good to use his time to take a quick drive over to Baylands Park, near the southern tip of the San Francisco Bay. He had never been before, and was told it was a good place to get away from the mayhem of nearby Silicon Valley. He parked his car on a side street, and was pleased to see the park was very quiet and peaceful on this Friday morning. Kyle felt this would be a good opportunity for him to clear his head after the craziness of the past few weeks. He couldn't believe things had changed so much for him in such a short amount of time. Only a month or two ago, he was feeling bored with his weekly routine and the monotony of his job at the lab. Now, somehow, he was on the verge of a potentially life-altering breakthrough.

As he walked along a path that followed around the massive tip of the bay, Kyle found his attention drifting towards his recent outings with Travis. He had not really seen him again since that night a few weeks back in San Jose, when Kyle had gotten into a fight with a stranger at the house they were visiting. Initially, Kyle had actually felt somewhat proud of the way he'd handled himself during that altercation. After all, it wasn't him who went overboard with the antagonizing. And Kyle had been impressed with how he'd handled himself physically, scoring at least a draw against a stronger opponent whom he was sure had much more fighting experience. But in the end Kyle had still been unable to walk away at the right moment, when doing so would have prevented things from escalating. Kyle was starting to feel like he was losing touch with himself, and he was becoming alarmed at his impulsiveness the past couple times he'd gone out and partied with Travis. It was becoming apparent that Kyle might want to try and minimize his contact with Travis during this important upcoming phase in his life. As hard as it was for Kyle to admit, Travis was clearly not the best influence. And unless he was willing to change quickly, Kyle couldn't afford to be sidetracked with his unnecessary and destructive distractions.

Kyle looked out ahead from his vantage point on the north end of the trail. He could see in the far distance the endless rows of state-of-the-art buildings, housing the best and brightest of the technology world. At times he still couldn't believe he'd made it out here and was becoming integrated into this ecosystem. This was one of the most privileged and sought-after areas in the entire country, if not the world, and Kyle was right here in the middle of it. If things went as well as he hoped with the new discovery, he could realistically be setup for life to stay here and spend his time doing almost anything he wanted. Millions of people would kill for that opportunity, and Kyle often felt he didn't deserve it. He had to remind himself that he'd worked very hard to develop a plan that would give him the freedom to have choices in life, and that he had earned his current status. He also was beginning to realize that he could easily screw it all up if he wasn't careful.

Walking on the return path towards his car, Kyle checked his watch and saw that it was only 12:17 PM, and he still had over an hour to kill before the rest of the team would be returning to the office. He began to contemplate where he could grab lunch near the lab, when he felt his phone vibrate in his pocket. He pulled it out and saw a message from Frank: *Hey stranger, Nicole said you guys were all out taking a long lunch. I'm at a place up in Palo Alto if you want to meet up.*

Perfect, Kyle thought. He had not seen Frank in a while, and was wanting to spill the beans a little further on their recent success, perhaps even bouncing a few ideas off of Frank for technical advice.

Kyle arrived at the Middlefield Road Diner several minutes later. It was a 1950's retro-themed diner, and at the moment it was rather jam-packed with college-age kids, mostly from nearby Stanford University judging from their attire. Kyle entered the diner and saw Frank sitting in a booth near the front entrance.

"Hey man, glad you sent me that text, you have good timing," Kyle said as he took a seat across from Frank.

"And it looks like we just barely beat the rush. It's the small victories in life ya know," Frank joked. "Well I've never been to this place but I've heard they have some of the best burgers in the city. I hope that's good with you."

"Absolutely," Kyle said. "I'm starving actually, a nice big bacon cheeseburger with fries sounds great right now."

"Great, let's order up," Frank replied, as they flagged down the waitress and placed their orders.

"So what's been going on with your 'Total Recall' project lately?" Frank asked. "I got the invite you sent out earlier this week. Appreciate you thinking of me, I was swamped at the time or I definitely would have come by."

"Oh no problem, I understand. It's...it's getting really interesting actually. I have to kind of be careful how I say this, but we had a legitimate breakthrough this week. We have a few more experiments to do before we go public with the results. But what we accomplished on Tuesday was pretty unbelievable. A giant step ahead for us in the right direction."

"Wow, listen to you! I don't think I've ever heard you sound so spirited about work! So what's going on man, what's got you all hot and bothered? Come on you can tell me, you know I won't blab," Frank insisted.

"I don't know how much I should be telling anyone at this point. It's really my whole team who should get the big reveal when everything's ready to present. But I guess I can tell you the gist of it. I was actually thinking I might be able to use your help somewhere down the road since you seem to be one of our resident experts on hardware systems integration."

"Definitely, you know I've always offered to help your team out whenever you need me. So spit it out man, what've you guys got?!?" Frank asked again eagerly.

"Alright...and again this doesn't leave this table until we're good and ready to bring it upstairs," Kyle reminded him. "As I've been publishing in my reports, we've had a lot of success lately in locating target synapse patterns that correspond to a particular memory. We've pretty much got the neuro-headset as optimized as I think we're going to get it. And we've been able to use our neurotransmitter mapping tool to generate a 3-D model of the specific neuron pathway being utilized during a memory recall."

"Okay...so far I'm aware of pretty much all of this. I've seen a couple of the 3-D models in the reports, pretty damn cool stuff. But this has already been accomplished by other laboratories around the world. I mean, I think we were even licensing parts of that mapping software from the Basel Institut, for God's sake! You know if B.I. was willing to let us get our hands on something they'd developed, that means they probably have something light years ahead of it already in place," Frank stated, as a server brought their plates over to the table.

"Yeah you're right. I know for a fact there are at least five labs in the world that are using a version of the B.I. platform. We've done a lot of modifications to it since we've had it though, and pairing that with the proprietary technology we have in our neuro-headset and our monitoring systems...I think it's safe to say we're now a step ahead of the competition," Kyle beamed.

"Well aren't you something special? The project I'm working on, we're at least three years *behind* the competition from a development standpoint. So...if you think you've got a leg up, what's been holding you guys back?" Frank asked earnestly.

"Really, it's that we haven't been able to make progress on securing the neuron pathway for extended periods of time. We've only been able to hold it for a few seconds...and then trying to get back to those same pathway endpoints later is nearly impossible. We've tried to alter acetylcholine levels, hoping to somehow enhance the targeted neurotransmitters. But nothing so far has produced the results we've been looking for. That is...until three days ago."

"Wait, hold on for a minute," Frank said, now visibly intrigued by what Kyle was telling him. "I'll admit I probably don't fully understand a couple of the things you just went over...but are you telling me you guys found a way to make photographic memory a real thing."

"Haahhh!" Kyle exclaimed. Hearing someone phrase it that bluntly out loud sounded absurd to him. "I think that might be taking it just a little bit too far. I mean you're smart enough to know this, I don't have to tell you that these things don't work like you see them in science fiction movies. It's much more rudimentary than that."

"I'm sure it is. But still, what you just told me sounds like it could have huge implications! I'm not gonna make you give me all the details right now, but I can tell something has you legitimately excited over there. All I'll say for now is that if there's any way I can be a part of it, I'm happy to help out." With that Frank grabbed the check off the table, and stepped over to pay the cashier.

"I appreciate the offer. And again I hope we can go public with this soon and maybe start bringing more people like you on board to help us accelerate," Kyle replied as he stood with Frank in line. "Thanks for lunch by the way, you didn't have to do that."

"My pleasure. I'm really just trying to get on your good side so I can jump on the gravy train when it eventually leaves the station," Frank joked.

"Smart man, always thinking. Alright well on that note I'm going to get back to the office so we can get the tracks built for that train as soon as possible," Kyle said.

A short time later Kyle arrived back at the lab, where Ryan, Michael and Farida were just starting to get back into the swing of their respective itineraries. Kyle took another look at their formidable To-Do list. "How is this list not getting any smaller?" he asked. "We've been at this non-stop for days, and there's still a ton left to do."

"I know. I was looking at the list too, and I actually had to add a few things we'd forgotten. I know we haven't talked about it yet, but I'm thinking we might want to come in again tomorrow," Farida said.

"That's the second Saturday in a row. I really hate to do that to you guys," Kyle responded.

"We don't mind boss," Ryan said. "We just want to get this thing ready to rock as quickly as possible."

"Yeah, and anyway even if I was at home this weekend I'd be sitting there thinking about this. I'm good to go for tomorrow too," Michael added.

"Well alright then I guess. I really appreciate it. You guys are definitely the best," Kyle said, as he prepared himself for the long afternoon, and another long Saturday to come.

CHAPTER 15

"No way! That's terrible to hear..." Kyle exclaimed as Ryan delivered the bad news. They had been working almost nonstop for the past few weeks since Ryan's successful run, and had finally been able to make some real progress on getting prepared to conduct the next confirmatory experiment, this time at a 60 minute duration. They all agreed that enabling this extension would go a long way in demonstrating the robustness of the system they'd designed, and the extended duration could prove invaluable down the road in increasing the potential applications for their technology. Now, at 8:30 AM on a Wednesday morning, it was Ryan's duty to inform Kyle that Michael had fallen ill, and would be out of commission for at least the next few days.

"I went over to his apartment to see him last night, and he was in rough shape," Ryan had said. "He's afraid it's the flu, so he's going to try to get one of those fast-acting antivirals from his doctor today. But I gotta say, judging from the noises I heard coming from his bathroom last night...I'd guess that he's going to be out until at least early next week."

"Poor guy. What terrible timing too," Kyle reiterated. Kyle couldn't help but feel partially responsible. He was driving this project pretty hard lately, trying to get over this last hurdle before the team could finally solicit some help from the rest of the institute. Now he was down a man, and he had to come up with a plan rather quickly. The last thing any of them wanted to do was sit around and wait for days until Michael fully recovered. Kyle thought about just using himself, Ryan or Farida as the confirmatory subject. However, now they were down to only three people to operate the experiment, which was below the minimum number needed to run it under proper protocol. During Ryan's pilot run, Kyle had largely taken the role of supervising the process and taking notations. Now, in Michael's absence, he would need to provide hands-on assistance in order to operate the equipment with Ryan. But that assumed they could even find a viable test subject.

"We're screwed. Damn...we are screwed! We don't have enough people to run this with one of us as the subject. And it would take me at least a week to train another technician here to do Michael's part," Ryan said. "I guess we're just going to have to suck it up and wait until he gets back."

"I can't believe this," Farida lamented, distraught by the prospect of losing all that time. "I knew we should have just done another 30 minute run when we had the chance. We got too ambitious, and now look at where it's put us!"

Kyle was beyond frustrated with their current situation. They were so close to success, but bad luck had just thrown a seemingly insurmountable obstacle in their way. There was no way they could continue on schedule, unless they could find a person willing to volunteer for this experiment at the very last second. But where could they find someone who'd be willing to do that?

All of the sudden, Kyle had an idea. He quickly reached into his pocket, took out his phone and started dialing as he exited the lab area. The phone rang several times, and eventually a voice at the other end of the line picked up.

"Well look who it is, 'The Invisible Man'!" Travis said sarcastically as he answered the call from Kyle. "Now why in the hell would you be calling me this early on a Wednesday morning? Hmmm, let me think...you must need something, but I can't think of what. Whatever it is, I'm inclined to say no, given that you've been too cool to hang out with me for like the past month now."

"Hey listen, Travis I'm sorry," Kyle said. "I know I've been kind of shitty to you lately...and I know I don't give you enough credit for being a really good friend. I've been busy as hell lately, but I know that's no excuse. I feel really bad about it, and I want to apologize." Kyle had decided to throw on a little extra remorse up front, which he hoped would put Travis in a tough position to keep grilling him. This was a tactic that had worked well for him in the past in dealing with Travis, and he desperately hoped it would work again here.

"It's...it's okay man. I understand you're busy and shit. It happens," Travis eventually responded. "Why ARE you so busy all the time now anyway? What the hell do you have going on over at your office?"

"Well actually...that's part of the reason I'm calling you right now. There's something we could really use your help on over here, if you'd be willing to check it out. Do you think you could get over here around 6:00 PM tonight so I can show you what I'm talking about?" Kyle asked, still partially in shock that he was really planning to go through with this.

"Really? You want me to come by your lab? That's awesome man, I'd love to check it out! Yeah, I get off at 5:30 today so I can be there close to 6:00."

"Great, I'll text you the building address, so just call me when you get here tonight. Thanks a lot man, you're saving my ass right now. You really are a great friend," Kyle finished. He hung up with Travis, and reentered the lab to share the news with Ryan and Farida.

"Wait, who is this we're going to be testing today?" Farida asked. "Your buddy? Does he know anything about eidetic memory or what we're working on here?"

"He knows at least a little, I try to keep him in the loop on some of the stuff I'm involved with here," Kyle fibbed.

"I'm just amazed you were able to find someone who'd even consider volunteering for this on such short notice. I think given our options, we're going to have to give this a try," Ryan said. "Do you think he'll sign off on the experiment? And will he actually go through with it once we tell him what it is?"

"You guys can just let me worry about that. But for now, let's assume he's a 'Go', and get these protocols updated to reflect the changes." The team followed Kyle's lead, and spent the remainder of the day updating their documentation in preparation for Travis' visit.

When 6:06 PM finally rolled around, Kyle received a phone call from Travis. "Hey I think I'm outside your building. It looks dead from the outside, can you come let me in?"

Kyle retrieved Travis, and led him directly into the lab area, where he awkwardly exchanged introductions with Ryan and Farida.

"Cool place here man, lots of fancy machines. Must have cost someone a lot of money," Travis observed. "So it doesn't exactly look like we're all about to head out to happy hour. What are you guys working on here? And what made you finally invite me over?"

"It's very complicated to explain...but in a nutshell, here it is: Our team has recently uncovered a way for people to go back in time within their memories, and recall specific events from their past almost like they're living them over again," Kyle summarized as directly as he could.

"Ha! You're fucking shitting me man! Nice one! I give you credit for the imagination, but next time you might want to tone it down a tad," Travis said in disbelief. He continued to scan around the room, noticing that the three faces staring back at him did not appear to be joking.

"Wait...you're actually not kidding? You're fucking serious about this?" Travis asked. The revelation was astounding to him, and in an instant he was willing to forgive Kyle for all the times he had blown him off because of his job.

"I'm being completely serious buddy. We all are," Kyle answered. "So the main reason I called you in here in such a rush today is that we're up against a huge deadline. We need to run another experiment on someone to confirm that our system really does allow a person to photographically recall an event from their past. And we need to do it as soon as possible. And---"

"---And you want me to be your guinea pig. Hell yeah I'll do it! Where do I sign? Can we start now?" Travis asked eagerly.

Kyle looked over to Farida and Ryan, and without hesitation the three of them immediately got to work on finishing preparations for the system. Before long, Travis was being seated into the experimentation chair to begin his trial run.

"Okay Travis, so here's how this is going to work: We're going to put this headset on you, then have you sit back and try to relax your mind as much as you can. We're going to have you think of a memory from far back, preferably a happy memory from your childhood. And while you're staying relaxed, try to maintain focus on a specific detail you remember from that event."

"A happy memory from my childhood, eh? You know damn well I don't have a whole lot of those," Travis snarked at Kyle.

"Hey, it's what's worked best for us so far, so just try to think of something," Kyle said, as he sized the neuro-headset for Travis.

"Okay…think I've got one. It's going to sound weird, but it's actually from a family barbecue we had at my cousin's house in Kansas a long time ago, like a family reunion type thing. I remember it being a good day and my parents were always talking about it before they both turned into pieces of shit. But I only have flashes of it in my mind really," Travis said.

"Good choice, that should work perfectly, let's go with

that. Okay so when the system gets fully started you're going to feel a lot of vivid stimulation. Again it's like you're really going back there and reliving the memory in real-time. I just want you to relax and talk through it if you need to. Your mind will be able to wander a little, and you'll know that in reality you're in a lab strapped to a machine. But the system should keep bringing your focus back to the memory. We're going to try to go for 60 minutes, if that's cool with you," Kyle stated.

"Sounds great to me. Hell yeah this is exciting!" Travis responded.

Kyle looked over to Ryan and Farida, and received the thumbs up to start. "Okay you're all set to go. We're going to try to talk as little as possible at this point, so go ahead and sit back and relax, and just try to focus on what you remember from that day," Kyle instructed.

Travis made himself as comfortable as he could in the chair, sat back and began taking slow deep breaths. He allowed his mind to wander back to that day in Kansas. He remembered it was hot, somewhere around summertime. He tried to picture the yard…..

Tall green grass. Taller than I can ever remember seeing. It's so humid out! To my right I see two young kids playing in a small creek, trying to catch little fish with their bare hands. A puppy is bounding happily towards me with its tail wagging. The puppy is sniffing at my feet. My feet, look at how small they are! I'm in those little white loafers my mom always made me wear to family gatherings. I remember the tassles snapped off of them one time, and my dad showed me how to fix them. That memory must have happened sometime after this one.

I'm following my cousins down towards the creek bed. It's so full of life. Frogs are hopping around the wet rocks. Golden fish are swimming to the surface and trying to catch water bugs. The cattails that line the sides of the creek bed are taller than I am. I forgot those things even existed.

Now I'm walking towards the house. I'm throwing sticks for the puppy to fetch. How long did they have this dog for? I can't remember. It's hard to focus on other things. Now I'm walking towards a big tree that has a tire swing attached to it. I see two girls who look a couple years older than me. There's my cousin Melissa, and...oh my God, that's her friend Anna! She was my first kiss! Oh God, how much did I have to beg her for that? It was so worth it though. I used to think about that girl all the time. What an endorphin release that just gave me. This is absolutely incredible.

I'm walking up the hill towards the house. My relatives are hanging out on the driveway. Look at how well they're all getting along! I don't remember it ever being like this when my family got together. There's Uncle Nate grabbing a handful of beers out of an old Coleman cooler. How sauced is everyone gonna be here by the time they have to drive home? Oh the good ol' days.

There's my dad standing over by the TV with my uncles. They're all watching a baseball game. My dad looks great, I can tell the years of alcoholism and a two-pack a day habit haven't caught up with him just yet. He looks strong, and he's in a good mood judging from his reactions to the game. He sees me now, and he's telling me to come over. I walk up to him and wrap my arms around his leg. He pats me on the head with his free hand. Where was this during the rest of my childhood? Was this really too much to ask for?

I can't believe how vivid this experience is. I can even read the box score of the game on that small ass TV they brought outside: Royals 4, Tigers 2. Incredible. Now my mom is standing with us. She throws her arms around my dad, and she gives him a big kiss on the lips. I can't believe the affection they're showing each other. It seems genuine. Fuck. Things could have been so much different.

"How are we looking over there?" Kyle asked Ryan and Farida.

"So far so good," Ryan replied. "Vitals are fine, EEG signal is in the normal range."

"How about you, how does the 3-D model look? System recording everything correctly?" Kyle asked Farida.

"We're looking fine over here," Farida responded. "He actually went under more quickly than Ryan, believe it or not. I'll let you know if I see anything unusual. Looks like we have about 48 minutes left."

My family is now sitting together at the dinner table. I'm in a seat at a small folding table with my cousins. Everyone is still getting along so well with each other. Unbelievable. My mom is talking to my aunt about a book she read recently, something about a medieval princess. I wish I could understand more clearly what everyone is talking about. I want to hear everything. It's hard to focus. I'm going to have to come back here again someday. This can't be the last time.

I'm finished eating, and now I'm walking out into the living room. Behind me I see two of my uncles entering with two of my older cousins. They take a seat on the big L-shaped couch. They're talking about how great the meal was and how stuffed they all feel. I remember always thinking one my uncles was a nice guy and the other one was kind of a jackass, but now I can't even remember which is which. In the corner of the room I see an old man sitting in a wheelchair. He's slowly packing a black wooden pipe. He lights it up like a man with decades of experience.

My Uncle Brian turns to the old man. He says: "Hey Grandpa Vinny how have you been? I haven't seen you in years! In fact, I think the last time was when our Theresa was born and we had everyone over to the house."

"Ahh well, my stream is still strong and I can still wipe my own ass, so I guess no complaints!" the old man responds. Everyone on the couch is cracking up. Is this old dude my great-grandfather? I don't remember him at all.

My Uncle Larry nudges my cousin Patrick, who looks to be in his mid-teens at this time. "Hey, did you know you have Hollywood royalty in your bloodline? Grandpa Vinny here used to be a big-shot producer over in Tinseltown back in the day. Even acted in a few of them right? I've tried for years to get some good stories out of him but haven't gotten a whole lot. Come on Grandpa Vinny, you gotta tell us what it was like? Give us a good one while we've got the family here together!"

"Great-grandpa was in the movies? How did I never hear about this before?" Patrick asks.

The old man lets out a cloudy puff of smoke from his pipe, and takes a moment for himself before speaking: "The story of how I became an Executive Producer at one of the biggest studios in

Hollywood is one that's too long for today, I'll tell you that. And I could go on all day about how things were different back then. A man gained respect by working hard and taking risks, not by playing politics and trying to bring others down."

"Amen! Man I agree with you, I feel like I was born in the wrong era sometimes," my Uncle Larry, who's clearly drunk, belts out loudly. "I see how it's just getting worse for these boys too and it makes me sick. Poor little Travis over there probably doesn't stand a chance in hell!"

"Yeah, well it was certainly a different time back then...back when my buddy Albert and I made the trip out to Los Angeles at the ripe old age of 19. You all know I loved your Grandma Judy very much...and even though we chose to live separately for the last few years, I always considered her the love of my life. But I'll tell you what...Hollywood back in the 1930's was a young single man's paradise! Dames like I've never seen before or since!" the old man chirps, and I see him give a devilish glance towards the men on the couch.

Wild laughter fills the room, and I can tell the other guys are trying to envision what he's talking about. The old man continues: "On one particular picture, I believe it was around 1937, Albert had worked his way up to Casting Director, and had gotten me on the film as a producer. The film was supposed to be a biblical epic from the Old Testament, and the script called for a budding romance between a religious prophet and young woman. The line of women auditioning for the lead role was out of this world! Just BEAUTIFUL women! One of them in particular caught my eye right off the bat. I begged and begged Albert to cast her in the lead actress role. Eventually he finally gave in, and as production on the film began, I fell hard for her. Long brunette hair, striking green eyes, stems for days, oh the whole works. To this day, the most beautiful woman I've ever seen!"

The men are now leaning forward intently, eyes transfixed and sipping from their beers in eager anticipation. I'm finding myself completely drawn in to this story as well, and I can't wait to hear what the payoff is. I can't believe my whole life I've gone through thinking that no one in my loser bloodline has ever amounted to anything. Now I'm learning that my great-grandpa was a Hollywood hotshot!

He continues: "As filming was about to begin, it became

apparent that this girl just didn't have the chops to pull off a leading role in a blockbuster picture like this. I spent hours a day with her, attempting to focus on getting her ready for the film, but mainly just fawning all over her," the old man confessed. "I don't know if it was the compassion I was showing her or just dumb persistence, but eventually she began to grow fond of me as well. Now a gentleman never tells details...but let's just say we were able to take advantage of the nearby producer's trailer a few times."

This sends the room into a frenzy. Uncle Larry is lurching back in his seat and laughs himself to the point where he starts coughing violently. Patrick is clapping his hands together so hard that he spills half his beer on himself. This is so cool to see. I love this.

"Come on let's hear it, there's got to be more!" Uncle Larry booms.

It seems like recounting this story in front of an audience is giving the old man some renewed energy. He rolls his chair closer to the couch, sits up straight, and continues: "Well a few weeks into filming, Albert comes up to me one day. He says 'Vin, we might have a big problem here. I think I picked the wrong gal to play the lead in this film.'"

"I say to him something like, 'I don't know, I think she's doing an alright job. She certainly looks the part.'"

So Albert looks at me, and I can tell he's having a tough time getting this out. Eventually he says 'If it was just the acting, I could probably send her down for an easier role. But it's not that. It's that...I just found out from our cameraman that she's been sleeping with members of the crew!'

Uncle Larry slaps his leg in excitement and leans in. "Oh man, you must have been shitting your pants! What did you do?"

"So I'm thinking about how I'm going to come clean to Albert, my best friend. I don't want to ruin this movie, and I certainly don't want to blow my big chance in Hollywood. And I know we can't have the lead actress in this epic religious movie shrouded in rumors of being a hussy on set. So I ask Albert, I say 'I can't believe this. Do you know yet which guy she was with?'"

"Albert has this exasperated look on his face, and says 'Which guy? WHICH GUY?!? Vinny my friend, I hear she's slept her way across almost the entire set!'"

Now Uncle Larry falls forward off the couch and is literally rolling around on the ground. Even Uncle Brian, who I'm realizing was the more conservative one, is beet red from laughing so hard.

My great-grandpa continues: "So, initially I was a little hurt that she didn't harbor feelings only for me. But I quickly got over it. She was unfortunately dismissed from the cast several days later. Do you fellas want to know the best part?"

"Hell yeah we do!" shouts Uncle Larry.

"The best part is...this girl eventually learned how to act. And act very well. So well in fact, that she was able to land the leading role years later in an epic movie called….."

"And he's out," announced Farida. "Just need him to keep the headset on for another 20 seconds to finish the recording and we're all set!"

"WAIT...WAIT...DAMN YOU!" Travis attempted to scream as the memory faded and he steadily regained his awareness.

"Hey buddy, how you feeling? Just hang tight there for another couple seconds and I'll get this thing off of you," Kyle instructed Travis.

"Holy shit did that really just happen? Was that for real?!?" Travis asked in total disbelief. "That wasn't one of those virtual reality things right? That's not what you guys really do here, is it?"

"Yes my friend...believe it or not, it was for real. And you did great man. So tell us about the memory, what did you see?" Kyle asked as he slowly removed the neuro-headset from Travis' head.

Travis had to compose himself for a moment while he tried to form a sensible description of what he'd just experienced. "It was like you said. It was like I was really back there, six years old or however old I was at that time. I saw relatives I had completely forgotten about. I saw my parents...and they were happy. And nice to me! Can you believe it?"

"I know. I've heard it's incredible in there. You're lucky, I haven't even gotten to take it for a spin yet! You and Ryan over here are basically the only people in the world who have had this opportunity so far," Kyle informed Travis.

"I'm so pumped that just worked!" Ryan declared loudly. "You guys know that years from now, people are going remember where this amazing technology all started. Right here in this place. Shit yes!" Ryan exclaimed as he put his arm around Farida and gave her a big celebratory hug.

"I certainly hope you're right. Well I don't know about you, but I'm wiped now. Let's see if we can finish up here real quick, close down shop and all go get a drink somewhere nearby to celebrate. Sound good?" Kyle asked.

Everyone was in agreement, and a short time later the four of them triumphantly marched out of the lab, each certain that today was a day that would change their lives forever.

Chapter 16

It had been a whirlwind two weeks since the Eidetic Memory Team had submitted their summary report, which contained the results from both Ryan's and Travis' experimental runs. Kyle had decided to break the news at that month's Senior Management staff meeting. He had dazzled the audience with a well-prepared visual demonstration of the experimental procedure. The real "wow" moment came when he displayed a split-screen showing an earlier trial run, where the test subject's synapses fired at random, contrasted against a display of Ryan's and Travis' perfectly structured synapse patterns. This had left quite a few of the senior scientists in the room speechless. Kyle took advantage of the moment to call up another video, this one demonstrating recursive functions in mathematical programming. Kyle then communicated how recursion had been the real breakthrough in getting their system to work, and gave Farida her much-deserved credit in being ultimately responsible for the discovery.

Senior Management had requested the team attempt to prepare a live demonstration to align with the Cognitive Sciences Seminar, taking place on campus in three days' time. This would mean they would have spectators present from all over the University of California system, as well as visitors from some of the most respected universities on the East Coast such as MIT and Yale. Kyle had agreed to the challenge, and his team was honored, if not a bit trepidatious, by the prospect of doing a live demo in front of the brightest minds in the field.

"We all knew this day was coming eventually," Kyle had

said. "We just have to trust in our process and trust in the technology. We've already had two experiments that ran almost flawlessly. Well three, if we count Farida's. This is really our chance to finally shine."

"Kyle's right...we have nothing to worry about," Michael added, back from his recent brush with the flu and finally feeling close to 100%. "This is where all our hard work pays off. We get a chance to make history in front of some of the most accomplished scientists in academia. Let's give them a day they'll talk about for the rest of their lives."

"Amen. So...who should we put in the chair?" Farida asked anxiously.

Before anyone else could begin to debate an answer, Michael stepped forward to make a rather compelling case for himself. "Sorry guys, but I think this time it has to be me. Not only is it kind of my turn...but I have a special memory in mind that I'm planning to use."

"Well what is it?" Ryan asked anxiously.

"It's, umm...well I don't know how to say this. It's actually the death of my mother," Michael confirmed. A few moments passed in silence, with no one in the room sure what exactly to say next. With a heavy heart, Kyle searched for the appropriate way to put this risky suggestion to a vote.

"I'm sorry Michael. I didn't even know your mother was gone," Kyle said. "I'm sorry if this sounds a little insensitive, but are you sure you think this would be the best time to recall this memory? In front of the type of audience we're going to have here?"

"Actually, I think it's the perfect time. I think it's meant to be this way," Michael answered. "My dad gave me a call two nights ago, and he was balling his eyes out over the upcoming 25 year anniversary of my mom passing away from pancreatic cancer. I tried to calm him down like I always do, when the sadness gets too much for him to handle. We talked about my mom for a while, what we missed most about her and why we both loved her so much. You know what he told me his biggest regret was? He said to me, 'I wasn't there in the room with her when she passed. I was weak, and I had left you and your sister with her so I could get away for a second and have a couple smokes. I think you were both too young to even comprehend what was happening back then. None of us got to say goodbye, before she slipped away.'"

"So it's those final moments you want to try to recall?" Kyle asked.

"Exactly. My older sister still swears to this day she heard my mom whisper something in that room, before the doctors and my father came in and she was pronounced dead. I know it's a long shot, but this could be a chance to provide my family some sort of closure. And further than that, I'm sure it'll put on a riveting show for our esteemed guests," Michael concluded.

There was no dispute about what Michael had said from anyone in the room, and the team went forward with attempting to make the most of their three day window. One of their main focuses was to pump up the system's graphical output and link it to the bank of monitors outside the lab area, so that the estimated 30+ guests they were anticipating would have the full range of available information displayed right there in front of them.

When the morning of the demonstration came along, the Keane Institute for Learning and Memory was abuzz with more excitement than it had ever seen. It was finally showtime, and they felt ready for it.

As the large group of visitors rounded the corner towards the lab, Stan was finishing up his rundown on the lab's history and the recent breakthrough they'd had in eidetic memory research. Stan then pressed the intercom button in the viewing area to alert Kyle, who was inside the lab, that they were now ready for the team to begin.

"Good morning everyone, and welcome to the Eidetic

Memory Laboratory at Keane," Kyle said through the intercom system. "I'm sure by now you've all received my synopsis detailing how our technology functions, and I'm sure Stan has given you a thorough summary of what we plan to do here today, for the next 60 minutes or so. So without further ado, I'd like to introduce the rest of the team. Constituting our Laboratory Science Technician staff we have Ryan Bisbee and Michael Jacobs, who are full-time employees here at UC Santa Clara. In addition we have Farida Eshed, who is on assignment with us from UCLA. Today we will be conducting a recall experiment with Michael as our test subject."

Michael gave a quick wave of acknowledgement, and the crowd briefly applauded Michael as the volunteer. When the applause ended, Kyle made sure to capture the appropriate tone for his next reveal.

"Our experiments up to this point have focused on recalling what I would classify as 'positive childhood memories'. Fortunately these types of memories usually prove plentiful, and are often easy to detail. However, in this case we are choosing to challenge our system by focusing on a different type of memory. Michael has elected to give us all a view into his last moments with his dying mother, who passed away from cancer almost 25 years ago."

The audience seemed surprised by this revelation, but was nevertheless still hanging on Kyle's every word. Kyle was now starting to feel less concerned about their decision to involve such a grave topic. He continued: "As Michael was only seven years old on the day she passed, he currently only possesses a general sense of that day. Michael has in addition chosen to try to narrate as much of the detail he is witnessing as possible. This should hopefully provide a framework for what he is seeing in his mind. We appreciate your respect and full attention during this process. And we all thank Michael for being willing to share such a personal moment from his life."

The audience gave a polite and respectful applause as Kyle finished his introduction. Now the team was loading Michael into the experimentation chair and connecting him into the system.

"You still sure you want to go through with this?" Kyle asked Michael. "I respect the hell out of you for it, but I'm sure nobody will fault you if you want switch your memory to something else."

"Thanks Kyle, but I swear I'm fine," Michael replied. "If there's even a remote possibility of providing some answers for my family, I want to give it a try as soon as possible. I feel grateful for being given this amazing opportunity. And this is going to make such an impact for our project. Thank you again for allowing me to take this chance."

With that, Kyle assumed his position with Ryan next to the monitoring equipment. Still anxious, but forcing himself to stay composed, he proceeded to give Farida the nod to start the system.

Over the intercom, Kyle instructed Michael to relax and breathe slowly. The crowd watched in high anticipation as the lab fell silent. They watched Michael close his eyes and begin taking in deep breaths, exhaling as slowly as he could. In and out, Michael continued to breath. Then, less than a minute later.....

"My dad...he's sitting in a chair next to mom's bed. Amy's sitting on his lap. She's...she's touching my mom's arm, my dad is petting her hair. Mom looks so sick. This isn't how I remember her. It's a bright and sunny day outside her window. I wish she could wake up and see it."

Kyle looked at Farida, who remained focused at the 3-D modeling workstation. Ryan took a deep breath, exhaled, and continued to monitor the brainwave activities on the EEG screens. Kyle stepped up to the nearby microphone, and quietly asked if the crowd outside could see the replications of the lab displays they had set up on the monitors in the viewing area. A few members of the crowd gave Kyle a thumbs up, as all eyes appeared to be glued to the two main screens in the center of the viewing area.

"Now my dad is getting up. He's wiping a tear from his eye. He sets my sister on the ground, tells us to stay with mom, and that he'll be right back. Me and my sister are playing with some coloring books, on the floor at the foot of my mom's bed...it's quiet in the room now...I can hear people in the distance walking by in the hallway...it's still quiet..."

The team continued to monitor Michael's status as he fell silent for the next several minutes. Ryan recorded a few figures from the EEG onto a form, and handed it to Kyle to give it to Farida. Farida took a moment to review the figures, then quickly input them into her model. Kyle used this brief opportunity of downtime to walk up to the observation window near the viewing area. The visitors, still with looks of amazement on their faces, were continuing to watch the monitors attentively. Kyle approached the right side of the area where the management team from the institute was seated. He made an "ok" signal in their direction, to which several of them smiled and confirmed that everything was good on their end.

Kyle then retook his seat near Michael, who was remaining deeply focused in his memory, but continued to give sporadic updates on his interaction with his sister.

Finally, with 6 minutes and 37 seconds left in the session, Michael began speaking faster.

"I hear something...sounds like...like a groan coming from my mom. My sister and I look at her...there's no movement. We both sit down again. There's another groan. I hurry over to my mom...I knock into a piece of equipment. My sister follows me...she stops. She's crying. My mom's head moves slightly, towards my direction. Her eyes are still closed. Her lips are moving, she's now whispering something. I lean in. She's still whispering, softly. I can't hear her. I lean in more. More. Now I can hear. She...she

says 'My family...is what I'll miss most. Make me proud...all of you.' She stops. She's not whispering anymore. My sister runs up to her, grabs her arm. She calls out for my mom. No response. She asks me what mom said. I say I don't know. My sister runs out, trying to find my dad. It's just me now. I'm holding my mom's hand..."

Michael became silent for the remaining moments of the session. When the clock on the monitors finally hit zeros, Kyle looked out into the audience. The entire crowd was visibly stunned by what they had just witnessed. The emotional impact of reliving this experience with Michael, combined with the awe-inspiring marvel of technology that had enabled it, was too much for some in the audience to handle. There were more than a few tears being shed as Ryan slowly helped Michael out of the chair. Kyle himself was struggling to hold back his emotions. Michael, out of the four of them, actually seemed to be the most at peace with what had just occurred. When Michael appeared reoriented, Kyle walked over to him, giving him a big hug. "That was really something. I hope you got what you needed."

"I think I did. Thanks again boss. This technology is going to change the world."

The two embraced again, and the crowd burst into applause as Michael approached one of the intercom microphones.

"Thank you all again...for coming today to witness what we've accomplished here. I know that was an extremely difficult experience for me, and I'm sure it was probably tough for some of you as well. Hopefully though, this was effective in demonstrating what this incredible technology is capable of achieving. I just want to say I'm very proud to be a part of this team, and I'm looking forward to what lies ahead for this project. Thank you."

"Thank you as well, Michael, and the rest of the team," Stan chimed in from the viewing area intercom. "We are all very proud of what this team has accomplished, and we plan to work as hard as we can to ensure we provide you with all the resources you need going forward, to continue to move this project to the next level, wherever that may be. I think someone may be giving the Basel Institut a run for its money at the next International Conference!" Stan boasted, followed by another round of cheers from the crowd. "For now, I think we'll be heading back to the seminar. Though I must say, it's tempting to play hookie and stay here after witnessing something as exciting as this." The crowd politely laughed along with Stan, then started to file out of the viewing area.

"Kyle, I know you guys probably have some wrap-up to do with the experiment. Do you have time tomorrow morning for a quick debriefing with some of our department heads?" Stan asked.

"Sure do. Send me an invite and I'll make sure I'm available."

As the last of the visitors left, the team sat together in silence, reflecting on what they had just achieved that morning in such a short amount of time. Michael's bravery had paid off, and though the experience had been tough on him, he was rewarded with a degree of closure for his family that couldn't have been obtained any other way. And with the seniority level of the industry professionals who had just witnessed their experiment, the four of them had all but guaranteed job security for the remainder of their careers.

"Let's all take a well-deserved break for a couple hours, and plan on meeting back here this afternoon to talk about what we want to do next," Kyle suggested. The team agreed, and went their separate ways, each member feeling extremely satisfied with the direction that their treasured project was headed in. None of them could have anticipated what was about to come.

Chapter 17

"Hey everybody, let's go ahead and get started," Darren said, as the rest of the group settled into their seats within the circle of chairs. It was a lighter crowd than usual at the San Marcos Counseling Center, with about a third of the 25 or so seats empty in the room. Travis took a seat next to a younger woman who was new to the group, and tried to strike up a conversation with her, though she didn't seem terribly interested in making small talk about how much it sucked to spend your Thursday night talking about what's making you miserable with a bunch of strangers. She had however appeared to enjoy when Travis muttered to himself that one of new guys in the group looked like he had fallen out of the "I like to touch kids" tree and hit every branch on the way down.

As the session commenced, Travis looked around the room and did not see Jamie present. She had been off-and-on with her attendance for a while, and had missed the past few weeks, even after telling Travis during their meet up for coffee that she would start attending again. Travis couldn't help but wonder if something might be wrong on the home front between her and Manny. He'd been thinking about her pretty regularly since their last meeting. And even though Kyle had told him to keep it under his hat, Travis was eager to tell someone about his unbelievable experience with the memory recall device. He figured that even his minor involvement in such an astonishing discovery would be enough to impress most women, hopefully including Jamie.

"Today I thought we'd do things a little differently," Darren continued. "Here's what I had in mind: I'd like us all to take a couple of minutes, and try to think back to a specific event in our past."

"Wow, think about our past, what a trailblazing idea!" joked one of the guys in the group. "We've never done that in here before!"

"I know, I know, it's all we do every week," Darren joked back. "But this time...I'd like you to try to think of something that happened to you in your past that you've been unable to let go of. Something that you've found yourself going back to in your mind time and time again. Something that you feel has had a hand in shaping the pathway of your life. I can go ahead and share first, and maybe my experience will trigger some experiences of your own."

"So back when I was using, I used to have this weird habit where I would go hang out in cemeteries by myself after I'd shot up."

"Really? Man you are a freak!" shouted Jamal, one of the relative newcomers to the group. A few of the other members chuckled as well, as it was strange to hear something like this come out of Darren's mouth, who came off as a pretty straight-shooter most of the time.

"Ha, believe me, in retrospect I still can't believe that that used to be my idea of a good time. But drugs make us do strange things. Anyway back to the story...So I had this large cemetery about a half mile away from my house, and I would often shoot up crystal meth and head over there after. Normally I'd just kind of stumble around, checking out some of the elaborate monuments and headstones that were there. I'd fantasize in my mind about what these people's lives might have been like, some of whom had died over a hundred years ago."

"On some days, if I was lucky, I'd happen upon a burial service. I know that sounds nuts, but these were absolutely mesmerizing for me to witness when I was stoned. I'd usually try to lie next to a tree in the distance, close enough to where I could hear what was being said. I couldn't help but be fascinated by the show of emotion that was always on display. Grown adults crying their eyes out, sometimes physically collapsing under the weight of their sadness. I'd become so numb from the drugs and the denial that I was dealing with in my life, that this sadness served as a sort of contrast that I was oddly drawn towards."

"One day I had shot up a particularly potent concoction of heroin and meth, and had made my way over to the cemetery on a sunny Saturday afternoon, which was usually the best day to catch the burial shows. It turned out I was in luck on this day, as there was a very large burial service being held in the middle of the cemetery. So I took a seat on a park bench nearby and listened in as the minister spoke about the deceased. He was apparently a father who appeared to be only in his late 30's or early 40's, judging from the portrait they had displayed next to the casket. He must have been a very good man based on the minister's kind words and the impressive attendance. I continued to watch the service come to a close, as they eventually lowered the casket into the ground. As the attendees started to file out, I saw a group of three people near the middle of the crowd, being consoled by nearly everyone who passed by. There were two young children, one boy and one girl, and a pretty woman standing with them. I assumed this must be the widow of the deceased man with her children. Slowly the crowd started to make their way back to the area where the cars were parked, which was not far away from where I was seated. Now normally, I probably would have gotten spooked by getting this close to the strangers I was eavesdropping on. But my buzz that day was strong enough to conquer any amount of unpleasantness. Or so I thought."

"As the crowd continued to leave, I felt my heart start to beat very rapidly. I started feeling extremely nauseous, like I was having bad trip. I was starting to worry I might be having an overdose, and that worry kept compounding in my brain until I almost began to black out from it. I tried to make myself get up from the bench and run away, but my legs, they felt like they weighed 1,000 pounds each. So the best I could do was just kind of fumble off the park bench and wobble a few feet. But I couldn't hold myself up, so I fell down on the ground."

"While I was laying there, trying to catch my breath, ahead of me I could see the family of the dead man only about 40 feet away. The woman and the daughter were still bawling, crying into the arms of a relative. But the little boy...he must have seen me struggling on the ground there, and he started walking towards me. I was panicked at this point, and doing everything I could to get to my feet and get the hell out of there. The boy was now close enough to me to where I could see him very clearly. His eyes were still swollen red from crying, but now he carried on his face more of a concerned look. He slowly continued towards me, and then I heard him call out back to his family: 'Mom, mom, this man needs help! Mom, come help him!'"

Most eyes within the group were now fixed towards the ground, having trouble focusing on Darren as he continued his harrowing story.

"Hearing these words being shouted from this little boy must have jolted me back to my senses, and I was finally able to get up off the ground and stumble back home from the cemetery, never once looking back. For days afterwards, I was beside myself with guilt from what I had done. I couldn't get it out of my head, what I saw from that little boy that day. There I was, a complete waste of life, a worthless junkie who found entertainment out of witnessing other people's misery. And there was this little boy, who had just lost his father and whose life was being changed forever. And he was the one who had reached out to help me! I couldn't believe how impossibly selfish I had become during that time when I was using. I was completely incapable of thinking about the welfare of anyone besides myself."

"From that moment on, my love affair with drugs started to steadily decline. I still shot up here and there for the next couple months, but it was never quite the same for me. Within a year I was completely clean, and aside from one relapse I've been clean ever since."

The group, unsure of how to respond, offered a polite applause before they were quickly cut off by Darren.

"I appreciate the sentiment, but I definitely don't deserve any praise for any part of this story. In the end I consider myself very fortunate to have made a positive outcome out of all this. It's what drove me into discovering the healing powers of therapy, and eventually to start leading groups full of wonderful people like yourselves. But I've never really been able to forgive myself for that day. Much too often, when I'm starting to feel that my life has discovered its purpose, and that I've done more good in my time on this earth than bad...my mind inevitably goes back to that day. I believe people are capable of extreme acts of kindness and forgiveness. And I believe that if I met that boy again today, he would probably forgive me for disgracing his father's funeral. But I truly don't know if I'm ever going to really be able to forgive myself..."

Darren allowed a few moments to go by for the members of the group to reflect on what he'd said before continuing.

"Well, that's probably enough from me for one night. Would anyone else like to share a memory from their past?"

Harold, the former gang member from Oakland, volunteered to speak, and began to tell the group about a shootout he'd had with a rival gang when he was younger, that had resulted in innocent bystanders being wounded. As Travis listened to Harold's story, he noticed the side door open, and he saw Jamie slowly walking through. She quietly closed the door behind her, standing in silence in the back of the room as Harold continued his story. She looked unsure if she should join the circle, and from her appearance she looked very upset about something. Travis decided to sneak away from the group and go back to see what was going on with her.

"Hey Jamie, how's it going?" Travis asked, seeing that Jamie's eyes were red and puffy as he got closer to her, as if she'd been crying recently.

"Oh hey Travis," Jamie said, seeming embarrassed and trying to dry her eyes with her jacket sleeve. "Sorry I'm a bit of a mess right now. Been a rough day."

"Oh crap, I'm sorry to hear that," Travis replied. "Well I don't know if joining group is going to make you feel any better, we're talking about some pretty heavy stuff today. If you want to go outside or something and talk about it...I'm all ears."

"Okay. Thank you Travis, I really appreciate it," Jamie answered as they exited the side door.

They were both silent as they went outside into the chilly evening weather. It was now Fall, and the temperature was already starting to drop noticeably at night. Travis was nervous to broach the subject of asking what was bothering Jamie, but he didn't want to let the silence become uncomfortable.

"So what's got you all worked up? Did something go wrong at the hospital or something?" Travis asked.

"No no, it's not that. I just...I've been in a really weird place mentally these past couple weeks. I don't know how it got so bad either, I was doing pretty well the last time I saw you. I just can't seem to get out of my own head. I feel like something is eating at me, it has been for a long time, and I'm just too stupid or something to figure it out."

Travis lit up a cigarette and took a slow drag, blowing a cloud of smoke into the crisp evening air. He offered Jamie the pack as a friendly gesture, figuring she'd quickly decline. To his surprise, she took out a cigarette, and leaned towards

Travis so he could light it for her. They sat for another moment in silence, staring out into the distance as the sun completely disappeared from view over the trees and buildings.

Travis again broke the silence. "I didn't peg you as a smoker. I figured you were one of those vegan healthy-living Northern California types."

"Ha, well you've got the avoiding meat part right. But I wouldn't exactly say I've been living a healthy lifestyle lately. I hate to say it, but I think Manny and I might be through."

Travis did his best to not appear excited by this development. "Oh really? What happened there?"

"We've just been fighting over the same crap for a really long time, and I think he's finally had enough of it. I know most of it was definitely my fault. I couldn't take him criticizing me anymore, and he couldn't handle the negative outlook I was taking on most things. I feel really bad about it. He's such a nice guy and a good person, and I know he cared about me a lot. I wish I could have been the happy-go-lucky type of person that he wanted and deserved...but I'm just not even close to feeling that way about my life right now. Ugh, I'm so sick of even talking about it, I'm sure I'm already annoying the shit out of you."

"Hey, no way girl, let it all out! Everyone I know has got problems. Yours are no worse than most of the people in that room over there...just different. Lord knows I've got plenty of fucked up shit in my life. You've just got to try to take the good days with the bad, I guess. Something like that..." Travis said.

"Well I'd take ANY good days at this point," Jamie laughed. "Wow...just...wow... I never ever thought that my life would end up like this. Back when I was a little girl, I thought I'd grow up to be a famous singer, and I'd be touring across the country, uplifting people with my music and making their lives better. I remember I even dreamt about holding a big charity concert for the village my family is originally from in Mexico. I wanted the concert to last for days and days, so more and more people could come and we could raise enough money to lift the village out of poverty. Back then, I used to always think about how to make other people happy. Now I'm so self-absorbed and caught up in my own issues, I can't even remember the last time I went out of my way to do something truly nice for someone else. God that's terrible!"

"I hear ya... The world's kind of a fucked up place, you gotta do what you can to find a little bit of happiness," Travis said. "I don't know...sometimes I feel like there's something just really wrong with our generation. People either come off as spoiled whiny little bitches, or they take themselves so seriously that you can't even understand what makes them want to get out of bed in the morning. There's just so little guidance out there to tell us if we're heading in the right direction. It's really confusing shit. I don't know...I guess we shouldn't be so hard on ourselves for having a tough time figuring it all out."

"Yeah...you're kind of right. That's a good way of putting it actually," Jamie agreed, pausing to compose herself. "So enough about me already. How have you been doing lately Travis?"

"Me? Umm...I guess I've been doing pretty well actually. Haven't had any more run-in's with the law, so that's a start I suppose. Actually I've just been kind of trying to relax and take it easy lately," Travis finished. He thought for a moment about what he wanted to say next, realizing he wasn't going to be able to keep it a secret any longer.

"I did have something really exciting happen to me the other day. But I don't think you'd even believe me if I told you. It doesn't sound like it's even possible."

"Really, what?!? Tell me! Come on you have to tell me about it!" Jamie pleaded.

"I mean...I guess I'll try, but I'm warning you it's Star

Trek-sounding shit. So...you remember how a while back I told you about my buddy Kyle, who works at a research lab in Santa Clara?"

"Yep I remember."

"Well the lab there specializes in analyzing the human memory. And Kyle is managing a team there that's been working on this machine. I know it sounds crazy...but the machine is designed to enable people to go back in time within their own thoughts, and relive memories from their past."

"Wait what...are you kidding me?" Jamie responded. "You're right, that doesn't sound real at all!"

"I know I know, believe me I called Kyle a fucking liar when he came clean and told me about it a few weeks ago. But the thing is Jamie...I went over there to the lab to see what he was talking about. Actually he'd invited me in to be their next test subject, since the guy who was supposed to do it was out sick or some shit. So I got to go in and try out their machine...AND IT TOTALLY FUCKING WORKS!!!"

Jamie's jaw dropped to the floor. It was unbelievable what Travis had just told her...but the look on Travis' face, which typically held some semblance of a joking expression, appeared in this moment to be dead serious. Jamie couldn't comprehend that this could be a reality, but she did acknowledge that this moment didn't seem like an opportune time for Travis to try to pull one over on her. Was he really not messing around?

"It's an unbelievable experience Jamie. I mean words can't describe what it's like to go back there in your mind, back to your own childhood. It makes you realize so many different things, things you were too young to notice at the time. I feel like it gives you a whole new appreciation. Now pretty much all I can think about is going back in there and trying it out again. It's just...it's intoxicating..."

"Oh my God Travis! Oh my God I can't believe what you're telling me! That sounds so incredible! I certainly can't blame you for obsessing over it. Part of me wants to beg you to take me over there so I can try it out myself!"

"Well hey, maybe I could even try to make that happen. I feel like everyone I know should try this thing. I mean for people like you and me, who are loaded up with this emotional baggage, I feel like it could do a lot of good for us," Travis continued passionately. He could see Jamie's face fill with hope, as she stared into his eyes with excitement. He knew this could be his one big chance to make an indelible impression her, and he had no choice but to continue down the path he had started on.

"Yeah, you know what...I think I will try and get you over there! The more I think about it, the more I feel like this could really help you out with what you're going through. I'll tell you what, I'll talk with Kyle this week and see if there's any way he can get us in there as volunteers. I mean they're always looking for people, so they'd probably love to have us!"

"Wow, that would be so amazing Travis! Thank you so much for being willing to try that for me! Thank you thank you!!" Jamie screamed, shaking with excitement, as she grabbed Travis and kissed him hard on the cheek.

Travis could feel his heart melt as Jamie's lips met his face. He knew he now had some serious work to do on Kyle. He had to figure out a way to get back into that lab.

Chapter 18

Kyle hopped into the back of the Jeep, more than ready to get away from the city for a day. His team had been working almost nonstop up to this point, and he had mandated they take this Sunday off to get away from the office in hopes of maintaining their sanity. Given that Kyle had spent the better part of his time so far in the Bay Area either at his office in Santa Clara, or in his neighborhood in downtown San Francisco, he had done very little in the way of outdoor exploration, and was excited for this day trip. He was glad he'd been fortunate enough to bump into his neighbor Carlos, who lived three floors below him in his apartment building, a few days earlier that week. Carlos was organizing a day hike in the Muir Woods on Sunday, and offered Kyle the last seat in one of the Jeeps heading out in the morning. Kyle had been surprised by the impromptu invite, but it had only taken him a second to decide to sign up, and at this moment he was very happy that he had.

There were five SUVs in all, caravanning across the Golden Gate Bridge towards the forested area north of San Francisco. Kyle introduced himself to the three other passengers in Carlos' Jeep. They were all friends of Carlos who had met through the hiking club Carlos had started four years earlier. The club would usually schedule a couple of day hikes per month, and throw in a few overnight camping trips throughout the year. It seemed like a good escape from the big city grind, and as Kyle looked in awe at the giant redwood trees lining the road up to the trailhead, he thought to himself that this might be a hobby he'd enjoy doing more often.

The five vehicles pulled into the small dirt parking lot adjacent to the trailhead. Kyle jumped out of the Jeep and walked to the nearby cliffside to survey the landscape. The fresh mountain air filled Kyle's lungs as he took in the impressive scenery, and Kyle began to feel more relaxed than he had in months. He had to admit to himself, he hadn't been living the healthiest lifestyle imaginable the past couple of months. Sitting in the lab at work all day, then binge drinking and partying with Travis on the weekends to blow off steam, with an all too occasional trip to the gym thrown in. And ever since his life had been flipped upside-down with the breakthrough in the lab, he had been all-consumed with unlocking the potential of their discovery. Standing here in the mountains several thousand feet above the city, Kyle was finally feeling able to take a step back from everything, and attempt to gain a better perspective on what he hoped to accomplish in the coming months.

"Alright gang, as most of you know we start each hike with a pre-hike shot to celebrate our lives, and our ability to come out here and enjoy everything that nature has to offer. So if you're a fan of rum punch, come on in and grab one," Carlos instructed, as the group of around 25 people gathered around the folding table Carlos had set up. Kyle took one of the small paper cups, and waited patiently for the rest of the group. "Salud!" shouted Carlos, as the group echoed his cheers and took down the rum punch shots.

Everyone then began assembling their gear in preparation for the four hour hike. Kyle found Carlos preparing his backpack, and approached him. "Just wanted to say, thank you again for getting my ass off the couch and getting me out here. I really appreciate the invite."

"Of course my friend! We do this all the time, so hopefully you can start joining us in the future," Carlos said. "Although, if you want to become a serious hiker, we're going to have to get you some real hiking boots!" Carlos was referring to the shoddy white gym shoes that Kyle was currently sporting. He'd had the shoes buried in the back of his closet for a long time, and having been caught off guard by the hiking invite, had basically grabbed what he had available. As they began to ascend up the hill, he was realizing the bald tread might not be very conducive to climbing these steep trails.

The climb continued sharply uphill for about a half mile, before finally leveling off near a creek bed that snaked through the trees. Kyle was already somewhat winded from the challenging start to the hike. He was thankful for a brief reprieve near the beginning of the creek bed, as the group discussed which route would be the best to take to the mountaintop. He fumbled with the spare water hydration backpack Carlos had brought for him, finally getting the bite valve to function properly as he chugged down about a quarter of the pack in one steady stream.

The group decided to continue along the creek, which was shaded from the unusual heat by large redwood trees. As the lot where they had parked completely disappeared from view, Kyle realized this was probably the furthest away he had been from civilization in years. *Good, about time,* he thought to himself.

The trail continued on a slight incline along the creek, and eventually curved towards a wooden bridge which crossed the creek. Carlos informed them that following this branch of the trail would get them to the summit quicker, but was a little more strenuous. As the group continued across the bridge, someone spotted a school of Coho salmon swimming underneath in the creek. Kyle quickly took out his phone and snapped off a couple pictures of the fish as they swam by. Even during his rare forays into the wilderness back when he lived in Arizona, Kyle rarely saw much in the way of wildlife, so he was grateful to have the opportunity now.

The difficulty of the trail increased substantially for the next mile or so, and despite Kyle's recent attempts to get in a quick workout a couple times a week, so far he was getting about all he could handle from this hike. Kyle was also having some difficulty keeping his footing with his worn out shoes, so he decided to take a position near the back of the pack. He was still in great spirits though, and was enjoying listening to the other members of the group talk about their past hikes and the upcoming camping trips they had planned.

As they continued along the creek, Carlos announced that they were only another 40 minutes or so away from a scenic canyon that was one of his favorite stopping points. Kyle was finally starting to get acclimated to the pace of the hike, and decided to strike up a conversation with the group of three hikers who were with him towards the rear.

"How's the hike going for you all so far? I kind of thought I was in decent shape before coming out here, but I'm starting to think I was woefully mistaken," Kyle joked.

"Ha, well don't feel too bad. I was 35 pounds heavier than I am now when I first started with the club. It was a struggle for me the first couple of times out, but before you know it you'll be able to knock out a 15 mile hike with your eyes closed. I'm Caleb by the way. This is my girlfriend Trisha, and my buddy Joe."

"Kyle Drake, nice to meet you guys," Kyle responded. "So you've all been with the hiking club for a while then?"

"Yep, almost two years now. Trisha and I found it online through a site that posts social activities around the area. We loved it, and got Joe to start coming out with us about a year ago."

"I'm kind of a workaholic, so forcing myself to get away from my computer and get some exercise on the weekend is just what I needed. Ahhhhh, such is the glorious life of a patent attorney in Silicon Valley," Joe snickered.

"And Caleb and I both work from home, so if we didn't do something like this I'd be concerned we'd turn into those creepy hermit people who are afraid to leave the house,"

Trisha joked.

"Yeah, I'd probably start hoarding my own fingernail clippings, and become so afraid to communicate with outsiders that I'd only talk to people through the mail slot on the door. It would really just be a hassle for everyone, so I think it's much better that we found a way to get out of the house a couple times a month," Caleb added.

"I wish I could say I did better than that, but I've been kind of living like a shut-in lately myself," Kyle informed them. "It's crazy how hard it is to get away sometimes. A month will go by and you'll realize you've done nothing the entire time but work, eat, sleep, and repeat. It feels like such a waste when you live in a great place like this."

"Yeah I hear you. I've lived here my whole life and I still feel like there are things I want to try out, but somehow still haven't had the time!" Caleb said. "Whereabouts do you work?"

"I'm a researcher over at UC Santa Clara," Kyle said. "Been there just a little over a year."

"Oh no kidding!" exclaimed Joe. "I'm an engineer at a semiconductor company not too far from UC. So you consider yourself part of the biotech crowd then I imagine? That and the high-tech sector are what really run this town. You know they always say that this state is going bankrupt, which is just mind-boggling to me given the amount of corporate income tax that I know is pouring into the government coffers here. There must be just a ridiculous amount of mismanagement going on. But anyway, that's a different rant for a different day."

"Well moving to California from Arizona has been quite a changeup for me in that regard. Zona is pretty conservative compared to out here in most ways. Especially the part where I came from, definitely cowboy country…" Kyle added. "But I do appreciate the open-mindedness and progressive thinking of the people I meet out here. I feel like this is probably the right place for me at this point in my life."

"Well we're glad to meet you Kyle Drake, and hopefully you're not so exhausted by the end of this hike that you decide to never come back. We'd all like to see you again," Caleb remarked.

The group had finally reached the canyon, and most of them took the opportunity to find shade and take a break from the heat. Kyle found a seat next to Carlos, removed his shoes, and dumped out about a handful of dirt and rocks from each one.

"I think you might be right about the hiking boots," Kyle told Carlos. "I'll try to come better equipped next time."

"Ha, no worries rookie. So you still having a good time?"

"Absolutely," Kyle replied, looking out into the valley several hundred feet below. He could see the dirt lot where the cars were parked far in the distance, and the headwaters of the creek where they had begun the hike over an hour earlier. The canyon was a beautiful mix of colors, with red and green from the giant redwoods contrasting beautifully against the crystal-clear blue sky.

Kyle found his thoughts turning towards his late brother Ben. He would have absolutely loved coming out here on a trip like this with Kyle. Kyle was fairly certain his brother had never made it out to Northern California during his travels, though he had been almost everywhere else in the world, including South America, Africa and most of Southeast Asia. Kyle could still remember the day when Ben told his parents he was dropping out of college to join a non-profit organization and travel the world. Kyle was probably only 12 or 13 years old at the time, but he still recalled the terrified looks on the faces of his parents. Save for a quick trip or two to some nearby Mexican beach towns, no one from their family had ever traveled outside the United States, let alone to the exotic places Ben had mentioned. His mother had tried relentlessly to talk him out of signing that first one-year commitment, saying it was too long for a person to be on his own in a foreign land where English was barely spoken. But Ben had been able to convince them, through his typical fearless demeanor, that there was nothing for them to worry about.

When Ben finally came home to visit after that initial assignment was completed, Kyle had never seen his parents as excited as they were to hear about their son's adventures. Kyle remembered sitting on the living room floor with the rest of his family on the couch, his brother's luggage not even brought in yet from the front porch. Ben had brought back several gifts for Kyle from his travels, including a collection of large exotic insects in a display case that Kyle had made sure his parents held on to when he moved out of the house.

Over the next few years Ben would eventually sign up for four more international assignments. He would always come back for a week or two between trips, and listening to Ben tell stories, it sounded like each trip and each destination had been better than the last. For some reason, though, Ben's return home after that first trip is what really stuck out in Kyle's mind. His brother had seemed so changed after that trip. So inspired. He even looked different physically, sporting longer shaggy hair and a light brown goatee that he continued to fashion on each ensuing visit home.

Kyle often thought of how hard it must be to drop everything in your life and suddenly move to a foreign land, with the purpose of helping people less fortunate than those from where you came. That was a novel concept to Kyle, and he had a high admiration for anyone who was willing to make that sacrifice.

The group packed up their gear and continued up the mountain towards the summit, which was now only another hour or so away. To pass the time, Kyle struck up a pleasant conversation with a slightly older couple who had joined the hiking club a few months earlier. They had struck it rich with a startup tech company, and were now partially retired and looking for something healthy and social to occupy their time. Kyle told them about his position at the lab, though he continued to find it difficult to avoid broaching the subject of the wild memory recall sessions he'd recently been involved with. Kyle then chatted with Carlos for a while, mostly about Carlos' sister recently giving birth to triplets. Before he knew it, the group was approaching the summit of the mountain. Kyle was now near the front of the pack, and as they rounded the corner around the final switchback, he could see other groups of people sitting on top of the giant rocks, posing for pictures with the endless redwood forest in the background. One of the guys in their group quickly sprinted ahead and deftly climbed up one of the empty rocks on the peak, yelling and beating his chest like a gorilla when he reached the top.

Kyle didn't quite have the energy left to display that level of enthusiasm, but he indeed was very excited to have successfully conquered the hike and been able to witness the incredibly scenic views in person. Kyle joined the rest of his group as they posed on top of one of the large boulders to take a picture. Carlos then explained that they would be taking a 20 minute break at the top to remain on schedule, as members of the group wandered around to explore the different views the summit had to offer. Kyle walked around the perimeter of the peak, stopping to take a few pictures and observe some of the landmarks he could pick out in the distance as he looked out to the southeast towards Sausalito.

To Kyle's left, he noticed a small path leading down to a moderately steep drop, the end of which was barely disappearing out of his view. As he still had time to kill before the group started the descent down the mountain, Kyle decided to explore the path. After only a few steps down he again found that his footing was becoming difficult to hold. He contemplated the best way to make the drop down to the next level, eventually deciding to turn around and repel down the drop backwards, using the long branches from some of the nearby bushes to control his rate of descent. He soon found this method very effective, and was quickly able to make his way down to the section of the pathway that was previously hidden from view.

Kyle looked out over this lower path and saw a similar drop, this one being slightly longer and steeper than what he'd just successfully negotiated. He decided to use the repelling method for this drop as well. Kyle slowly and carefully stepped out over the ledge, using a branch from a small tree to steady himself as he found footing. Slowly, he continued to climb down the hill. He got about halfway down, and paused to survey the remainder of the path and consider his options. Estimating he had another 15 feet or so to go, Kyle decided to stay on his current route. He let go of the branch that he was holding on to for support, and slid to his right to catch an embedded rock with his right hand. Coming to a stop again, he corrected his course and continued down on the original path.

Suddenly, the rock he was holding on to gave way, and Kyle sprang off the path and quickly slid down the mountainside past the landing point he was targeting. Falling rapidly for several seconds, Kyle grabbed desperately for anything he could hold on to to slow his descent. Finally Kyle was able to dig his feet into a soft patch of dirt, enough to slow his momentum and come to a stop about 10 feet below the end of the pathway. Fearing the worst, Kyle slowly turned his head to see where he had ended up on the mountain. Kyle's fears were justified when he realized he was now dangerously close to a sheer cliff that dropped out more than a hundred feet below. His heart now racing, Kyle realized he quickly needed to find something more solid to support his weight, before the soft dirt his feet were entrenched in came loose and he slid further towards the cliff. Using all the upper-body strength he could summon, Kyle dug his fingers into the gravelly terrain, and pulled himself up towards the flat area of the path. He then made another exhausting effort and was able to pull himself up a few more feet.

Gasping for air, and with his arms burning more than he could ever remember, Kyle decided to take a risk and attempt to propel himself upward with his legs, using his momentum to advance far enough to where he could grab on to the base of the large bush that sat directly in front of him. Kyle rested for a brief moment, trying to focus and gather his remaining strength for the burst of energy he would need for this maneuver. As his mind raced, he was surprised to find his thoughts were now on his lab at UCSC. He found himself thinking about how pissed off he would be if he screwed up his chance at seeing his project come to fruition, by doing something as dumb as getting hurt trying to scale down the side of a mountain. *Stupid ass, you should have never tried to climb down here alone*, Kyle scolded himself. *Now you're going to have to man up and get yourself out of this.* He took several deep breaths, tried to remain calm, and focused on what he needed his body to do successful complete this move. Deciding it was now or never, Kyle counted down from three, then pushed as hard as he could with his legs to quickly shoot up the precipice. He felt the fingertips of his right hand wrap solidly around a branch, as he quickly swung his torso so he could grab the base of the bush with his left hand. Pulling himself up to the small plateau where he had originally intended to stop, Kyle collapsed from fatigue and laid in place for several minutes, loudly attempting to catch his breath but feeling extremely thankful to have escaped his little mistake alive and mostly unscathed.

Finally able to gather himself and finish off the short climb back to rejoin the group at the summit, the embarrasment of what had just occurred finally started to set in. Kyle quickly made an attempt at brushing the dirt off his shirt and his legs, hoping he would be spared the indignity of having to come up with an excuse as to why he was now covered in it. He decided that if anyone asked, he would just say that he had a quick slip while trying to get a better angle for a picture, but would make no mention of his rock climbing expedition.

Kyle made his way back to the summit as the rest of the crew were starting to put on their packs and prepare for the hike back down.

"There you are," Carlos remarked when Kyle approached the group.

"Yep, just went for a quick lap around the top so I could see the view from every angle. What an amazing place this is! Took a little spill near the south side but no big deal. It's these damn shoes, I'm throwing them away when I get home," Kyle said decisively.

"Yeah let's get you some real boots before the next hike. One of these days coming up I'll take you over to the sporting goods shop I get my gear from, they'll set you up real well," Carlos said.

"Deal," Kyle quickly replied, eager to begin the return hike down the mountain, put this near-death experience behind him, and get back to the organized chaos that had become his new life.

CHAPTER 19

"I don't know about this," Kyle repeated to himself neurotically, still very much on the fence regarding his decision to let Travis bring one of his rehab floozies into the inner circle of the most important project he had ever been involved with. There were still hundreds of things that could go wrong. Even with all the safeguards the lab's engineering team had been required to put in place before they could start human testing, there was still always a chance something bad could happen. The mind is a fragile instrument, Kyle reminded himself, and with as deeply as they were diving into it, there remained a chance they could irreversibly screw something up and leave a subject mentally damaged forever. Kyle had heard about many case studies over the years of mental experimentation gone wrong, mostly back in the earlier days of behavioral therapy research. Though this wasn't "One Flew Over The Cuckoo's Nest", and he wasn't Nurse Ratched, every member of the team was constantly aware of the fine line they were walking, and they knew it would be in their best interests to apply a high-level of discretion in selecting subjects for their experiments.

It was perhaps divine intervention then that presented the situation in which both Kyle and Travis could get what they were aiming for. The Executive Board at the Keane Institute, now barely even attempting to mask the "favorite child" status of Kyle's team, had fast-tracked several bureaucratic approvals that they viewed could possibly remove obstacles for the team. One such task was to automate the data analysis from the experiments, and automatically tag the data so it could be summarized and presented as quickly as possible. In fact Kyle had been able to steal Frank away from his existing project for a couple days to work on implementing the new process. And Frank had done a superb job, showing a keen interest in the science of mind-mapping. He was able to streamline the data collection process far beyond what they'd previously achieved. Farida had initially been a little nervous about giving up some of her control over the final output. But with what Frank had accomplished, the team now barely even needed to intervene with the software after the experiments were completed.

Stan had informed the team earlier that week of management's intentions. "The Exec Board wants to make sure we have all our ducks in a row in regards to standardizing the way we're conducting these experiments. The more automation we can use and the more data integrity we can guarantee, the smoother things will go once we start publishing these results outside the lab." Kyle couldn't really disagree with this line of thinking. Though it would be hard to give up some of the hands-on influence they'd had in the experiments up to this point, Kyle knew that enabling this technology to be run with as few highly-skilled technicians as possible was an eventuality.

The other item the Legal department was able to fast-track was a rather air-tight Release of Liability waiver that would aid the lab in continuing to recruit subjects for their experiments, as long as the subjects were able to give properly informed consent. The Exec Board was now targeting a grand reveal of the lab's breakthrough at the International Conference on Cognitive Neuroscience at the end of the year. ICCN was being held in Zurich, Switzerland this year, right in the backyard of the Basel Institut, generally considered as the worldwide leaders in cognitive research. Stan had bragged to the team: "We want to show the world what kind of research the greatest state in the greatest country in the world is capable of!" With the conference as their marching point, the team had begun to map out the full series of experiments they would need to accomplish in order to have time to prepare for creating a dazzling display at the conference.

Which is exactly how Kyle found himself in the lab with Travis once again, this time being introduced to one of his newest friends.

"Hi I'm Jamie, nice to finally meet you Kyle. Travis has told me so much about you," Jamie said with a friendly, bashful smile. "Well not too much, I mean nothing really about the lab or what you guys are doing here. Well maybe just a little bit...," Jamie confessed nervously, worrying she had just blown their cover and put Travis in a tough position.

"Nice to meet you too, Jamie. It's all good, Travis barely knows the half of it, so I'm sure whatever he's told you is fine," Kyle said, shooting Travis a semi-frigid glare for likely being reckless with the confidential information he'd been entrusted with. "I just want to thank you again for coming by during the week on such short notice. I'm sorry if this is making you miss work or anything like that. What is it you do?"

"I'm a pediatric nurse at a hospital. I've actually already worked all my hours for the week and I have today off. So no worries there! And thank you so much again for letting me come in here. I must admit I could barely believe it when Travis let me in on what you guys were researching here, and what you've been able to accomplish. It's unbelievably exciting, and if there's any way at all that I can be a part of it, I'm willing to do whatever it takes!" Jamie added, sounding genuinely enthusiastic. Kyle was so far impressed by her. This wasn't the type of girl Travis usually went after. He was normally more into the extremes: the wild-child crazy girls, or the overly timid girls who would prefer to follow his lead on everything. Jamie seemed more balanced than either of those options. She was also quite attractive, Kyle admitted to himself. No wonder Travis had begged Kyle to let him bring her in as a volunteer. He was certain Travis was trying to impress her with pretty much every move he was making.

"Well MY ass is probably gonna get fired for taking today off, but this is just way too exciting to miss out on," Travis chimed in. He seemed antsy to Kyle...overly eager to begin the experiment. Jamie hadn't even begun her debriefing yet, but Travis was already trying to herd everybody down to the examination room. Kyle was sure there was something Travis wasn't telling him. He would have to be careful as they proceeded with preparing for the experiment.

"So Jamie, seeing as how you're in the healthcare field, you probably already have at least some familiarity with the types of equipment and monitoring systems we use here," Kyle told Jamie, as they entered the lab and approached the experimentation area. "We monitor your vitals right here to make sure nothing is going out of the safe range, and the only other piece of equipment we'll really have directly hooked up to you is this neuro-headset, which maps out your synaptical activity. From a physiological standpoint, it's a very safe process. Although obviously, the manipulations we're performing with your mind could be difficult for some people to handle. So far, we haven't even been close to having any real issues with our subjects. But this is why we normally recommend attempting to recall something simple and pleasant from your past for the first attempt. Travis tells me you might have something different in mind though?" Kyle asked, as he opened the door to the row of cubicles near the back of the lab.

Jamie paused, searching for the right words to communicate what had brought her there today to this person that she had just met. It had been such a long road to becoming willing to even attempt recovery for Jamie. Month after month, her emotions had spiraled further out of control, and this constant up and down had taken its toll on her. Jamie briefly thought about all she had missed out on the past decade of her life because of her emotional issues, and struggled to fight back the urge to cry. *Don't blow this Jamie, this could be your chance!* she reminded herself. At this point, Jamie was convinced she had a terrible secret buried deep somewhere inside of her. Over the span of the last several years she had, only very slowly, finally begun allowing herself to unravel this bundle of self-consuming pain.

For most of her life Jamie had been clueless about virtually everything surrounding her family's sudden departure from their hometown. And for the longest time, she felt this event may have even been what initially sent her on the downward spiral of anxiety and dramatic mood swings that she was currently battling with. She'd held on to resentment towards her mother, unfairly, for years after the move. It was only recently that she had finally felt far enough removed from it to begin assessing things from a more rational viewpoint. There was a reason behind her mother's decision to relocate their family. And Jamie was terrified of what the answer might be. Today was her chance to chase it down, once and for all.

"Yes, I did have something quite different in mind actually," Jamie began, trembling as she tried to maintain enough composure to get through this explanation. Jamie turned towards Travis, who seemed to have picked up on her change in mood, moving closer towards her. "Travis, I want to thank you again for all you've done for me. You've been nothing but supportive, and I know you and Kyle had to pull a lot of strings to get me in here today. So I feel it's time to be completely honest with you…"

Travis tensed, feeling in this moment genuine concern for Jamie. His pessimistic instincts braced him for what was probably about to come.

"What I've told Travis so far is that I wanted to come here today, and use this technology to try to figure out some things from my past that might have caused me to become the mess that I feel like I am today," Jamie said, the tears starting to visibly well in her eyes. Kyle, completely caught off guard by this sudden admission, realized the three of them were still awkwardly standing in the back area of the lab with the door wide open. He quickly ran to shut the door, and rolled a chair over to Jamie for her to sit as she continued her story.

"Thanks," Jamie said quietly, taking a seat and grabbing a tissue from the box on the desk. "For years now, I've literally racked my brain trying to figure out what event in my life could have caused all this. And every time I've tried, I've come up empty. I used to be such a happy person...I really did. And I've tried to get help from therapists, but even they haven't been able to uncover the great 'Mystery of the Disappearing Jamie'. But the therapist I'm seeing now, he's really got me thinking about the period in my life when things changed for me. It's been hard focusing on that time, fighting through all the walls I've put up in my mind. But I think I finally know what I need to tackle today. It's a memory that involves my neighbor when I was living in Chico as a young teenager. He was my mentor while I was growing up. His name was Mr. Harris."

Kyle shot Travis a confused look, unsure what to do with this confessional Jamie had just delivered. Travis approached Jamie, gently patting her on the back as she continued to fight back tears.

"What do you think happened between you two, Jamie?" Travis asked earnestly. "I don't wanna stick my nose where it doesn't belong, but I think it probably helps Kyle help you if you're as specific as possible. Right Kyle?"

"Yeah it helps...but we don't have to know a whole lot of detail. We just need you to establish approximate beginning and end points for the memory before we analyze."

"Okay...," Jamie said, attempting to gather her focus as she tried to mentally prepare for the experiment. "And how long can I be in there? How long does your experiment run?"

"We currently have it qualified for a 60 minute session. So that's how long we'd be targeting today," Kyle answered. He was now starting to feel guilty at the thought of putting Jamie through this process, and decided to offer her one more out. "I really just want to say again that I appreciate you coming in here today. I can see that you're taking this process very seriously. However I do want you to know that I completely understand if you don't want to go through with this. It certainly has seemed to be a pretty life-altering experience for the few of us who have tried it. And even though in this case it sounds like that's what you're looking for, it can still be very difficult to process mentally. But if you think you do still want to move forward with the experiment, you'll notice in the waiver I gave you that your results may potentially be used in some of our reports and presentations in the future. We try to maintain anonymity through all of this, but I wanted to make sure you were aware in case that's something you're not comfortable with for this particular memory."

"No...no it's fine. I've lived with secrets for way too long. Let's do it. I'm ready."

Jamie quickly signed the waiver and handed it back towards Kyle, a renewed sense of resolve apparent in her. Kyle again shot Travis a look of uncertainty. He wished right then that they could get a quick moment alone together so they could talk over what was occurring. After taking all the information he had into account, Kyle decided they should go ahead and move forward with the experiment as planned. He excused himself from the room to inform the rest of the team, and get them prepared to get started.

Alone now with Jamie, Travis pulled a chair up next to hers and continued to try his best to console her. She was sitting with her eyes closed, taking long deliberate breaths and trying to remain as calm as possible. He watched through the clear glass walls as Michael, Ryan and Farida prepared the experimentation area. The lab was now buzzing with complex monitoring instruments. There was noticeably more gear involved now than when Travis had done his trial run a couple weeks earlier, and it was definitely high-end stuff. They must have seriously increased the lab's budget based on the success they'd had so far, Travis figured.

Slowly pacing now in the back room trying to relieve his nervous energy, Travis thought back again to his experience in the chair. He had thought about it every day since. The dramatic connection he had felt with his former youthful self. The connection to his family. He thought about how invigorated he'd felt afterwards. He desperately hoped that Jamie could have the same experience today.

After what seemed like hours, Kyle finally emerged from the lab. "Alright Jamie, we're ready for you now," he said, trying to put on a smile and maintain an air of reassuring professionalism. Inside, Kyle was nervous like he was for every experiment they had run so far. Even though they'd been able to produce consistent results up to this point, this was undeniably still unchartered territory they were venturing into, and a lot of unpredictable things could happen. Especially in this particular case.

Minutes later Jamie was being seated into the experimentation chair, and Ryan took a seat next to her, connecting the remaining attachments on the neuro-headset.

"You excited?" Ryan asked casually, himself having little idea what Jamie's intentions were. "Only a few people in the world have experienced what you're about to go through, and you're looking at pretty much all of them. It's a mind-opening experience. Have fun out there," Ryan offered, oblivious to his faux pas.

Ryan gently placed the headset on Jamie, and Farida quickly began the calibration sequence. "Wow this new server can really fly! I'm almost finished with half of the checks already. How's the EEG looking over there Michael?" Farida asked.

"We're all clear over here," Michael responded. "Ready for launch as soon as you guys are."

The room became quiet as the team waited for Farida's system checks to finalize. Jamie continued to lay quietly in the chair, breathing slowly as instructed by Kyle. Kyle and Travis stood near Farida, waiting for her to give the go-ahead to start. Finally the system checks completed, and Farida gave Kyle the nod to get going.

"Okay Jamie. Keep breathing in slowly and deeply with your eyes closed. Let your mind start to focus on the first thing you can remember from the day you're targeting. Keep focusing on that as much as you can. You'll feel the system kick in, and when it does, just stay relaxed and let it guide you through your memory."

Silence again. Suddenly, the system activated, and Jamie let out a loud moan. Watching the monitors, Kyle saw her blood pressure and brain wave activity spike dramatically, before quickly lowering closer to normal levels.

"She almost blew a gasket, haven't seen that happen yet!" Ryan said excitedly.

"Very funny," replied Kyle. "Keep an eye on her vitals and make sure she gets back within the normal range." Kyle took a look at Travis, who was staring ahead intently, grinding his teeth, and knew he must be feeling pretty worried about how this experiment was going to turn out. Kyle placed a friendly hand on his shoulder.

"I'm still not quite sure what you've gotten me into here, but this is going to be interesting...," Kyle said quietly.

"Yes, it certainly is. I just hope she gets what she needs out of it. Girl is more fucked up than even I am. Man...I could really use a drink right now," Travis confessed.

"Let's try to get through this with no surprises, and then I'm right there with ya," Kyle confirmed.

I'm at my house, in the sunroom. My mom has just come home from her job, and she's carrying two bags of groceries. She calls my name to come help her put them away. Unbelievable! I can almost feel the box of cereal in my hands as I place it in the cabinet. My sister is helping me. She looks so young. I haven't seen her in far too long.

I ask my mom if it's okay for me to go down the street to Mr. Harris' house for a bit. I say he's helping me with my geography assignment for school. She says sure, and I run out the door. I count six houses that I pass on the way to his place. I always thought it was only four.

I knock on his door, using the big brass knocker that he let me help him install. I had forgotten about that. I wait a few seconds, and I hear him coming down the stairs. He opens the door, and he greets me with a soft "Madame" as he often used to do. It's so crazy seeing his face again! How many years has it been? I hadn't tried to picture him in a long time. I'd forgotten what he even looked like. I follow him into the kitchen. He's making himself a sandwich. He asks me if I've eaten dinner yet. I say no, but I need to be home in two hours to eat with my family. I go over and open his pantry. He has a glass jar of gummy bears in there that he always keeps stocked. One of his few vices, he always said. I grab a handful and go back to the table. He laughs at me, but doesn't attempt to stop me. We sit at the table together and talk about Africa. I ask him questions from my homework assignment, and he knows most of the answers immediately. He always knew so much about everything. When he can't answer questions, he grabs an encyclopedia and flips through it with me, showing me pictures and giving me explanations. He's talking to me like an adult, like he always did. I remember how much I liked that. It always made me try harder to comprehend what he was teaching me.

I ask if we can take a break, and we walk over to his living room. I sit down at his piano and try to play a few keys that he taught me. He sits down next to me, and he opens the song book to one of the tunes he knows how to play. He can only play a couple of songs, but he plays them very well. He plays a few lines, and I quickly try to follow. I mess up, and the piano makes a terrible clunking noise. We both laugh hard at this. I need to focus. I need to remember why I came here.

Kyle checked the monitors, and everything looked okay to him. Jamie's vitals had returned to normal, and her synapse pattern had mapped beautifully. Whatever she was looking for in her memories, it seemed she had found it. Kyle looked over at Travis, who was laying on his back on an empty desk, throwing a whiteboard eraser into the air and catching it repeatedly.

The stopwatch on the monitor in front of Kyle passed the 25:00 marker. "We've got about 35 minutes left," Kyle called out to Travis.

"Sounds good," Travis said nonchalantly. Kyle could see he was still attempting to play it cool.

Mr. Harris asks if I want to see his coin collection before I go back home. He tells me he thinks he may have some coins in the collection from Africa that I could talk about in my assignment. I follow him into the basement. I sit on top of his washing machine while he carefully removes boxes from his shelf. It seems like he's taking a very long time. He keeps stopping. He's breathing very loudly. Something is wrong here. Oh God...is this it? Is this where it happens?

He turns his head over his shoulder and looks back at me. His face is sad. I ask him what's wrong. He says he's been feeling very lonely lately. I ask him why. He says he's been missing his deceased wife a lot the past couple of days. He says there's been a lot of things that have reminded him of her. I say I'm sorry. He says he misses his children, and his grandkids, and he doesn't get to see them often enough. I tell him that's very sad. I ask him why they won't visit more often. He asks me if I want to help him. I say of course I do. He walks across the basement and reaches up into a cabinet. He pulls out a camera. It looks just like the one my grandmother has, where the picture prints right out of the bottom. He asks me if I can do something for him. If I can keep a secret. I tell him I'm good at keeping secrets, even though my mother tells me it's a bad thing to do. Oh no. This isn't happening.

"BP and heart rate are up a tad," Michael called out to the team. Kyle walked over to the monitors to observe.

"Still within range," Kyle said. "Let's make sure she's not pushing the upper limits though before we bring her out. Not that much longer to go…"

Mr. Harris says when he feels really lonely, it helps him to look at pictures of his grandchildren. He says he doesn't have very many pictures though. He tells me he loves me very much, and thinks of me like one of his grandchildren. This makes me feel happy. How disgusting.

He says he used to like it when his grandchildren would come over and play around in the sprinkler in his front yard. He asks me if I would pretend to do that now. I say I can't get wet though because I don't have a bathing suit. He tells me underwear is pretty much the same thing. He says he's sorry if he's making me feel weird. I tell him it's okay, and I squat down to remove my shorts. I'm standing in my shirt and underwear now. He sets the camera down, and walks over to where the light switches are. He flicks them on and off a few times. Oh Jesus, he's trying to get the lighting right for his camera. There's a bright light hanging right above my head. He keeps turning it on and off. It's blinding me. I don't like this. I want to leave. Suddenly, I hear a loud knock at his front door, directly above us. Four more knocks. "Mr. Harris, your medical delivery is here. We need your monthly payment before I can leave your medication." Knock, knock. "Mr. Harris, are you home?"

Mr. Harris looks up at the ceiling. His face looks frightened. I'm so confused. He stands still for another minute. Then he turns, and he begins walking up the staircase. I hear him slowly go to the front door and open it. He's talking with somebody outside. I decide I want to go home now. I walk up the stairs. Mr. Harris is at the door talking to a deliveryman. I walk to the hallway and watch him. The man he's talking to looks over his shoulder, I think he sees me. Mr. Harris asks him how much he owes, and starts to write out a check. I remember I left my shorts and shoes in the basement. I run down the stairs to grab them. I then grab my homework from the kitchen, and leave out the back door. I start running home. I feel like I disappointed Mr. Harris. It makes me feel sad.

I walk inside my front door. My mom asks me if Mr. Harris was helpful with my homework. I mumble "yes", and I go to my room. I lie on my bed and stare at the ceiling. I don't understand what just happened. I don't understand what he was trying to do. I think about if I should go back over there and make sure he's okay. I can't decide what to do. I can't decide if it would be a good idea to ----

"Can you hear us? Jamie can you hear me? Time's up and we're going to disconnect you from the system. Ryan's going to remove the sensors from your head, so just lie still and relax," Kyle instructed.

Travis popped up from his spot on the desk and ran over to rejoin the group. He watched Ryan carefully unplug the sensor wires, and gently lift the neuro-headset off of Jamie.

"She's covered in sweat!" Travis observed loudly, as Ryan inclined the experimentation chair into the sitting position.

"Yeah she had a tougher time in there than any of us have. Must have been a whale of a memory," Michael declared, expressing his impatience with the level of privacy Kyle was handling this operation with.

Jamie opened her eyes, and began to regain her acclimation with the present. Travis helped her out of the chair, and together they walked slowly over again to the back offices. Kyle remained briefly in the lab to make sure the team had the closing protocol down for the new equipment. After approving the protocols, Kyle started back towards Travis and Jamie. He was excited to hear from Jamie what exactly had happened, but he felt he should probably brace himself for another potential emotional outpouring.

Kyle approached the lab's rear office, and through the glass wall he was surprised to see Frank standing there, alone in the observation deck. Kyle hadn't noticed him during the experiment, and wondered how long he'd been watching. Though he felt he should probably dismiss Frank and get down to business on debriefing with Travis and Jamie, he was having a hard time finding the motivation to throw himself into that gauntlet just yet.

Frank was now animatedly waving at him, so Kyle decided to get on the intercom.

"Hey Frank, how's it going?"

"Pretty good man. I gotta say the show you just put on was more subdued than what I expected. At least from up here it was. I think more theatrics are in order for next time. How did the new equipment work out for you guys?" Frank asked.

"Like a charm. Farida is compiling the preliminary report as we speak, should be done before the end of the day. You can come on down if you want, we're pretty much wrapped up here," Kyle offered, regretting the invite as soon as the words left his mouth.

Frank scurried down the staircase into the lab, and joined Kyle as they finally entered the office. Inside Jamie was hunched over in a chair, with Travis sitting on top of the desk. Neither of them spoke. Kyle felt awkward introducing them to Frank, but felt he needed to break the silence with something.

"Hey guys, this is my coworker Frank Bernstein. This is my buddy Travis, and his friend Jamie."

Frank eagerly shook Travis' hand, and gave a friendly wave to Jamie, who was still sitting with her head down staring at the ground.

"So are you two an item, or how do you guys know each other?" Frank asked Travis out of nowhere.

Travis gave Kyle a surprised look. But the question seemed to snap him out of his trance, as he put on a clever grin. "Actually yeah, we've been dating, oh what is it honey, about three months now? We met at a market over in Sausalito. She asked me for help with the produce because she thought that I worked there. We struck up a great conversation, and it's been love at first site ever since!" Travis lied enthusiastically. Kyle could barely hold in a laugh as he shook his head. He could always count on Travis to save an uncomfortable moment with a good fabrication. He'd been a pro at things like that for as long as Kyle had known him.

"Oh wow that's crazy! You guys are so lucky to just kind of stumble upon each other like that. I wish I could find someone that easily. Not all of us are born with the Don Juan looks like your buddy Kyle over here," Frank said to Travis, pointing his thumb conspicuously in Kyle's direction.

"Ha, I know right?" Travis said, appearing to have officially regained his energetic smart-ass demeanor. "I love this guy! We need to bring you around more often!" Travis said, throwing his arm around Frank. "So what do you guys think about getting the hell out of here and grabbing a beer somewhere?"

Kyle was certainly all in favor, but wondered if Travis had forgotten they had someone else with them who had just gone through possibly the most mentally exhausting experience of her lifetime. Kyle glanced over to Jamie, who was now looking up and appeared to be following the conversation.

"That sounds fucking great actually...I could really go for a drink. Will you walk with me out to the car, love?" Jamie fired back at Travis, seeming to pick up perfectly on his deception.

"Let's go, first round is on me!" Travis exclaimed, as he took Jamie's arm and headed out of the lab. Frank and Travis followed behind as Kyle led the small caravan over to a sports bar a few blocks off of campus. Today had already been one of the weirdest days Kyle could remember in recent history, and from the looks of his current mix of company, it was probably about to get even weirder.

CHAPTER 20

"Seriously, that's the shirt you picked to wear out tonight?" Travis asked Kyle mockingly, not wasting any time trying to chop Kyle down a peg before the ladies arrived. "You look like you should be shredding files in Gordon Gekko's office before it gets raided by the feds."

"What the hell does that even mean?" Kyle asked, responding as nonchalantly as possible. He could already tell Travis was worked up about the prospects of this "double date" that he had developed in his mind, when in reality it was nothing more than a few casual drinks with Jamie and her friend. It was rare that Travis let his nerves show so transparently through his play-it-cool veneer, and Kyle enjoyed taking advantage of these opportunities by fucking with him as much as he could get away with. That's part of the reason why Kyle had decided to don one of his most stylish shirts for the evening, knowing it would get under Travis' skin and make him worry that he'd gone too casual. Truth be told, Kyle did feel a little overdressed in his dark blue tailored French cuff dress shirt. The restaurant they were all meeting at, a higher-end gastropub in Sausalito, had been suggested by Jamie's friend Casey, who would be joining them there tonight. It seemed to follow the design of most of the new craft brewpubs that had popped up recently in Kyle's neighborhood, albeit with what was portrayed to be a more local hangout vibe.

Kyle and Travis sat together at the table, continuing to enjoy throwing friendly barbs at each other, sipping on IPA's as they watched a college football game on the flat screen TV that hung over the bar. In a way it was a nice moment for them, reminding Kyle of the old days when the two of them would hang out like this all the time, before all the complexity of recent months had entered their lives. Neither of them knew where this memory recall innovation was going to take them. But both knew it could potentially be life-changing. In the back of both their minds, they also knew the potential for heartbreaking disappointment could be just around the corner.

Looking over his shoulder towards the TV on his left, Kyle saw Jamie entering the restaurant and approaching the table. Kyle and Travis both stood and gave Jamie a friendly hug.

"How've you guys been this week? Thanks again for coming out here to meet us for dinner," Jamie said.

"No problem, thanks for putting this together. This is a pretty cool part of town, I guess I've never really spent much time over here," Kyle responded.

"Same here. I think this might be my first time in Sausalito actually. Casey's office has a location pretty close by so she got a recommendation to try this place out from one of her coworkers. She actually just called me and said she's going to be running a little late."

"No worries. We've got no other plans for the night. I'm just happy to sit here, relax and drink a few beers. Haven't gotten out of the office much lately as you can imagine," Kyle admitted.

"Dude, I don't even know how you can go into that place every day and keep acting professionally when you know what a goldmine you're sitting on," Travis told Kyle. "If I was you, I'd be using that machine on myself all day long. Or I'd probably try to steal it from the lab and sell it to the government for millions."

Jamie laughed. "Yeah, I'd probably do the same thing. Hey Kyle...I know I've said it a hundred times, but thank you again for helping me out the other day. I know that was a lot to ask from you, but it was really important to me to at least give it a try."

"No problem. I'm just glad I could help out. So I have to ask, how are you feeling now that you've had some time to think?"

"I'm...better. I'm really feeling better about a lot of things actually. It's like I can finally understand why things ended up the way they did. I don't feel completely weighed down by my past like I used to feel."

"That's really great Jamie," Travis said authentically. "Actually, I can already notice a change in you. You seem different."

"Oh I do do I? Well umm, thanks Travis?" Jamie laughed, unsure of how to handle the compliment.

Travis blushed slightly. "No not in a bad way. I mean you just seem more relaxed...less preoccupied. It's really good. I'll tell you one thing, you were in pretty good spirits at that bar we went to afterwards!"

"Yeah, you certainly were," Kyle added. "I think you put down four cocktails in like the first ten minutes we were there! Not that I can blame you though, after going through that experience."

"And I think Frank is completely in love with you now. After he tipped a few back that guy went into full flirt mode. Careful, you might have a stalker. Actually...that's not him over by the bar is it?" Travis joked.

"Oh shut up you guys, neither of us was that bad," Jamie refuted. "From what I can remember at least. I did kind of tie one on that night. I still can't believe that day though. I can't believe something like that really exists. And it actually works!"

"I still can't believe it sometimes either," Kyle admitted. "We've been working on that project for such a long time, and we hardly had anything to show for it. Then all of the sudden, one breakthrough and here we are. Pretty lucky to have gotten to this point. I just hope we can bring it home successfully."

"So what exactly ARE you guys going to do with that technology? What do you think it'll be used for?" Jamie asked earnestly.

"There are all sorts of potential applications: Understanding the memory capacity of the human mind, and trying to optimize it. Helping people with degenerative memory conditions, like Alzheimer's Disease. Law enforcement, solving unsolved crimes and interrogating criminals. I certainly see a lot of potential in helping people like yourself who are having difficulties with repressed memories. Recovered Memory Therapy is a booming field right now, and if our device could help out in that arena, it could be huge."

Jamie seemed blown away by these possibilities. "Wow...that's just so amazing! What an incredible thing to be a part of. I'm not even a real part of it, and it's still pretty much all I think about every day now!"

"Are you kidding, all I can think about is that my best friend is gonna become a millionaire!" Travis confessed. "I mean you're going to make some serious scratch off of this thing, right? This is probably the coolest thing that's been invented since...fuck I don't know, the internet?"

"Glad you're so confident I'm going to get rich off of this," Kyle said. "I honestly have no idea how that's all going to play out. The university pretty much owns all the intellectual property. I'm sure my team will get plenty of credit for what we've done, but how that translates monetarily, no idea."

"Well shit, you could write a book about it and make the New York Times bestseller list. Do a couple of nationally televised interviews, give a couple of keynote presentations. I'm telling you man...you're coming out of this thing a celebrity, whether you like it or not."

Jamie's eyes briefly shimmered as she looked at Kyle. For a moment, Kyle allowed himself to revel in this possibility. What if this could be his big break? What if this could set him up for life, to do whatever the hell it was he wanted to do with his life? It was tempting to get carried away with the possibilities, but he couldn't let himself think too far ahead. Not yet.

Several minutes later, Jamie's friend Casey finally arrived and joined the group. Casey was a slender, pretty girl with blond highlighted hair, who seemed to dress very trendy. She offered a friendly handshake to Kyle and Travis as she apologized for being late to the restaurant.

"Sorry I'm so late guys. Things have been nuts at work lately. Fridays always seem to be the worst for some reason," Casey said.

"Hey not a problem at all. So what line of work are you in that makes you stay late on a Friday?" Travis asked, attempting to come off as sincerely interested as he could manage. Casey was probably hotter overall than Jamie, Travis thought, but for some reason if he was forced to pick between the two, Travis was sure he would still opt to go with Jamie.

"I work at an ad agency near the Financial District downtown. It's a cool gig, but by Friday I'm usually pretty beat. Actually I could really use a drink, what're you guys having?"

"Going with beer for now. This place brews their own IPA, pretty good. Probably switch to the hard stuff in a little bit though," Travis replied.

"Mmm a beer sounds good actually. I think I'm gonna have that," Casey decided. Travis' interest piqued a bit upon learning that this pretty new girl was a beer drinker. Travis was also noticing that Casey was the type of girl who maintained almost constant eye contact as she spoke with you. He found it challenging to hold her gaze, and as he worked his way through another pint, his imagination was starting to run wild about just how good of friends Jamie and Casey might be with each other.

"Gosh it's really good to see you Jamie, it's been too

long!" Casey proclaimed. "I can't believe we don't bump into each other more often at the apartment. We really need to do a better job of making time to hang out."

"I know, I know, you're completely right. And I hope you don't feel bad about it or anything, it's completely been my fault. Work is no excuse for me." Jamie couldn't help but feel remorse over neglecting to reach out to Casey over the past few months. Especially after what had happened the last time they tried to go out together. Mercifully, Casey didn't seem to harbor any resentment over that little episode at the restaurant in Tiburon, and Jamie was extremely grateful for it.

"Well I wish you could have come with us to Lake Tahoe a few weeks back. What an amazing trip. I think Tahoe's a place everyone needs to visit at some point in their life."

"I know, I really wanted to go when you told me about it," Jamie said. "But obviously I couldn't get it worked out. Part of the reason was that I didn't want to go there my first time without Manny. You probably haven't heard yet, but we actually broke up a few weeks back."

"Oh no, that's too bad!" Casey said sympathetically. "I'm sorry to hear that. He seemed like a really nice guy."

"Yeah, yeah, he definitely is. He moved out of the apartment about two weeks ago. So sad to see him go... But anyway, I don't want to bring everyone down talking about that. Let's get something to eat!"

"Thank God, I thought you'd never say that. I've been wanting to order the jumbo steak nachos for the past hour!" Kyle joked. Jamie and Casey both found this comment hysterical.

"I'm serious! Sorry I guess I'm just a fat ass... but would you guys have some if I ordered them?"

"Sure! Beer and nachos, definitely on my diet!" Casey cackled. Travis desperately searched for an equally witty line to drop to keep pace with Kyle, but was coming up empty.

Conversation flowed smoothly for the next hour or so, while the drinks kept coming in steady supply. Kyle was starting to feel pretty loose, and he knew Travis couldn't be too far behind. *We should probably slow down a tad, don't want this to turn into a prototypical Kyle and Travis rampage night*, Kyle thought to himself. He set down his beer and took a big drink of water, as Casey continued telling them an entertaining story about a friend's recent trip to Mexico.

"So anyway, I guess if you're searching for a place to take a vacation next summer, just keep that in mind," Casey finished. Jamie laughed as she polished off the remnants of her drink, and asked the server to bring her another.

"So what's everyone doing for the holidays coming up? You guys going home or just hanging here?" asked Casey.

Travis snickered. "Psshhhh, hell no. It's a pain in the ass traveling home during the holidays. I'm staying right here and enjoying my time off of work. Gonna sit on my ass, drink beer and watch football for four days straight!"

"Ha, how noble of you Travis," Jamie joked.

"Indeed. Though I am envious of you being able to just hang out and relax," Casey said. "I've got to travel all the way back to Kansas City for Thanksgiving to see my family."

"Not worth it! You should just bail on that and party here with us!" Travis exclaimed. Kyle could see that Travis was on the verge of falling into his M.O. of becoming drunkenly overbearing, so he decided to cut in before Travis could embarrass himself.

"Don't worry buddy, I'm staying in town too, so we can keep each other company. Maybe I'll even whip up a Thanksgiving turkey and stuffing dinner for us."

"Oh that sounds so romantic, you guys! I can just see the two of you sitting together over a candlelit dinner, drinking red wine in your pajamas," Casey joked to Kyle.

"Oh totally. Then after dinner we'll just curl up on the couch together and watch 'Home for the Holidays'. Sounds like the perfect little evening, huh buddy?" Kyle asked. Jamie and Casey laughed hysterically at the prospect of these two sharing such a moment.

"Yeah yeah yeah, just the way I'd always dreamed it would be. Well I'm only going through with it if I can be the big spoon," Travis relented, followed by more laughter from Jamie and Casey.

"You guys are too much. Wow, I haven't laughed this hard in a while. Now I really have to pee," Casey admitted. "Do you have to go too Jamie?"

"Yeah, I might as well. Ok guys we'll be right back, don't go ordering shots or anything while we're gone," Jamie instructed.

"Ay ay captain!" Travis snapped back.

Fixing her makeup in the bathroom mirror, Casey couldn't resist asking Jamie about the nature of her relationship with Kyle and Travis.

"So I know you told me you met Travis at a meeting a while back. How many times have you guys hung out before tonight?"

"Just a couple times, probably like three or four total. He's pretty funny huh?" Jamie asked.

"Travis? Yeah he is, he cracks me up. Definitely doesn't hold anything back. And what do you think about Kyle?"

"Umm...I don't know. This is only like the second or third time I've been around him. He's a really nice guy I think. Seems really smart too from what I can tell."

"Not too hard on the eyes either," Casey added. "I know you just broke up with your boyfriend not that long ago, but he seems like a pretty good catch. I think you should go for him."

"*I* should go for him?? I was going to say the same thing to you!" Jamie said in surprise.

"Ha really? Oh, well I appreciate that Jamie. But I'm

definitely not looking for a boyfriend or anything right now. Anyway I'm telling you, you're the one he has eyes for. I can tell by the way he looks at you when you're speaking. There's something there for sure."

"Really? Hmmm, I hadn't even thought about that," Jamie fibbed. "I mean I guess he is kind of attractive. I don't know though...I just got out of a relationship. And I'm friends with Travis, so that might make things weird."

"Nice try Jamie, I can tell you're into him too. Well do whatever you want, but I'm just telling you: If you're interested at all, don't let that one get away. From what I can sense, I think the feeling would definitely be mutual."

Kyle and Travis waited patiently for the girls to come back to the table, eyes fixated on the football game above the bar. Kyle could sense that Travis probably wanted to put the full-court press on Casey as soon as she returned, and was trying to think of a way to talk him out of it. However, the combination of the alcohol and general fatigue from a killer week was making it hard for him to phrase it in a way that wouldn't piss off Travis. So for the time being, Kyle bit his tongue and decided to let things play out as they may.

Jamie and Casey returned from the restroom, and Casey suggested they make a change of venues. "This place is getting kind of loud. There's a cool little wine bar next door. How about we grab a drink there, and then I'm probably gonna be done for the night."

"Sounds good to me," Kyle replied.

"And don't worry Travis, they have good beer there too. Probably even have the football game on TV just for you," Casey joked.

"Oh, well in that case: fuck this place, let's drink some chardonnay!" Travis cracked back. The four of them exited the restaurant, and made their way into the downstairs wine bar next door, which was lit up purple with an array of chic retro chandeliers. Live music was playing from a reggae-soul band, as Kyle grabbed the last open table near the back wall of the room. Casey ordered a bottle of the house malbec for the table, and Travis requested an amber ale for himself to drink. Kyle was pleasantly surprised by how good the band was that was playing. Jamie and Casey seemed to be loving it, and even Travis was tapping his toes a little, though he seemed frustrated by not to be able to continue working on Casey. After finishing off an impressive extended medley, the band announced that they would be taking a quick break.

"Pretty good huh? How are you guys liking it?" Casey asked the group.

"It ain't bad! Not what I usually listen to, but I like it!" Kyle responded.

"Me too, I love it!" Jamie exclaimed. "This is so much fun. You hanging in there Travis?"

"Hey, I've got a cold delicious beer in my hand, so I ain't gonna complain too much. But if you wanted to suggest that we bail and head over to that dive bar across the street to knock back some shots, I'm not saying no."

"Ha ha, maybe some other time," Casey said. "I'm actually just going to stay for a couple more songs, then I've got to start heading home." Kyle could see what looked like defeat wash over Travis' face.

The band struck up another song, this one a slower number than what they'd played so far. As he took another sip from the wine, Kyle began feeling extreme gratitude for this moment. This was the most relaxed he had been in longer than he could even remember. Sitting there, the four of them, having a nice respectable evening out in this new part of town, rather than just he and Travis being the shit shows that they usually acted like when it was just the two of them. He looked over at Jamie, watching her for a moment as she basked in the band's soothing melodies. She looked very attractive in this romantic lighting, her dark hair and eyes shining with an almost exotic radiance. At that moment, as if almost connected by mind, Kyle felt Jamie take his hand and place it in hers. It was a sudden, subtle move, and Kyle wasn't expecting it at all. He felt at the same time excited and nervous that Travis would see what was happening. He tried to act as naturally as he could, as Jamie held his grip into the next song.

Kyle glanced over at Travis out of the corner of his eye, careful not to turn his head or draw attention to himself. He appeared to be covered for the moment, as Travis had his face buried in his phone, likely surfing for the sports scores. Kyle felt Jamie's grip on his hand tighten as she turned her head, looking into Kyle's eyes with a seductive gaze. There was no mistaking it now: she was definitely coming on to him. Kyle's mind thought back to the restaurant when Jamie and Casey had disappeared into the restroom together for what seemed like an unusual amount of time. They must have hatched this plan together, to set the mood like this. And Kyle was certainly feeling in the mood, the wine making him even more so. But what could he do here in a crowded bar, with his jealous best friend sitting right next to him?

Suddenly, he had an idea. He subtly leaned over to Jamie, and in her ear he whispered for her to walk over towards the restrooms. She nodded, and quietly snuck away along the back wall, following the signs down the stairs to the basement level. Kyle watched Jamie leave, then waited about a minute before pulling out his phone. He put it to his ear, pretending he was getting a call, and ducked out from the bar area, quickly walking down the staircase. There he found Jamie, who grabbed his hand and whispered "Back here" as she led him through an additional bar area that apparently was closed for tonight's performance.

They found an empty storage area that was out of view from the staircase, and quickly Jamie pressed her lips to Kyle's. She kissed him eagerly, wrapping her arms around his head and pulling him in as close to her as she could. Kyle was again caught off guard, but completely aroused by her intensity. He couldn't believe that this quiet modest girl whom he had just met days before was now making such a strong move on him. And he was clearly sharing her same feelings, as he backed Jamie up against a wall and began slowly working his body against hers. They continued to kiss passionately, working their hands along each other's bodies. For a moment Kyle felt that they might go all the way right there in the basement.

Abruptly, Jamie pulled her head back. "We can't do this here right now. It's not right. It'll kill Travis."

Kyle immediately knew she was right. "I know. Travis really likes you. We can't do this yet. And look at us, we're in the back of an abandoned bar for God's sake!"

"Okay, let's hurry up and get back to the table. Do I look like a hot mess or am I okay enough to head back in there?"

Kyle fixed a few wayward strands of hair, then gave Jamie the go-ahead. "You go in first, I'll pretend I'm still on the phone for another minute then head in after you."

Jamie leaned in and kissed Kyle again, then quickly sped off up the stairs and back to the table. Kyle's head was spinning, but he attempted to gather himself and get ready to pull of his con. He held the phone to his ear again as he ascended the staircase, pretending to hang up a call and retaking his seat at the table.

"Sorry guys, randomly got a call from a buddy," Kyle attempted to explain.

"Really? Who was that?" Travis asked, sounding detached with his phone still held up to his face.

"One of the guys from that hiking group I'm in. Wanted to see if I want to go up with them on Sunday morning."

"Ha, Sunday morning. Well have fun with that tree-hugger, doesn't appeal to me in the slightest," Travis disdainfully replied. By Travis' reaction, Kyle wasn't sure if they'd gotten away with their little tryst. But it certainly could have gone worse.

Casey leaned over and whispered to Jamie that she was going to head out after the next song ended, and Kyle handed his credit card to the server to close out their tab. As the song came to an end, the group quietly stood and exited up the stairs to the sidewalk. The November evening air was chilly and crisp, and Kyle was unsure of what was going to happen next. For a moment, everyone looked around at each other, waiting for someone to make the next move. Finally Casey spoke up.

"So uhh, Jamie, I'm heading back to the apartment now. Happy to give you a ride if you'd like."

"Oh...okay. Yeah I guess that makes sense. I'll just head back with you now then," Jamie said awkwardly. Kyle was starting to feel that Travis had to have noticed what was happening by now. Or maybe he was just too drunk to notice anything, and they would get lucky.

"Sounds good. Okay well in that case, good night guys! It was great to hang out with you tonight. Hopefully I'll see you again soon!" Casey said, as she hugged Kyle and Travis goodbye. Jamie gave them both a hug too, and made it a point to thank Travis for helping to arrange the fun evening.

Watching the girls walk towards the car, Kyle felt at once relief and disappointment in how the night had ended. He knew it was the only possible outcome though, and resigned himself to as much as he offered Travis his spare bedroom for the night.

"Alright I'm pretty cashed, let's head back to my place and crash out."

"That's okay man. Thanks but I think I'm gonna head back to my place tonight instead. Not feeling so hot...probably gonna chill the rest of the weekend and try to rest up," Travis replied.

"Shit, really? Sorry to hear that buddy. Okay well hit me

up later, and I hope you feel better," Kyle said, as he exchanged his customary handshake with Travis.

Standing on the corner waiting to hail a cab, Kyle watched Travis as he slowly plodded towards the train station to catch the late train back to Hayward. Kyle felt sad for him, going back to his quiet apartment in the middle of nowhere with no one around to keep him company. He was definitely starting to worry about how things would go if he and Jamie ended up hooking up. He wasn't sure if that was a blow Travis could take.

CHAPTER 21

There was a distinctly putrid smell emanating from somewhere inside the house as Travis attempted to pry himself off the faux leather living room couch. The hot sweats he was currently experiencing made his skin stick to the couch, as he slowly rolled over in an attempt to get into a sitting position. Feeling nauseous and extremely light-headed, he paused for a few seconds to gain his equilibrium before attempting to stand. It was at this point where he noticed the myriad of stains scattered across his dark grey sweat pants. *Jesus, what the fuck is that?* Travis thought to himself. Fighting back the urge to vomit, he slowly stumbled across the living room and into his bedroom, where he was greeted with a veritable crime scene of broken glass and splintered wood strewn across the floor. Two of the three blades on the ceiling fan were dangling precariously from the base. A glass water bong sat on the nightstand by his bed, amazingly still intact but showing heavy signs of use from the day before. Travis looked at the sheets piled up on his bed, and immediately identified the source of the stench that was filling up the house. A puddle of dried vomit covered the area where his pillows would normally be located. No wonder he'd woken up on the couch.

I must have drank and smoked myself retarded last night, Travis thought, as he grabbed an open bottle of cheap bourbon from the top of his dresser, taking a hefty belt in hopes of postponing his brutal hangover for as long as possible.

Unable to remember if he'd eaten at all the entire day before, Travis slowly made his way into the kitchen. He opened the refrigerator and pulled out a large jar of chunky peanut butter. Grabbing a spoon from the cabinet, he began shoveling it directly from the jar into his mouth, washing it down with a freshly opened beer. On the kitchen table he noticed what appeared to be a piece of paper with a handwritten message. Travis walked around the table and picked up the note. He recognized the signature at the bottom as his housemate's:

Travis -- what the hell happened to you yesterday? I came home from Seattle last night and the house was destroyed! You were blasting heavy metal music so loud that two of the neighbors came over and yelled at me to make you stop. Then when I confronted you about it, you threw a bottle of liquor at my head! I'm not going to put up with that shit. When I get home tonight you better have a great explanation for all of this. Or else you're leaving me with no choice but to contact the landlord and see about getting your sublease terminated.

Travis crumbled up the note and threw it into the sink, then took another swig from his beer. He could honestly give two shits right now about what his stupid fucking roommate thought about him, or what he thought he could threaten him with. What did any of it matter anyway? At this moment, Travis would be happy to move out that house and find his own place in the middle of nowhere, where people might leave him the fuck alone.

Starting to feel a rebound effect from the alcohol, Travis quickly downed his remaining beer and opened another, bringing it with him over to the couch. His mind remained almost completely blank as he laid there on his back with his eyes closed, only moving occasionally to raise the beer can to his lips. Travis enjoyed this temporary numbness from the pain he had felt the day before. He knew it wouldn't last. But for a few moments, it was nice to just sit there with a buzz going, not thinking about anything.

Soon enough, the toxic combination of self-pity and self-loathing started creeping its way back into Travis' head. How hollow he felt inside. Purposeless. *The world is shit, and I am its litter box.*

I mean, you're already feeling low enough. You've been a fuckup your whole life, came from a fucked up family, and have worked so many shitty jobs that you've barely been able to make ends meet. You move across the country, fuck up a couple more times, then finally start to get some of your shit together. Then out of the blue, you meet someone, a girl, who you can talk to honestly about your life, and who has a fucked up enough background to identify with you. She talks to you sincerely, no bullshit, and you can tell her the truth about how you feel about the world. She opens up to you, and it appears for a moment that she might be different from all the shallow, self-obsessed bitches that you've come across so far in your life.

Then she meets your friend. Your only friend. Your smart, overachieving, good looking, safe but still has an edge-friend. And your dumb ass never even sees it coming. Next thing you know, they're giving each other "fuck me" eyes all night, they sneak away together in the middle of a bar to hook up, they come back to your table with sex hair and guilt-ridden faces, and then they have the audacity to pretend that nothing happened!

Who needs that shit? Who needs any of that shit? Travis thought to himself. He wanted to believe he'd just read things wrong, but he knew it was a lie. As in most instances throughout his life, it appeared that in this case the most cynical explanation would also turn out to be the correct one.

Travis walked back into his bedroom, ignoring the stink as he grabbed a plastic bag of marijuana from inside his nightstand. He packed the bowl on the side of the bong, lit up the weed and inhaled deeply from the top. Before he knew it, he was now also guzzling down bourbon in between bong rips, strumming his cheap acoustic guitar, and loudly combining lyrics from different songs into an incoherent babbling. Travis continued in this bipolar emotional state for the better part of an hour, alternating between feelings of euphoria from the weed and booze, followed by extreme depression from the repercussions he was going to have to face, and the painful confrontations he could only avoid for so long.

It was impossible for Travis to admit to himself, but over the past few months he'd been tricked into believing his life was finally heading in the direction he wanted. Between holding down a steady job for a couple of months, being able to pay for his own living expenses, and attending his court-ordered therapy sessions on a mostly regular basis, Travis was taking on more responsibility than he had at any other point in his life.

For a while there it had made him feel good, being able to present himself to other people as a contributing member of society, and actually being able to feel that it wasn't all complete bullshit. Combined with his excitement over his best friend being on the verge of an earth-shattering discovery, Travis had finally found a reason to think about his future, and wonder if it could hold something for him that was worth chasing. His whole life he'd been searching for some sort of guiding light, something that would give him some direction in his life. It didn't have to be anything astoundingly ambitious: just a reason to get out of bed in the morning and be able to smile, knowing that what you were doing that day had a purpose, and could someday lead to even better things. In reality it had only been a few weeks since Jamie and Travis had developed their friendship, but this had been enough time for Travis to open his mind and his heart to new possibilities.

It wasn't even necessarily that he and Jamie had to become romantic. Maybe they would just become authentic friends who would be able to depend on each other. Maybe she would see Travis for who he could really be. Maybe someday she would introduce him to one of her girlfriends, and say "This is my best friend Travis. He's one of the most funny, thoughtful, genuine guys I know." It was daydreams like this that had carried Travis through the past few weeks on a relative high. And now, surprise surprise, he was back to wondering what he even had to really live for.

Sitting on the floor of his bedroom, Travis took another deep hit, coughing loudly as he leaned his head against the wall. It was strange. In his current haze, he found himself thinking about Frank, Kyle's coworker from the lab. Travis remembered Frank's playful ribbing of Kyle when they'd gone out for drinks together to blow off steam after Jamie's traumatic recall session. Frank had brought some much needed levity to a very distressing situation, and his interloping presence had allowed Jamie time to process her experience before discussing it, which appeared to be the correct move in the end. Travis thought back fondly to that random night out at that sports bar in Santa Clara. The riveting mix of emotions all stirring at once: being eager to discuss what had happened, yet feeling satisfied enough with what had already been accomplished, and deserving of taking a few hours to leave their worries behind. As it turned out, that moment might have been the height of Travis' optimism. He remembered, in that moment, truly believing that great and exciting things were on the horizon.

And the memory recall system had made it all possible. That unbelievably glorious machine. It offered so many exciting things. It offered the unbridled joy from reliving a happy childhood memory. The youthful optimism from remembering what you used to dare to dream. The closure of finally understanding why things in your life have worked out the way they have. Travis knew that if he stood any chance of getting out of this fucked up headspace he was in, he desperately needed one of these life-altering experiences to happen for him. And he knew only that machine could offer it. He needed to get back into the lab.

But how could he make that happen? He couldn't stand

the sight of Kyle right now. And even if he could, it would probably be months before his turn to go through another recall session would possibly come up again. Travis then remembered, when they had left the bar that night, Frank had insisted that Travis take down his phone number. Frank had actually gotten pretty drunk by the end of the night, and he'd joked with Travis that if he ever had an emergency where he desperately felt the need to rip on Kyle, he should probably have his number handy. Travis had obliged without putting much thought into it at the time, figuring he'd probably never see Frank again. What if he could somehow talk Frank into letting him get back on the system? Frank worked at the lab and seemed to know Kyle well, he must have some idea how to operate it. Maybe Travis could tell him that Kyle wanted to try running a test when he wasn't present, to evaluate how easy it would be for a non-expert to operate the system? Travis knew that story had tons of holes in it, but he had to try something. It was worth a shot.

Attempting to sober himself up before making the call, Travis went to the kitchen to grab a glass of water. He scrolled through his phone and was able to locate Frank's recently entered number. Travis took a few deep breaths, trying to focus his scatterbrained mind as he quickly attempted to plan his first few lines to Frank. Finally deciding it was now or never, Travis dialed the number and pressed the phone to his ear. After a few rings, a loud voice on the other end picked up.

"Hi this is Frank Bernstein, who is this?"

Travis fumbled as he tried to introduce himself. "Hel--hi Frank. Hi this is Travis, uhh, Kyle's buddy from the other day, remember?"

"Oh yeah Travis, hey how's it going man! Good to hear from you, I was hoping you'd give me a shout one of these days. You calling to take me up on my offer to talk shit about Kyle? That guy's such as asshole right?" Frank asked.

Travis, even in his current mental state, could detect a certain degree of legitimate agitation in Frank's voice over what would've otherwise seemed to be a playful wisecrack.

"Uhh...yeah man. Totally an asshole. That's why I'm calling you right now instead of him."

"Ha, I hear that man. Let me guess, he's trying to cut you out of his pet project just like he's doing to me, right?"

Caught off guard, Travis paused for a moment, unsure of what to say next. "Yeah...right. That's shitty of him isn't it?"

"Totally is! I mean you volunteer to go under the knife for him, so to speak. You let him get you interested in his dangerous mind-fuck device without him giving you the slightest clue of what effects it could have on you. And he just uses you for your skills or your data, and proclaims it all in the name of science. Then, just when you're really getting into what he's working on, he cuts you off completely. Just leaves you hanging out to dry. What kind of bullshit is that?"

Travis couldn't believe what he was hearing. Had he missed something completely with Frank? Here he was, petrified to call Kyle's coworker behind his back in hopes of getting back on the recall system. And without him even having to press at all, Frank was now taking the words right out of his mouth. This might end up a lot easier than he ever could have imagined.

Travis quickly gathered his focus, now resolved to close the conversation and get what he needed from Frank.

"Absolutely my friend. Couldn't have said it any better myself. That guy has no loyalty whatsoever. And I know it better than anyone, I'm the idiot who's been his best friend for almost seven years. Screw him. You know what would really piss him off: What if we snuck into that lab of his and used the machine behind his back? Maybe we could even learn some shit about it that he doesn't even know yet! Can you imagine, having the upper hand on him on the one thing he's most obsessed with?"

"Hey Travis...would you believe me if I told you I was already one step ahead of you? I'll tell you what, why don't you come over to the lab late this coming Tuesday night. 11:00 PM is perfect if you can make it then. I'll sneak you inside and show you what I'm talking about. I think you'll be quite pleased."

"Are you serious?!? Count me in! Where do you want me to meet you?" Travis asked.

"There's a parking lot behind the building with a big soccer field next to it. We'll be the only ones in the lot at that time so you can't miss me."

"Okay, I think I know where that is. So, uhh, Frank...are you going to be able to get me back into that machine?"

"Well how about this...you come prepared on Tuesday with a memory in mind, and I'll promise you one thing: You're not going to leave disappointed."

CHAPTER 22

"I can't believe I'm back here already. This is so awesome," Travis admitted to Frank as the lights came fully on inside the laboratory. The last three days had been brutal for Travis. After he'd hung up with Frank that Sunday afternoon, he'd temporarily regained enough motivation to try and scrape his life back together. He'd spent the next five hours cleaning up the entire apartment, doing such an impressive job that his housemate had approached him that night and offered to take back his threats about pursuing action with the landlord. Monday and Tuesday at the office had been riddled with anxiety. He could focus on nothing but his potential upcoming recall session. By the time Tuesday evening had come around, Travis had lost all capacity to play it cool, and had arrived at the lab almost an hour ahead of when Frank had said to meet him.

After what seemed like an eternity of waiting, Travis finally saw the headlights of a silver Saab pull into a parking space close to the entrance. Travis watched as Frank got out of the car, and followed him towards the building entrance.

"Hey Frank, how's it going man?" Travis whispered loudly as he quickly approached Frank, who was removing a key card from his wallet to activate the back door entrance.

"Hey bud, glad you could make it. You know you didn't have to park so far away though. There are plenty of people on campus working overnight in the other buildings. You don't have to worry, no one is going to suspect we're up to anything."

"Oh okay okay, that's good to know. I kind of have a bit of a checkered past with the law so I just try to be extra cautious these days. Glad to hear you've got things under control," Travis admitted.

"I've been coming in here at night for, what, a couple weeks now at this point? And no one at this university is the wiser for it. Just make sure you don't wander off or touch anything important without checking with me first," Frank instructed as they entered the narrow hallway leading towards the lab area.

"You got it, will do. So what do you have in mind for tonight?"

"Come on inside and I'll show you," Frank said as he opened the glass entry door to the lab. Travis beamed as the recall system came into his view. It was strange now, seeing everything powered down. It looked so simple. Just a reclining chair with some wires and equipment attached to it. It couldn't be THAT difficult to manufacture another one sometime in the future, for personal use. If one were so inclined.

Travis set his jacket on a chair near the back of the room, and took a seat on top of a nearby desk. Frank approached the mainframe computer located to the side of the recall chair, and removed a small mobile computer from his backpack. The computer quickly booted, and he connected it to the mainframe with a long cable. Travis then watched in amazement as Frank quickly moved around the room, expertly powering up the various pieces of equipment in sequence. Travis was blown away by how easily Frank was able to do this. He remembered coming into the lab for the first time, watching Kyle's team slowly and deliberately bringing the system online, diligently recording notes and checking various measurements as the system equilibrated. What took them a good amount of time to accomplish, Frank seemed to be able to do in a matter of seconds. "I'm going to take a wild guess and say somebody's done this before!" Travis exclaimed as Frank took the neuro-headset into his hands and began preparing the sensors.

"Yeah I guess you could say that. In order to do all of this undetected, I had to come up with a way to replicate the system applications without using most of the lab's equipment. It was quite a challenge at first, I gotta admit. But I soon found that I was actually able to improve on many of the boot sequences, and capture more data than Kyle's team probably knew even existed. If that passive-aggressive jackass had just enabled me to get more involved with his project, all of this knowledge could have been his. Oh well...his loss."

"So how long HAVE you been using the machine for?"

"Oh...probably about six weeks now."

"Six weeks!" Travis exclaimed. "Six weeks and you're still getting away with it! How the hell has nobody noticed anything yet?"

"I told you, I'm smarter than them and I'm being plenty careful. But I'm obviously taking a big risk here by bringing you in on this. So I hope that if and when the time comes, you can remember where your loyalties lie."

Travis was stung by the inflection of Frank's comment. It had officially set in that there was no turning back after tonight. He really would be betraying Kyle's trust beyond repair if he went through with this. His relationship with his best friend would be severed forever, and Travis squirmed as this reality sunk in. He hated himself for having this weakness: this self-serving need to get back into the recall system as soon as possible, in the never-ending hunt to find something positive from his life to hold on to. No matter what the costs were.

"Don't worry, I'm aware of the risks you're taking. This means a lot to me and I certainly won't forget it."

"Great. So do you have a memory selected?"

"I do," Travis answered. He had spent much of the last two days digging through his memory archives, trying to find the last point in his life when he had felt exceptional. When he'd last felt that he was as talented and had as much potential as anyone else. He had to dig far back into the annals of his past before he could finally come up with what he was looking for.

"Good. Now, there is just one other thing." Frank pulled out from his backpack what looked to be a plastic grocery bag. He began to remove several smaller bags from inside that appeared to contain a wide variety of different sized pills and bottles. They looked familiar to Travis, and as he stepped closer he realized what they were: Frank had brought with him a shitload of illegal and prescription drugs.

"WHOA...what's all that for? I didn't exactly peg you for a junkie?"

"These are psychotropic drugs. That's what I meant when I said I had a surprise for you. I've...well...we've discovered a way to drastically enhance the recall experience."

"Shit man, you've gotta have almost a thousand bucks worth of amphetamines on that table. And what's in that bottle? Is that like...LSD?" Travis asked, his own not-too-distant foray into the world of substance abuse suddenly coming back to him.

"Oh I'm sure it's much better than any street-grade crap you probably tried when you were younger. These are highly-engineered hallucinogens and amphetamines. I'm being extra cautious with them, especially since up until now I've been doing this by myself, and I have no intention of overdosing on drugs inside the lab that employs me. But these drugs are crucial to providing an enhanced version of the recall experience. What they do is, they're able to dramatically improve the sensory retrieval mechanisms of the hippocampus and the pre-frontal cortex."

"Jesus dude...I have no idea what that means. But where did you even buy this stuff? I mean I have some connections around town, but it would have taken me a while to build up this stockpile for sure."

"I was actually lucky enough to have some outside help. It's amazing what you can accomplish anonymously on the internet these days. But I hate taking this crap, and the hardest part for me has been figuring out how to dose myself. I'm not too great with needles," Frank admitted, as he showed Travis an area of small purple bruises located on his upper forearm. "Sounds like you might have some experience in that area though?"

"It's been a little while...but yeah, I think I can help us out. So how do you have any clue what you should take?"

"Like I said, I've had some outside assistance with that. It's not all that complicated, surprisingly. So, we should probably get started soon. Are you good to go?"

Feeling ashamed, Travis nodded and began unpacking the kit, helping Frank organize its contents on a nearby table.

"So the way this basically works is, over the course of two recall sessions, you'll take one of two distinct drug combinations, which have opposite intended effects. These dosages are based on your Body Mass Index, which I can measure with this portable meter. Depending on how your experience is enhanced during each of the two sessions, you reconfigure your personal dosage for the third session, and then fine tune from there if needed. This will be my third enhanced session so I pretty much know what my dosage will be. For you, I recommend we start with this combo on the left. It's the one that didn't make me puke my brains out afterwards."

"High praise indeed. Alright, I guess that'll work. So is this stuff as fast-acting as the 'street-grade crap' I've taken before?" Travis asked.

"Well the hallucinogens will hit you almost as soon as you inject, so you'll need to pop the amphetamine pills a few minutes before."

"Gotcha. And just to make sure...you've taken this already and you're sure it won't kill me?"

"Yeah man. This is pure-grade. And it's specifically engineered to enhance the power of the mind's memory. The lucidity this stuff gives you...I can't even describe it. You can literally remember which thoughts went through your mind from a particular moment of your life. And you can relive exactly how you felt as if it was really happening to you again. Touch, feel, smell...all that stuff comes back to you."

"Alright. That's good enough for me. Let's fire away," Travis agreed, as Frank instructed him to take a seat inside the recall station.

"I'll get the syringe prepped for you, but you're probably going to want to shoot yourself up if that's okay?" Frank inserted the syringe needle into the vial of clear liquid, and slowly withdrew the prescribed amount into the syringe, placing a sterile cap on the end of the needle as he set it on the table. Frank hooked Travis into the neuro-headset, and ran a calibration cycle via his computer. A little over a minute later, when the calibration was complete, Frank then slid a set of three pills over towards Travis and instructed him to ingest them. Travis abided, using a bottle of water to help him swallow the dry, chalky pills.

Turning his head to the digital clock on the wall, Frank began counting down the prescribed time between taking the next dosage of drugs. Travis laid back in the chair, not yet feeling any effects of what he'd just taken. After a few minutes had passed, Frank instructed Travis to inject himself with the syringe. Using an elastic band Frank had included with his kit, Travis quickly wrapped his lower bicep, forcing his veins to protrude outward. It had been over five years since Travis had last used intravenous drugs, but the techniques from a seasoned history quickly returned to him. He located a large vein, and he slowly inserted the short needle into his skin. He steadily depressed the plunger and watched as the medicine entered his system. Moments later he was finished, and he placed the empty syringe inside a plastic tray on the table. Frank then quickly capped the tray and placed it inside a pocket on his backpack, continuing to be thorough about making sure no identifying evidence was left behind.

The sedating effects of the drugs immediately began taking their toll on Travis, as he laid fully back into the chair and felt a wave of tension wash away from him. Frank talked softly to Travis as he monitored his vitals. He began coaching Travis on how the new process would work.

"You should be feeling very relaxed right now, yet still mentally sharp and alert. As the adrenaline rush from the amphetamines kicks in soon, you will start to be able to target the beginning point of your memory. The sensation will feel euphoric as the system pulls you into your memory path. Just let it ease you in, and try not to fight it. You're about to have an experience like nothing else in the world..."

I never realized how beautiful my mother used to be. Her eyes are radiant as she looks back at me from the front seat of our car. She asks me if I'm excited. I say yes. She asks if I'm nervous. I say no, but I'm lying. We continue driving towards my school. A classic rock station is playing softly on the radio, my dad's favorite. The sunset is gorgeous as it slowly descends over the mountains. So beautiful. Feels like it's exploding towards me.

We enter the parking lot, all around us are excited children and parents. Kids are already wearing their costumes, and parents are chatting to each other as they make their way towards the auditorium. My dad opens the car door for my sister, he takes her hand as she exits and I follow. We walk with the crowd towards the entrance, where I see my teacher directing the foot traffic. Next to us I see two fathers sitting on the trunk of a car, passing back and forth a flask of liquor with little regard for their current surroundings. Nice. The good old days. I love their style.

I realize that I can now feel the thoughts and emotions of my younger self much better than I could the first time I entered the recall experience. My senses are heightened, and I revel in the clarity of the sites, smells, and textures of what I'm experiencing again.

I can smell the lacquer from the wooden bleachers as we enter the auditorium. So many memories from just that scent. We had gym class in this room. Back when I was tall for my age, and was one of the best athletes in class. That didn't last long enough, but man was it great while it did. My mom is now taking me over near the stage with the rest of my classmates. Other parents are giving me a thumbs up and words of encouragement. I feel so reassured now. I don't feel nervous at all anymore. I'm the lead in the school play, and I'm not nervous. How have things changed for me so much?

Now we're in a classroom near the back of the stage, and we're putting on our costumes. The first group of kids are being led out to backstage to get ready for the opening of the play. I'm in the center of the room, and most of the attention now is on me, as a teacher puts me into the jacket of my tuxedo while another puts the finishing touches on my hair. They ask me if I feel good about my lines. I answer with a confident 'yes'. Across from me I see the two prettiest girls in my class getting their makeup done. One is my co-star in the play, and I remember that I get to dance with her at the end. I can remember now exactly how it made me feel to be with her during rehearsals. There was no place else in the world I wanted to be but in that moment. A paradise that only a naive child could know. I'm certain I've never felt that good in my life since.

We're now being led up the stairs to the backstage curtain. I can hear the music playing and the kids running around the front of the stage, with ripples of laughter coming from the bleachers. My grand entrance is coming up soon. I make sure my hat is on straight as I run through the first few lines in my head. I'm ecstatic in this moment. For once, I'm the star.....

Frank was quite pleased with the data he was seeing. Though he still couldn't visually interpret most of the model readings, he was getting better at looking at the raw numbers, and he knew this was going to be a very successful run. He thought of the group who had contacted him and sought his help in granting them access to the lab's confidential information. How pleased would they be to see this additional data validating their parameters? Frank thought about transmitting the data packet right away, right there in the lab. *No idiot, way too dangerous,* he told himself. *Wait until you can get onto a secured network.*

My lungs burn as I continue running around the stage, chasing the imaginary dog who has just stolen my allowance. I'm weaving in and out of the other kids, making sure not to accidentally knock any over. I hit my mark in the center of the stage, and someone backstage tosses me a cane. I catch it on the first try, and use it to hook the imaginary dog around the collar, starting a pretend tug-of-war with him that makes the crowd roar with laughter. The sound is delightfully deafening, and as the song comes to a close, I'm in awe of what I've just pulled off. I'm certain I'll now be famous around the school for decades to come. I'm bursting with excitement and raw energy.

I hear the soft tapping of the piano keys, and realize my dance is coming up next. I run to my position at the back of the stage behind the line of children. There I see my co-star, looking as beautiful as ever under the glimmering stage lights. I take her hand in mine, and immediately feel the sensation in my mind again of the first time I ever touched her skin, over 20 years ago. My heart is pounding with adrenaline as we slowly walk forward in unison. The other children are singing, and a gap in the middle of the line slowly forms as we emerge to the front of the stage. A round of applause fills the auditorium as we turn towards each other. She places her left hand on my shoulder, and my right hand goes softly to her hip. With our other hands extended out towards the audience, we begin our slow dance. We slowly spin along the front edge of the stage, then begin making our way back to the other side. It is pure bliss for me. I cannot remember ever feeling this good. I would right now trade anything, do anything to be back in this moment in time for the rest of my life. What a gift, to be able to see through child's eyes, but feel and experience through an adult mind.

As our dance comes to an end, we turn to face the audience and take our bows. As planned, I pretend to fall over, and the crowd erupts in laughter and applause as the curtain closes in front of us.....

"Travis? Travis how are you feeling? Blink at me a few

times if you can hear me," Frank instructed.

Travis mumbled a few words as Frank slowly inclined the chair and began detaching the headset. Eventually Travis opened his eyes, and felt that his pounding heart was quickly settling. Frank handed Travis a bottle of water, and he slowly sipped from it as his vital signs began to return to normal.

"How was it?" Frank asked directly.

"I...I can't even begin to describe it. It was like dying and going to heaven. I can't believe something like that exists on this planet." Travis shook his head in disbelief at everything that had just occurred in the past hour of his life.

"I know. I told you it's like nothing else in this world. Nothing else. So how are you feeling physically? Little sick, but hopefully not too bad?"

"Yeah, pretty much. I'm feeling better quickly though. The half-life on that shit must be pretty short."

"Told you, it was engineered for this purpose by people much smarter than you or I. So hopefully in about ten minutes or so you'll be feeling back to normal, and we can get ready to set up for my recall session. I want to show you how to do a couple of quick things on my computer first, but you really won't have to do very much."

"Okay, sounds good," Travis said. He took a seat in a nearby chair as Frank continued the preparations. As conflicted emotionally as he was at this moment, between the ecstasy he had just felt traveling back in time, and the remorse over so deeply betraying his best friend, Travis found the net result to be almost complete numbness. Too much of his destiny had already been chosen to start second guessing himself now.

CHAPTER 23

Kyle's team remained busy at the Keane Lab with the laundry list of enhancements they were hoping to knock out before the end of the year. In only the past few weeks, Michael had already eliminated the need for half of the sensors making up the neuro-headset. It had quickly gone from a device that looked like it would have been used during electroshock therapy sessions in the 1970's, to a sleek one-size-fits-all adjustable headband. Ryan and Farida had teamed up to eliminate several redundancies in the system calibration, cutting the time down from a little over five minutes to just under three. They'd also been able to reconfigure the graphical output of the key system indicators to display together on one screen, providing an essential summary view that could be monitored by just one person if need be. Farida had even in her minimal spare time managed to streamline the input layout of the mind mapping user interface down to only one screen. These were mainly surface-level improvements, but they would go a long way in demonstrating the team's capabilities to proliferate this technology to researchers and medical professionals down the road.

"Okay...now we're officially working ourselves out of a job," Michael had commented that morning while showing Kyle the latest improvements to the interface. "If we're not careful, this machine is going to end up turning into a glorified tarot card reading. This thing is gonna be so simple to operate, shops will be popping up everywhere where you can go in to get a quick mental reading to determine if you're 'truly at peace with your inner demons.' All for a nominal fee, of course." Kyle knew Michael was mostly joking, but he had sensed a growing unease come over his team in regards to what the end game should be for this technology. Kyle himself had only been privy to bits and pieces of information regarding the lab management's overall roadmap, picked up mainly from his weekly check-in meetings. He didn't want to simply placate his team by giving them the typical generic answers of an upper-level manager. But he also wanted to help them stay focused on the things that they could control.

"Well when you put it that way, it doesn't sound so terrible. At least we'll sell a ton of recall systems and we'll all get rich!" Kyle joked back. "I mean I hope you guys know this, but we're selling out at the very first sign of a buyout offer. I don't care what the offer is, we are taking the money and RUNNING with it!"

Farida was enjoying the alternate reality Kyle was imagining, and decided to play along. "Oh we are, are we? And what exactly do you plan to do with all that cash? I know I'm using it to bring my entire family over to the States to live. I'm buying a huge mansion right on the coast where we can all live together, happily ever after."

"Well I'll be using it to quit this job, join NASA and become an astronaut," Michael quipped. "Or maybe if I'm loaded enough, I'll start another one of those private space exploration companies and own my own spaceship. And I just know Ryan over here, he's probably already scouting locations for where he can start his religious cult dedicated to online multi-player RPG gaming."

"Hell no man, cults have too many rules. This place would be more like a commune, where everyone chips in and does their part to help build the greatest role-playing game of all time, and we split the rewards equally. That would totally work out, right? Ahhh, paradise. So how about you boss, when we're all multi-millionaires what's next for you?"

"Are you kidding? Isn't it obvious that I'm buying a yacht, loading it up with hot chicks and sailing through the Caribbean like a rapper? I'll start up a nightclub on a private island out there, where the party literally never stops. Fun and sun, 24/7," Kyle joked. "Ahhh, paradise..."

Ryan let out a laugh. "Sold! I like your version of paradise better than mine. I'm coming with you."

Kyle wanted to prolong this fantasizing exercise with his team, but over Ryan's head he spotted Stan making his way down the corridor towards the lab. He knew there must be something relatively important on Stan's mind for him to come all the way down here to address the team while they were gathered together. This was not usually his style.

Stan waved excitedly at the group upon entering the lab. "Good morning everyone. Farida, Ryan, Michael, Kyle. How are you all doing this morning?"

A muttering of "Oh, not bad's" and "Pretty good's". Though Kyle's relationship with Stan had certainly improved during this recent period of innovation, the rest of the team dreaded his visits, which usually came with some kind of arbitrary request that added to their workload. They had yet to meet a Director-level manager at Keane who understood the principle of 'value-added work', which in the end endeared them to Kyle even further.

"Hey gang, so I know it's been a while since we've had a chance to chat about the ICCN conference coming up here next month. I don't have to tell you again how critical this conference could be for the future of this project. If we're able to really knock the socks off the investors who are at the conference, it could put us in a position to land all of the funding we'd ever need to take this project to the next level!"

Kyle could sense the disdain his team had for Stan's transparent focus on securing investors. While Kyle knew enough to know they were a necessary evil, from a researcher's standpoint, they almost always put their own interests before the interests of proper scientific method.

"I know you guys have all been working hard the past couple weeks to get the system as finely-tuned as possible for the big announcement. From what I've heard you're even ahead of schedule at this point, which is a remarkable accomplishment you all should feel very proud of. This is a big part of the reason why we've decided to go ahead and submit this project for the keynote presentation at the conference."

Kyle's eyes lit up as he heard the words coming from Stan's mouth. *The keynote presentation at the ICCN conference!* Kyle hadn't yet attended the conference in person, but he'd heard enough about it in recent years to know what a big deal this was. Incredible scientific breakthroughs had been revealed at the keynote over the years. Within the last five, Kyle could remember a research team from Denmark demonstrating a new hypnosis method that could potentially be used to eradicate violent tendencies from children at an early age. Another year there was a team, out of Canada as Kyle recalled, that presented a method to correlate a person's ability to quickly comprehend the meaning of written passages with their likelihood of demonstrating financial responsibility later in life. These had all been exciting advancements in the field of neuroscience that had demonstrated significant relevance and staying-power within the industry. Kyle knew his team's discovery certainly had the flashiness to generate a great deal of attention at the conference. This wasn't his main concern. His worry was that they were running out of time to prepare. Keynote presentations could run as long as 2-3 hours sometimes. And based on the laissez faire attitude that Stan and the other members of senior management had demonstrated in the past, Kyle knew the brunt of the prep work would fall on his shoulders. What could he talk about for two hours in front of hundreds of spectators? If only they could replicate the memory recall system to have one stationed in Zurich in time for the conference. That would give Kyle's team the firepower they needed to deliver a legendary keynote. That was a pretty tall order though, unfortunately.

The team looked at each other with shocked expressions. This was about the biggest honor that could be achieved in their field, and while they were completely flattered to even be in the running, the amount of work they knew had to be done to go into the presentation was almost overwhelming. Farida took a seat as she let the reality of the situation set in.

"I'm honored to even be considered to partake in the keynote at ICCN. I really am. But the conference is, what, five weeks away?!? How on earth are we supposed to get everything prepared in such a short time? And wouldn't they already have a keynote selected by now?"

"I certainly empathize with your concerns, Farida, and please rest assured we are going to dedicate every resource to this team that we're able to in order to help you feel as prepared as you possibly can be. And as far as the keynote selection process, the committee actually prefers to give the candidate institutions as much time during the year as possible to build up their candidate portfolio. As your team was already submitted for a station at the grand expo, much of this work is already completed. We just need to spiff up our sales pitch with the latest and greatest, and we should be fully submitted in plenty of time. And let me tell you guys, I've seen some of the competitors this year, and I really like our chances! If we come away with the keynote this year, it could be the catalyst that launches you all to international stardom in the neuroscience community. You could be running your own labs this time next year!"

Stan let the gravity of the situation sink in as he offered some final words of encouragement before pulling Kyle off to the side.

"So what do you think? You think you guys are far enough along that we can do this thing?"

Kyle paused, contemplating his response. In most cases he would just tell Stan what he wanted to hear to get him off his back. But with what was now the most important deadline of his life looming, Kyle couldn't afford to mess around. He knew his team had accomplished something remarkable, and he knew the science was there to back up the claims they would be making. They just needed to figure out how to most effectively communicate their findings to such a large and varied audience. And this is what Kyle did best. The more he thought about it, he wanted the glory that this international stage would provide them. For his team, but also for himself. Why wait another year? This was their time to shine.

"It's gonna be tough, but yes I think we can do it," Kyle replied. "I mean you saw how that visiting group from the Cognitive Sciences Seminar responded to Michael's recall session with his dying mother. This is obviously a discovery that will get people talking. Our jobs are going to be to convince them that this isn't some sort of magic trick. This is a stable, repeatable process that's backed by sound scientific research. I'd be lying if I said I didn't wish we had more time to put together a game plan for the presentation itself. But I'm confident we can put together something that will effectively communicate what we've accomplished here."

"That's great Kyle...that's just what I was hoping to hear. We'll keep things progressing with the selection committee on our end, and we'll keep your team apprised of what we hear back. At the management meeting this week we should have a more detailed list for you of what the committee will be expecting. And like I said, we're willing to divert whatever resources are needed to help your team prepare. You just let me know." And with that, Stan shook Kyle's hand and marched back towards his office.

Kyle reentered the lab, where he found the rest of the team

eagerly waiting for his return.

"It sounds like we're pretty hot shit right now, eh boss?" Ryan joked. "It's a good thing the prospect of delivering the keynote address in Zurich in only five short weeks doesn't make me want to crap my pants. Oh wait...it does."

"Hey, if it means we get to keep the Basel Institut from taking center stage in their own backyard, sign me up!" Michael declared. "Those cocky bastards at B.I. could use a good humbling. If they lost out on the keynote to a couple of upstart Americans like us, that would piss them off beyond belief!"

"I mean, a couple of Americans and an Israeli. Sorry," Michael said, looking towards Farida.

"It's okay. And I agree with you. It would give me great satisfaction to headline ICCN, even more so if it spited B.I.," Farida said with a roguish laugh. "Can you believe they turned me down for an internship several years back? Me, the genius behind the discovery that enabled eidetic memory recall? What fools they are!"

Michael's laughter bellowed at the unexpected jab taken by Farida. "Wow Farida, you're kind of terrifying when you're vengeful. I'm going to remind myself never to get on your bad side!"

"Ha. Well I'll admit, sometimes I do have a hard time letting go of being slighted. I'm really only joking though. But honestly...if we're going to deliver the keynote at the conference, we really need to be able to give a demonstration. Do you guys know what that entails?"

"It means we need to somehow build another system we can take to Zurich. Or figure out how to make the system we have portable, and develop a way to recalibrate it after transportation. And we're supposed to do this in five weeks how exactly?" Ryan asked in astonishment.

"I'm not so sure we absolutely need to perform a live recall demo at the conference," Kyle said. "I know it'd be great for the 'wow' factor it would offer. But I think if we can effectively show what we've achieved here in the past few months, and what this technology has enabled...that would be plenty to convey our accomplishments and create a substantial buzz within the industry."

"You might be right...but wouldn't it be unreal if we were able to do a live recall in front that audience?" Michael asked. "I mean picture it...live on stage, in real time, with the crème de la crème of our industry in attendance. We could even use an audience member as our subject, to prove that we aren't faking anything. I know that might all be a pipe dream at this point. But I feel like we need to have some kind of visual element in our presentation to draw people in. Something to connect this recall experience at the human level. I just don't think a high-level scientific slide deck is going to be able to accomplish that."

"Wait a minute guys. We have these overhead lab cameras in here that we've never really used. Why don't we just record some video of one of our next runs, edit it up, and use that in our presentation?" Ryan asked.

Kyle contemplated the suggestion. "That actually sounds like a solid idea. It kind of hedges our risk. If we're not able to get a live system up and running in time for the conference, at least we can show the gist of how the process works. Plus, if we really are expected to be on stage for two hours, that would at least help us eat up some of that time productively."

"Totally," Ryan agreed. "We'll tape the session from every angle, then edit the thing to show how robust we've made the process. I'm pretty handy with video editing software, I could probably knock it out in a couple of days."

"Well shit, it's only...11:23 AM right now, what are we waiting for? Let's get on it!" Michael suggested. "And we all know whose turn it is next..."

Kyle noticed all heads turning towards him. "Is it really my turn already? I hadn't even noticed," Kyle kidded. In fact he knew quite well his return to the recall chair was coming soon. It'd been in the back of his mind ever since Michael had brought it up a few weeks prior. It had taken him almost no time to decide what he needed to recall. Really, ever since that hike he'd taken in the Muir Woods, he'd known where he needed to go with this opportunity. Kyle was finally on the right track to getting the fulfillment he wanted out of his life. But there were still a few things missing.

"I don't know guys, I'm kind of scared. I mean, how do we know if this thing is safe?" Kyle said sarcastically. Farida laughed as she grabbed her notepad, wasting no time in beginning to make preparations for the run.

"Nice try boss. Come on there's gotta be something that you've been dying to recall this whole time?" Michael asked. "Or maybe you already have it in your mind, but you're one of those superstitious types who won't tell us until afterwards?"

Feeling guilty still for continuing to mask his unauthorized self-experiment, Kyle downplayed his eagerness to get back into the machine. "I've got a few ideas in mind, sure. Let's go ahead and get prepped, and I'll make myself decide on something."

Michael powered on the system, and Farida began to run through her checklist of firmware improvements to make sure they had all been maintained. Ryan opened the interface for controlling the lab cameras on the nearby workstation, and one-by-one repositioned them to optimize their recording angle and clarity. There were now five separate high-definition feeds of the recall system being displayed on a flat screen monitor, as opposed to the single front-facing feed they typically displayed for visitors. Kyle had to admit the system looked sleek, and his turn as the movie star should at least show professionally at the conference.

Kyle could see Farida was nearing the completion of her checklist, as he slowly made his way over to the recall chair and took a seat.

"Now are you guys certain you can run this machine without my help?" Kyle asked, mocking himself for his mostly hands-off involvement in the actual operation of the system up to this point, but also trying anything to keep himself calm.

"Something tells me we'll get through it just fine," Ryan fired back. "Farida I'm going to put the headset on him, you ready to calibrate?"

Farida nodded as Ryan aligned the sensors with Kyle's head. Farida began the calibration sequence, which now could be completed in about half the time as it initially required. Sensing that Michael and Ryan were somewhat reluctant to ask, Farida decided to pop the question. "So, what memory have you officially decided on?"

"Well...believe it or not I actually do have something pretty important to me in mind. Farida, you probably don't know this yet. One of my brother's, my older brother Ben, died in a plane crash 15 years ago. What I'm planning to do is try to revisit the last time I saw him."

"That's terrible about your brother, I'm sorry to hear that Kyle. But that sounds like yet another wonderful opportunity to take advantage of what this technology has to offer!" Farida said earnestly.

"Man you guys are all so serious with your recalls. All I did was relive an afternoon at the waterpark with my cousins. I think I really blew it!" Ryan exclaimed.

Farida laughed, and gave Kyle a pat on the shoulder before returning to her station. She informed the team that the system was ready to go, and instructed Kyle to relax and begin to focus on the starting point of his memory. Kyle made himself comfortable in the chair, and began taking in slow deep breaths. He started turning his attention to his family's former house, the one he had lived in since he was seven years old. He focused on the front yard, with the big cottonwood tree he used to play in so often. He.....

"How fast can you get her going?" I hear my dad asking my uncle. We're standing in the front driveway of my house, all eyes transfixed on the brand new 2001 Chevy Camaro Z28. Black paint on black interior. I remember being blown away by this car when my uncle would occasionally let me drive it, but now I'm shocked by how dated it looks.

"I've had it up to about 120 on Highway 60. Thing drives like a dream. I sprang for the 5.7 liter so this baby is loaded with torque. It takes off out of the gate so fast, Kelly's afraid to drive it. I love it though. Always wanted one of these."

I rub my hand against the soft grain leather and take in the new car smell. I remember thinking at the time that I wanted to make a lot of money someday so I could buy something like this. A lot can change over 15 years.

My uncle pops the hood, and he and my dad start marveling over the V8 engine. My uncle asks me to grab him a beer from the cooler outside on the back deck, and tells me to get one for myself. I'm excited when my dad, who was always on the fence about me drinking while I was underage, doesn't say anything. I quickly cut through the front door and head out to the deck, which is crowded with my family and relatives, who are there for my graduation party. I try to go straight for the cooler, but my mom spots me and calls me over to have me say hello to some relatives. I don't recognize these people, though my mother introduces them as my second cousins whom I've allegedly met before. I stand there awkwardly in silence as their mother gives us a backstory on each child. I tune her out, and now I'm getting worried about how much time I have left in my recall session. I hope I entered in at the right point. I know that I talk to Ben on the front porch of our house. I remember it still being daylight outside. I just can't remember any other details. Who goes there first? How do I meet him there?

I finally break free from the group, and I quickly grab two cans of beer from the cooler and head back out to the driveway. My dad's now in the driver's seat, revving the car in neutral as my uncle claps his hands at me, asking me to toss the beer to him. I do, and he catches it, immediately popping the top and taking a swig. I walk back to the house and take a seat in the chair swing on the porch. This may be it. This may be the moment. How much time is left? I open the beer and slowly take a sip. I haven't acquired a taste for it yet, not like I did in college. I'm still on the porch by myself. I think this is when we have our talk. He better fucking come soon.

I hear the front door open. Voices talking to each other. The door opens fully, and out walks Ben. He takes a seat in the chair next to me.

"How's it going stud? You having a blast at your big party?" Ben asks me. "I see you're getting into the fun stuff at least," he says, nodding at my beer. "You're going to be drinking plenty of that I'm sure at Arizona State."

I laugh and say back, "Well I'm planning to use this summer to get even better at it. I finally don't have to worry about college applications or grades for three whole months! I'm ready to just kick back and have a helluva good time."

"Oh I can believe that. I felt that exact same way when I graduated. And don't forget, I did a year and a half at ASU before I dropped out. I know what college life entails."

"Well I can't wait. I'm so bored here," I say as I take another drink. "I'm gonna set myself up to have the best time ever in college. I hear that freshmen are supposed to rush as many fraternities as possible, so that you can get into all the parties and meet a ton of people. That's where all the girls hang out too." I can tell that I'm trying to sound cool around my brother. It sends an uncomfortable chill down my spine as I hear myself saying it now.

"Yeah man, you're going to have a great time in college. The big thing I'd recommend is to make sure not to stress too much about stuff that really doesn't matter. It's hard being that age, I certainly don't miss it. People around you are going to get all worked up about the stupidest things, but don't let them pull you in. Just stay relaxed and keep in mind that none of that shit matters in the end."

"I agree with that for sure. I hate all the gossip and drama I already see now in my high school. I know we're only teenagers, but it's insane how childish some people can act. I'm ready to move forward with my life and start hanging around more...I don't know...I guess 'sophisticated' people."

"Oh you are are you?" my brother asks me, smiling as he mocks my not so subtle judgement of my hometown.

"Ha, well, you know what I mean. I mean hopefully they're not too sophisticated, I still want them to get rowdy and party with me," I say as I toast my beer against my brother's. "But hopefully *the people I meet in college are able to think more deeply about their lives than just what's right in front of them. I really don't come across people like that much in this town."*

"Like I said, don't worry about it man. You'll get what you want out of it. Just try to keep an open mind next year, and try to expose yourself to as many new things and meet as many people as you can. That's really what the transition from being a teenager to becoming a young adult is all about. I mean that's how I got into traveling the globe doing this non-profit stuff. I just happened to wake up early one day, on a rare Saturday morning without a hangover, and I went for a walk around campus and stumbled across this sign for a meeting. I didn't know the first thing about it, just saw that it had to do with international travel. I took a risk and checked it out, and five years later, here I am, still with it."

"Do you ever regret not sticking it out through college and graduating? Or does that not even matter for what you want to do with your life?"

"Not for a second, man. I'd rather be doing what I'm doing right now than have ten million dollars in the bank. But every person is a little bit different. You know you've always been the better student and academic than me. I mean I did okay on grades but I never was able to really keep focused and stick to the game plan our parents tried to lay out for us. But that's okay. One thing I've found out as I've gotten older, is that people really only have so much control over where they end up in life. If you spend your life trying to mitigate every risk and overanalyze every decision, you're going to wake up one day and be 40 years old, and realize that your time to take risks and make mistakes in your youth has disappeared. And that's when you see people going off the deep end into mid-life crisis mode. I'm just hoping our esteemed uncle over there with the brand new sports car doesn't fall into that category," Ben jokes as he points out towards the driveway. I laugh, watching him and my dad still fawning over the car.

"So what are you hoping to do after you graduate college? You want to be a doctor or something? Are you interested in helping people for a living?" Ben asks me.

"Hell no, I pretty much hate being around people," I laugh as I answer back to Ben. *"I'm only planning to go into Biology cause I've always done well in the classes, and it seems like a quick way to start making some decent money. I know, I know...you're going*

to say I'm an idiot for selling out and not taking a risk at doing what I really want to do with my life. But the thing is...I really have no idea what that would even be yet."

"Lil bro, trust me that's totally fine. You're my brother, even if you wanted to become one of those Wall Street scumbags who scam people out of their life savings, I would still try to support you as much as I could!" I laugh at my brother's obvious sarcasm.

"It takes some people a lifetime to figure out if they're really doing the right thing with their life. And I'm not an expert in it by any means, but one thing I think I've figured out is that you're never going to know if you're doing things exactly right. A lot of people wait for that revelation, but it's never going to come for them. But if you're doing things completely wrong, you'll figure it out pretty quickly. That's why I recommend not worrying too much about getting everything perfect on the first try. If you're moving in the right direction...the speed at which you're moving just doesn't really matter all that much."

"Yeah...I think you're right Ben. I'll try to keep that in mind next year," I answer to Ben. I couldn't believe how right he was. Over the years, I'd tried hard to remember this advice exactly as my brother had given it to me. But every year, it seemed, I'd lose a little bit more of it. As I hear him say it again, I try my hardest to commit it deep within my memory.

"So, where are you off to next? Mom said you're leaving us again in a couple days?" I ask Ben.

"Yep, unfortunately I am. I'm heading back to South America. Bolivia actually. Working a nine month stint down there helping out a couple of the towns with some economic development work. I'm really excited about it though. It's my first time back to that area since I made my very first trip, to Peru five years ago."

"Wow that's awesome! Good for you man. Good for you. I'll be lucky if I see in my whole life 10% of what you've already seen. That has to feel amazing," I tell my brother. I continue to be amazed at the adventurous spirit he had, and I often wish more of it had rubbed off on me.

"It does feel pretty good, I must say. That lifestyle, it's a sacrifice though... I miss not being able to see you guys very often. I hope that Andrew doesn't have to grow up not knowing anything about me. I think about that a lot actually."

"I'm sure it won't be like that," I say, putting my hand on my

brother's shoulder. I had no idea at the time what was about to come in a few short months.

"It won't if I have anything to say about it. Well on that note, let's get back inside and spend some more quality time with the family. Maybe grab another drink or two while we're at it."

"Sounds good man," I say as I get up and follow Ben through the front door. We go out to the back deck again to chat with some relatives, but my mind is still on the conversation with my brother. The last real moment I shared with one of the most influential people in my life.

"So what'd you think, how was it?!?" Ryan eagerly asked Kyle. As the haze slowly lifted, Kyle sat up in the chair and collected his thoughts.

"Unbelievable. What an invention we've got here. If I wasn't already determined to succeed with this thing before, I don't think there's anything in the world that's going to stop me now."

"I like the confidence boss!" Ryan said exuberantly. "So what's next? How can we push this thing to the next level?"

"I'll tell you how we can do it. We're going to be the keynote team at the ICCN conference in a couple of weeks. And we're going to blow their fucking minds."

CHAPTER 24

After another brutal stretch of early mornings and late evenings at the lab, Kyle decided it would be good to get away from the office for a few hours and take Jamie out for a nice long lunch at one of his favorite restaurants in Santa Clara, The Hopping Pig. Kyle was a longtime fan of their braised short rib sandwich, and had a suspicion Jamie would like their menu too, given the surprising amount of things they were quickly discovering they shared in common. Kyle and Jamie had been out together a few times over the past couple of weeks, and Kyle was finding himself more and more attracted to her the more time they spent together. She not only fit the bill of what he was drawn to physically, but he was finding that her personality was actually a great complement to his. Deep down they were both brutal realists. Neither of them suffered fools very easily, and neither would be described as a 'people person'. But perhaps Kyle's favorite trait of Jamie's was her ability to keep things in perspective. He had already put her to the test on that a number of times.

Kyle arrived at the restaurant a few minutes early, hoping to beat the lunch-time rush and grab one of the available patio tables, which on this unseasonably warm day offered a picturesque view of nearby Agnews Historic Park. Kyle was pleased as the hostess showed him to a small table in the back corner of the patio. He took a seat and ordered an iced tea, waiting patiently as Jamie arrived almost exactly at the scheduled time of 11:30 AM. Kyle stood and hugged Jamie as she approached the table, enjoying the fresh scent of her hair as he felt her arms wrap around him. Though the embrace was short-lived, it was enough to make Kyle slightly aroused.

"This place is so nice, what a great idea to come here!" Jamie said cheerfully. Kyle continued to enjoy the transformation he was seeing in Jamie since her recall session. Though he had only known her for a very brief time before, it was evident that she was experiencing a sort of spiritual rebirth since that event. It was exciting to see her finally start to believe that happiness could be possible, and that she deserved to have it. It was a journey that Kyle hoped he could continue to be a part of for a long time to come.

"Yes, this is definitely in my top five restaurants in the Bay Area. I read a really good review about it when I first moved here and decided to check it out. I've never left here disappointed."

"Well judging from the crowd they must be doing something right! The ambiance is fantastic too. You sure do know how to impress a lady," Jamie joked, shooting Kyle a playful smile that he couldn't help but return with a satisfied grin of his own. The waiter approached, and Kyle was happy to hear him recommend the house specialty braised short rib sandwiches. They decided to order those as an entree, and start off with the antipasti plate as an appetizer. Kyle also ordered a basket of the homemade sourdough bread with roasted garlic.

"So how was working on the night shift the other night?" Kyle asked Jamie, referring to the graveyard shift she had picked up for a coworker the previous Sunday. Kyle and Jamie had made plans to see a movie together that night, and had altered the plans to an afternoon matinee after Jamie accepted the shift.

"It was interesting, I hadn't done that for a while. Usually things are a lot slower at the hospital on the late night shifts, but what you do see tends to be a bit crazier. We had a drunken teenager come in who had broken his pelvis trying to do a backflip off a parked car. I can't say that's something I see everyday! Anyway it screwed up my sleep schedule pretty bad for a day or two, but I'm basically back to normal now. How about you, are you still making the progress you need to with the recall system?"

"We've made some solid improvements the past few weeks. Believe it or not I actually got to take her for a test drive the other day finally! I went back and recalled a family party that I'd had for my high school graduation."

"What, Kyle that's great! You didn't tell me that! So what did you think?!? It's unbelievable, right?" Jamie asked enthusiastically.

"It is! It's incredible to witness what our team has accomplished first-hand. I mean it's not like I didn't believe you guys when you told me how vivid the experience really was. But it's just one of those things that you can't fully wrap your head around until you go through it yourself."

"I don't know what took you so long! But I totally agree with you. So...did you find anything important that you'd forgotten in your memories?" Jamie's demeanor appeared to become serious upon asking this question, so Kyle decided it was an appropriate time to give her the full answer.

"I did actually, Jamie. I chose to go back and revisit my older brother Ben, before he passed away during an accident on one of his mission trips. Ben's probably one of the most influential people I've ever had in my life. He was such a driven guy, and I've always admired the way he blazed his own trail and broke away from the boring cycle of living a middle-of-the-road life that I see so many people settling for. But Ben was able to be humble about it too. He wouldn't hold his accomplishments and experiences above anybody. For years after he passed, I can remember using him as a source of motivation when I was having a hard time with my life. I guess everyone needs some kind of role model, and he was the closest thing I had to one. That probably sounds crazy to some people because I saw so little of him during the last couple years of his life, when he was always traveling. What's even crazier is that as time's gone on, I'd forgotten a lot of the advice that he'd given to me. I'd thought that maybe he'd become in my mind more of an idealized version of my brother than a real person. So that's why I went back to talk with him again...I guess I wanted to complete the package of who Ben really was and what he really stood for."

Kyle still wasn't accustomed to sharing his inner thoughts like this with another person, and had a hard time looking Jamie in the eyes as he finished his thought. Though they'd only really known each other for a couple of weeks, Jamie was the first person he'd felt comfortable enough around to share something like this with since his brother passed. Kyle's hands fidgeted on the table as he waited for Jamie to say something.

Jamie gently reached across the table and placed her hand on top of Kyle's.

"Kyle, I hope you understand now why what your team has accomplished is so important. The opportunity that it gives people to go back in time and...not fix things from their past, but understand them more completely, and continue to learn valuable lessons from them. I think that's something that every human on the planet needs at some point in their life. It's like you said, as more time goes by you remember less and less of the real meaning. And I think you start to project yourself onto that memory to fill in those gaps. You start to trick yourself into thinking that the reality of the situation was different. I mean, that's really what 'nostalgia' is if you think about it. But I think in doing that, you lose the real value of the life lessons you're supposed to be gaining from those experiences. What's amazing is that this device you have has the potential to set the record straight for people, once and for all."

Kyle was thrilled by the strong vote of confidence Jamie had just given for the recall experience. She had made some excellent points which Kyle hadn't even thought as far ahead as to address yet. It was becoming apparent that as they progressed with this technology, Kyle was going to need some help in determining which direction they should take it. It was going to be good to have Jamie around to help him during this process.

Kyle had hoped he could dodge the next topic, but knew it was going to come up sooner or later, and he wasn't terribly surprised when Jamie sprang it on him.

"So how has Travis been? I don't think I've talked to him since we all went out together that night in Sausalito."

"I actually haven't talked to him since that night either," Kyle admitted regretfully. "I did send him a couple of text messages a few days ago, but haven't heard anything back from him since."

"Really? That's weird, isn't it? I thought you guys usually talked a couple times a week. Maybe he's just been really busy at work or something?" Kyle could tell Jamie didn't understand what was most likely occurring. And he wasn't looking forward to hitting her with the uncomfortable news. But there was no avoiding it at this point.

"I really don't think that's the problem, unfortunately. I think that Travis...I think he has a thing for you. I know he does actually." Jamie's expression turned puzzled, though Kyle noticed she wasn't exactly acting blown away by the revelation.

"Oh no," Jamie said with a sigh. "But...that doesn't explain why he would be ignoring us? How would he even know that you and I have been...you know, seeing each other?" It was a strange sensation for Kyle to hear Jamie say those precise words. It felt good, though at the moment Kyle felt guilty taking pleasure in it.

"I'm not sure. I guess he could have spotted us together that night at the jazz bar. I mean I thought we were being pretty careful. But he did kind of act weird when we all said goodbye to each other that night. And even before that...I don't know...I feel like he could tell something was up."

"Wow...now I feel kind of stupid for not trying to play it off better. I guess I knew there was a chance that he might have liked me as more than just a friend. But, I don't know...what am I really supposed to do about that? He's a really nice guy, and I just don't want him to be angry with us." Jamie's frustration was evident.

The waiter brought over the entrees, and the two of them ate their meals in relative silence, each pondering how to fix the situation they were in. Eventually they started to make conversation about some local day trips they wanted to take together in the coming months, and by the end of the meal, they were both feeling a little bit better about the Travis situation.

Kyle paid the check and glanced at his watch to see what time it currently was. He quickly ran through his head what his afternoon schedule looked like. Most of the management team was at an offsite meeting, so it would be relatively quiet back at the lab. His team had a few simulations they were planning to run in the next few days to debug their data collection software, which meant his afternoon would be busy, but not as brutal as it had been in recent days. He did not at the moment feel like being apart from Jamie.

"Hey, what do you think about coming back to the office with me? I can show you some of the upgrades we've made on the system since the last time you saw it. Might be kind of fun?" Kyle said with as much charm as he could manage.

"Really? Yeah...actually I would like that a lot! I wish there was something I could do to help you guys out with the project. But I guess there's really not, huh? I mean, unless you want me to jump back into the machine and remember something happy this time?" Jamie offered with dry humor.

"Oh don't you worry, I'm sure there'll be time for that coming up here soon. But let's head over there and I can show you a couple of cool new things at least," Kyle said. They jumped in their cars, and Jamie followed Kyle on the five minute drive back to the campus.

Kyle was hoping to take a few relaxed hours in the afternoon to show Jamie some of their system improvements, and maybe even get her thoughts on the structure of the presentation they were putting together for their station at the expo. As he and Jamie casually strolled into the lab, they found Ryan, Michael and Farida virtually at each other's throats.

"You've got to be fucking kidding me!" Kyle heard an enraged Michael shout as he entered the lab. "How the hell could this have happened?!?"

"Don't you even think about blaming me, Michael! Don't you dare blame me!" Ryan said furiously.

"Well you're the one who controls the firewall that's supposed to protect our shit, aren't you?" Michael fired back.

"Whoa whoa, what's the problem here guys?" Kyle asked, apprehensive about what he had just walked into.

"Kyle, glad you're back, we were just about to call you. We might have a big problem here," Ryan said, his eyes shifting quickly between Kyle and Jamie. Jamie surveyed the room and could feel the unease in the air with her being present in this crisis situation. For a moment, she debated faking that she was receiving a phone call in order to let Kyle have some time alone with his team. Kyle was completely unsure of what the problem could be, so he decided to start from the beginning. "Okay, so what exactly happened here since I left the lab a couple hours ago?" The team fell silent, waiting for someone to volunteer the complicated explanation. Finally, Farida stepped forward and began.

"A little after you left, we finished our first group of

simulations. Everything appeared to have run smoothly. The new 3-D model mapped the simulated synaptic pathway perfectly--"

"--And everything looked great from our end too," Michael blurted out, unable to contain his anxiety. He was squirming in his chair as he continued, his body language making Kyle even more nervous.

"The new analytical model ran just like it should. All the metrics were outputting beautifully onto the new summary display. At the time, we thought it couldn't have gone any better. And then Farida went into the file server to retrieve the master file..."

"And it was gone! Poof!" Farida said, throwing her hands up in the air and looking more exasperated than Kyle could ever remember seeing her. "I mean, Kyle...the panic that I felt when I couldn't locate that file. I've never felt anything like it. I searched everywhere I could think of on the system to find it, but it didn't turn up anywhere. I'll admit, I'm not the strongest when it comes to networking and servers, so I asked Ryan if he could help me take a look for the missing file."

"Initially, I had no idea where the file could have gone," Ryan said. "I ran a couple of scripts to search for if the file was corrupted during saving, but nothing came back. Then a couple of minutes after I ran the search...there the file was. Right where it was supposed to be the whole time."

"What? Really?" Kyle said, unsure of how this seemingly minute problem could have caused the shouting match he had just witnessed. "Well a slow network connection could have caused that, right? I mean we've had all sorts of problems with slow internet speeds around here from time to time."

"Of course that was my initial thought," Ryan responded. "Maybe the lab's network was just clobbered and performing slowly. But then I remembered that everything else had ran at the normal high-speed. It was only the master file that had an issue. I even ran a connectivity test shortly after, and the speed came back normal. It definitely looked to me like...I don't know...something shady might be going on."

Kyle felt confused as he replayed what he'd just been told in his mind. So far he wasn't seeing any big problem. If there were some technical issues with the system recording the data, they still had a couple of weeks to fix those. And Ryan was a whiz kid when it came to that stuff, so Kyle was sure it wasn't anything he couldn't handle.

"So I decided to dig deeper into what exactly had happened," Ryan continued. "I checked out all the properties of the new master file that had just magically appeared. Everything from that perspective looked okay. I opened the file and Farida did a quick scan of the data, and everything looked totally normal. So next I checked the system log to take a look at which location the system recognized as the source of the data. And besides the 8 minute and 33 second delay the system had in writing the file, everything on the log checked out. I then checked the backup file, which I'm directly managing here instead of the university IT group. Everything looked good with that as well. So I was almost out of ideas at that point, but I had one more idea in the back of my head. Have you ever heard of a term called 'slack space'?"

"Slack space?" Kyle repeated out loud. "I think I sort of remember hearing that term from computer programming classes I took in college. But that was a pretty long time ago at this point. No, I don't really remember what it is I guess."

"Well slack space is essentially the space that gets left behind on a disk when a file gets erased and overwritten by a smaller file. The way computer memory works is that when a file gets saved, it's broken down into a bunch of different clusters of a fixed size. When you erase a file, you're not always really removing all of those clusters. What you're really doing is saying that those clusters are no longer reserved, and now a new file can be written over the top of them."

Kyle again found himself racking his brain, trying to piece together where Ryan was going with this explanation. Did the recall system have a virus that was corrupting their data? Was the software they were using not powerful enough to properly handle the processing of their data? Kyle decided to let Ryan continue before he would venture a guess.

"What often happens with slack space is that if the new file is smaller than the old file, there can still be leftover clusters that contain fragments of the old data. Well, I went ahead and ran a disk check on the area where our master files are now stored. And this is on a brand new dedicated disk, mind you, that had only been installed nine days ago, and that had yet to ever have anything erased from it. Guess what I found?"

"You found slack space on the disk?" Kyle deduced.

"I did. Now this week we've run a total of four simulations, each of varying durations. And as I went through and analyzed the master files, each one had proportionally the same amount of slack space. I know from my days in the IT world that this almost always means that file compression is occurring."

"But how could that be? We haven't installed any compression systems yet," Kyle said, remembering the upcoming agenda for the next several weeks which he had just reviewed that morning.

"That's right, we haven't," Michael interjected, still visibly shaken up. "But Ryan and I checked, and the files are undeniably compressed. So that means one of two things: Either we don't know how to handle our own data, and are therefore complete fuck ups. Or somebody outside of this team has been accessing our data."

Ryan gave a silent, wide-eyed nod in the affirmative, and Kyle felt a knot in his stomach as he attempted to grasp the reality of the situation. He desperately searched for a rational, common sense reason that would explain why the data would have been manipulated by someone outside his team. Could Stan have authorized somebody from the lab's IT Department to access their servers, perhaps to ensure that their data was safely backed up? Kyle seriously doubted that. He knew Stan wouldn't want to do anything that could possibly jeopardize the team's standard routine this close to ICCN.

"Okay...say someone did try to access our data for whatever reason..."

"Not 'try to'. They did access our data!" Michael insisted. Kyle shot Michael a disapproving look, and Michael took the hint to try to compose himself.

"How could we find out who?" Kyle asked. "Could we try to locate where the data was sent?"

"Already tried that when I checked the system log. It doesn't show as being sent anywhere, other than the backup drive..."

Kyle suddenly remembered something that he had read recently. It was in an article about the difficulties in conducting intelligence tests online. Specifically, the article centered around word puzzles. The article had said that some people who wanted to falsely set the new high-score record were using programmed algorithms. These algorithms would simulate answers for a question by checking against various online databases, and converge all of the possible answers into the most likely answer. Kyle struggled to remember the name of the term for the algorithm. Finally, it came to him.

"So I'm guessing if we tried to read the data on the slack space, it would be very incomplete, and therefore incomprehensible to us, correct?"

"Already gave it a quick try, and yeah you're right, no such luck there yet," Ryan replied.

"So what if we used a probabilistic algorithm on the

slack space data?" Kyle asked. Ryan appeared surprised to hear Kyle make such a technically advanced suggestion as this.

"That's funny…I was actually just thinking we could try something similar to that," Ryan said. "I know that there are programs out there that can analyze slack space using a probabilistic model. That's basically the type of program that criminals use when they steal sensitive data off of a hard drive that's been thrown away in the trash after being reformatted. I'm always paranoid of that, every computer I've ever thrown away, I've smashed the shit out of the hard drive first before I put it in the garbage."

"So do you think you could get your hands on one of those programs, and give it a try on our data?" Kyle asked.

"Oh, I'm sure I can take a stab at it. There aren't exactly a lot of reputable sources where you can find programs like that out there. But fortunately I know a couple of backdoor channels still from my college days that I can check out. Give me some time and I'll see what I can come up with."

"Thanks Ryan. Take all the time you need."

Kyle took a seat with Jamie at a desk in the corner of the lab. They were working together to attempt to put together a design outline for their station at the ICCN conference, but it was proving tough to focus when the potential future of the entire project hung in the balance. If the system data had truly been compromised by an outside source, then a whole world of problems would be opening up at the worst possible time. Aside from the fact that for all they knew their proprietary data could be floating through cyberspace for anyone to get their hands on, it would likely take an act of God to fully understand what had happened and get the issue under containment in time for the conference. Jamie looked up and watched with eager anticipation as Ryan and Michael sat side-by-side at the system console, working together frantically to try and figure out what had happened to them today. She hoped desperately that they could come up with something soon.

Minutes later, when Kyle and Jamie had finally started getting into a rhythm on the outline, they heard a yell from across the room.

"It's done! No errors, I think it worked!" Michael exclaimed loudly, throwing his arm around Ryan and shaking him vigorously with affection. Kyle quickly ran over to the console to see what had happened, and Jamie followed closely behind.

"Let's take a look at this," Ryan said, shaking with excitement as he tried to operate the computer. "So I did like we talked about, and I located an algorithm that's supposed to be custom-made to analyze slack space on compressed files. I configured it for our system, then I ran a quick test on our server on a dummy file, just to be extra safe and make sure it wasn't going to infect our system with malware or any shit like that. It ran clean, so I turned it on our four recall master files and let it rip. Took about 25 minutes for it to run through all the data clusters and try to piece them together. Looks like this screen is the output from the run."

Kyle found himself staring at a black screen containing text in white font. The left side of the screen consisted of several sentence fragments.

INCOMPATIBLE SUBNET MASK. ATTEMPTING FILE TRANSFER PROTOCOL. REASSIGNING DEFAULT GATEWAY. RESOLVING HOST.

On the right side of the screen were several sets of numbers of varying lengths. Kyle scanned over them for several minutes, but couldn't make sense of any of them.

"Do any of you guys know what any of this means? That block of text on the left side sounds like networking jargon, but I'm not making any sense of it."

Ryan pointed to the section of text Kyle was referring to. "Those look to me like general protocols that a system goes through when trying to establish a network connection. Doesn't really tell us a whole lot at this point though."

Kyle turned his attention back to the list of numbers. "Farida, what about the numbers on the right side? Do those numbers represent anything to you?"

Farida took a position next to the screen and leaned in closely. She mouthed several of the number strings aloud as she scanned through them. The team watched as she continued down the list. Finally she leaned back and pointed to the screen.

"There. Those strings of one's and zero's right there. That's binary code. And look at how the numbers are arranged." Farida pointed to the series of numbers in the middle of the screen.

10101001.11101000.10000100.10110000
10111011.10001000.10011100.10111100

"Four sets of numbers, separated by three decimal points. It looks to me like that could be a binary representation of an Internet Protocol address. Ryan, can you go online and run that through a binary converter, and try to figure out where those IP addresses are located?"

Ryan quickly loaded a web page and copied the string of numbers into the entry box. The converter spit out the following series of numbers:

100.43.18.790
100.78.39.146

"The top one! That's the IP address for our lab!" Ryan shouted.

"Where the hell is that second one going to?" Kyle asked.

"Come on man, do an IP search and let's figure it out. Hurry!" Michael scolded Ryan.

Ryan searched for the location of the second IP address, and the following information was returned:

IPv4 Address 100.78.39.146
Country Code CH
Latitude 47.1667
Longitude 7.6
Located in Landschaft, Switzerland

"Oh my God!" Ryan cried out. "Landschaft, Switzerland! You guys know what's located in Landschaft don't you?!?"

Kyle clenched his fists as he answered. "The Basel Institut....."

CHAPTER 25

Stan could not have come at a worse time. Still trying to fully grasp what had happened to them that afternoon, the team was scrambling to come up with a plan. From what little they knew at the moment, it was entirely possible that their revolutionary discovery, for which they each harbored their own set of hopes and dreams, may have been compromised by the single most renowned institution in the neuroscience world. They wanted to do nothing else at the moment but figure out if the Basel Institut was really behind this, and what they might have on their project.

Jamie had fortunately suggested earlier that she take off and give Kyle some time alone with his team to work out their massive problem, which at least saved Kyle the added anxiety of introducing her to his boss in the middle of this chaos. For once, Stan must have to some degree been able to pick up on his unwelcomeness in the room, because he chose to deliver the big news in even briefer fashion than usual.

"How's my favorite lab team doing today? I trust everything is moving along smoothly?" Stan asked with his forced casual professionalism. Only Farida could manage to make herself acknowledge his question with a polite smile. "Well I have some rather big news, and I wanted to be the first to tell you all."

Kyle knew what was coming, and a feeling of dread washed over him.

"You're now looking at the keynote team for this year's ICCN Expo! Congrats guys, you did it!"

Again it was only Farida who managed a trepidatious

smile in receipt of the news. Kyle knew he needed to dismiss Stan as quickly as possible, so they could all get back to working on the problem at hand.

"Realizing we're only a couple of weeks away from the conference, I wanted to give you all a list of resources that are here at your disposal to help you prepare," Stan said as he handed out to each team member an information packet. "This will cover your travel itinerary, your rough agenda for the conference, provide technical help with getting the presentation prepared, and basically anything else you think you'll need. We're extremely excited, and want to give you our full support."

"That's exciting news, Stan. Really exciting," Kyle bluffed. "We all thank you for this opportunity, and we're certainly planning to make the most of it. Do you think I can I catch up with you later on the details? We actually have an important simulation coming up that we're running a little behind on."

"Oh of course, no problem, no problem at all," Stan bumbled, realizing that he may have unknowingly walked in on the team during an important experiment. "How about you swing by my office tomorrow and I'll give you the rundown. The conference is coming up quickly so I don't want to wait too long, but like I said, we've got plenty of resources to support you in anything you need."

"Thanks Stan, sounds good." And with that, the team again returned to the pursuit of their information leak. Ryan pulled up a new screen on the recall console, where he had further organized the data that the slack space scan had provided.

"Okay, so here's what we're looking at," Ryan began. "We have an IP address here from near Basel, Switzerland. And we have some fragments of networking and file transfer commands that sure do make it seem like there was data being transferred off of our server. The way our server is setup, there's virtually no way they could have acted alone in breaking into our system and ripping off the data. Someone with at least some knowledge of our configuration and the local infrastructure must have opened up a backdoor. But everything we have here is incomplete. We'd have to do a hell of a lot of connecting the dots to be able to prove definitively that something illicit happened here."

"I see," Kyle said. He mulled over the information they had reviewed earlier, trying to find the most logical course of action. "So it appears we have a couple of options here: We can dig into this master file issue and try to figure out what exactly has been copied from our archives. We can then take this to the executives at the lab and tell them everything we know, and enlist their help from a legal standpoint. And maybe if enough evidence is uncovered, we can pursue prosecution of whoever might have stolen our data, assuming that someone actually did. If our circumstances were different I'd probably prefer to go with this option, since it covers our ass from a liability standpoint."

"So what are your other options?" Michael asked.

"Well, really we have to keep in mind how soon ICCN is coming up here. And now that we KNOW we're giving the keynote, it's going to take all our time and energy just to get our shit together in time for this conference. I don't know if we can afford to spend time chasing this thing down a rabbit hole right now with all we have in front of us. Our other option would be to get on the defensive, and try to protect ourselves from anything that B.I. or any other group may have on how our system works. This means we need to be lock-tight on our scientific reasoning for anything we choose to present at that conference. Because for all we know, somebody attending might have taken our design and reverse-engineered it to try and attack us on our weakest areas, or maybe even try to take credit for our discovery. Maybe we even think about changing around our coding, so that the stolen information that's out there now becomes obsolete and inaccurate."

"I think I'd be on board with that plan," Farida said. "We have so much work left to do before we're ready to go up in front of that crowd. I don't think we can handle this distraction."

"I don't know man," Michael said. "It's going to make me paranoid as hell knowing that someone like B.I. might be out there trying to rip off our system. I mean what if they try and copy it, and they come to the conference with an identical system? And they're even located in the same country as the expo, it would be much easier for them to get a system set up for a live demonstration. They could completely steal our thunder!"

The group sat in silence, deliberating over what Michael had just pointed out. *What's the right play here?* Kyle tried to determine as unwaveringly as he could. After several minutes, it was Kyle who spoke up again.

"I have an idea," Kyle started. "What if we try to ping that IP address in Basel, and see if we can uncover what they know?"

Michael seemed bewildered by the suggestion. "What do you mean...like just say to them 'Hey we know you stole our data, tell us what you have or we're going to press charges against you?' I'm pretty sure I've heard multiple times that bullying doesn't work on cyber terrorists."

"Not bullying...we try to trick them into thinking we're the source. We keep it quick, and ask them general questions about what other information they would like to receive. Then maybe we can clarify what they already have."

Kyle now felt strongly about pursuing this course of action, but realized he didn't have the slightest clue on how to execute it. "The only thing is, I'm not sure how we'd communicate with them? I'm guessing there's some kind of high-tech version of chatting out there that we could use, pinging the IP address that we just found?"

Ryan was again on the ball to provide the technical

expertise. "Actually, we'd go low-tech for this. There's this thing called IRC, Internet Relay Chat. It's been around forever, I think it was like one of the first methods of communication for the earliest forms of the internet. Back in my amateur hacker days, I used to use it occasionally to communicate with other hackers. Anyway from what I remember, it's pretty universal and it's very much unmonitored, so it's still popular in the hacking community. I'd bet almost anything that this is the way whoever got into our system has been communicating with this group in Basel."

"I mean...you could at least try it, right?" Michael said. "Reach out to them on IRC, make a couple of general comments on the data transmission that's already occurred, and see if they bite? If you're planning to try it out now though, you better hope whoever's on the other end of the line is a real night owl. Because it's like 3 o'clock in the morning in Basel right now if I'm not mistaken."

"Well I still think it's worth a shot. Most hackers are insomniacs anyway. What do you guys think?" Ryan asked.

"I vote yes," Kyle responded resolutely, fueled by his desire to reach a solution as quickly as possible.

"Me too," Farida added.

"Me too," Michael concurred. With that, Ryan fired up the workstation, and installed a simple IRC program he could use to communicate with the IP address.

"Alright, all set. I'm ready to initiate the chat session, so let's figure out what we want to say," Ryan instructed.

Ryan entered the IP address into the connection window. Kyle read the commands as they popped up on the screen:

-Attempting to connect with Internet Protocol address 100.78.39.146-

There was a delay on the other end as the team waited tensely for a connection. Although it seemed like an eternity, less than two minutes had actually passed when the following response was sent back.

Hello there. U are earlier than usual. Must have got tired with video game. How r things? Using a new IRC client?

"Contact!" Ryan proclaimed. The team huddled into the screen and reread the brief message from the unknown sender, trying to determine how to properly respond while maintaining their cover.

"Let's keep it brief," Kyle reminded them. "Acknowledge the new client and put the ball back in their court. You guys agree?"

The team approved with silent consent, and Ryan shook nervously as he typed in the reply.

Yes. Having problems with old one. How r u?

"That's good," Michael said. The team waited with baited breath before a response appeared on the screen.

Tired since u woke me up. But ok. From latest transmission appears new dosages r working well. Will u have update later today?

Ryan again looked to the group for a response. "Be vague again," Michael recommended. "Tell him hopefully you will, but you can't guarantee it for sure."

Ryan nodded, and entered a reply.

I hope to. If not today, then soon.

The team again waited for a reply from the other end. This time though, several minutes passed and nothing was communicated. The team grew increasingly nervous that they may have said something that tipped off the other party.

"I don't like this. We need to escalate this somehow," Kyle said, trying to determine how they could obtain the critical information they needed through the course of such a brief conversation. "Let's ask them if they think we're still on schedule," Kyle suggested.

Ryan contemplated how to translate this into the tone of the prior messages sent.

R we still meeting your schedule? Anything u need more quickly?

A brief pause, then an answer:

Fine 4 now. Latest requests will need to be sent by EOY as discussed. Very important. I must go now. Thx for checking in. Out.

-Connection has been terminated-

"Wait wait wait!" Michael exclaimed. "Dammit! We could have had them!"

"God that was nerve wracking!" Ryan said, shaking out his arms as he stood up quickly from his chair. "What just happened there? Did we even learn anything from that?"

Farida wasted no time grabbing a nearby whiteboard and starting to document notes. "The way I see it, we learned a couple of things: First of all, we learned that the location of the IP address is almost certainly in another continent, since we apparently woke up whoever was on the other end. Basel would make sense in this case."

"And we learned they're expecting another transmission of data at the end of the year. EOY, that's end-of-year, right?" Michael asked.

"Yes, it must be. And that lines up with ICCN being at the end of the year. So far this is still pointing towards B.I.," Kyle deduced.

Michael leaned into the monitor again to reread the transcript. "Oh yeah, what was that video game comment about? And what are they talking about with the dosages?"

"Great questions...nothing comes to mind immediately," Kyle admitted. "But I think another thing we learned is that we weren't talking to a 'they', since the sign off was only 'I must go now'".

"Good point, I'll write that down," Farida added. The team surveyed the short list of items they had learned during the brief interaction.

Kyle focused in on the two unknowns that Michael had brought up. *What in the hell did a video game have to do with this project? And what dosages could they be referring to?*

The team discussed the conversation further, but couldn't come up with any firm takeaways that would help them decide a solid path forward. They were starting to feel like they were going in an endless circle, always coming back to the same list of vague points they had originally developed. After spending over two hours racking their brains, they all agreed that they should go home and try to sleep on it, and come back early tomorrow with fresh minds to try and develop a game plan.

"I think I'm gonna try to dig into the slack space data for a little longer before I call it quits. See if anything else comes up. I promise I'll go home after that though," Ryan informed Kyle.

"Okay sounds good, and thanks again for everything today. I'll see you back here bright and early tomorrow." With that Kyle headed out of the building with Farida and Michael. They tried their best to make small talk, but Kyle could tell their minds were still completely focused on solving the mystery of how they'd been hacked. They exchanged goodbyes and each headed their separate ways.

Kyle laid out on his apartment couch, completely exhausted from an emotionally draining day. What had started out so relaxing at lunch with Jamie had ended back at the lab in about the worst way possible. Kyle knew that he should eat something, but he felt too tired to make anything or even order delivery. He debated calling Jamie to update her on what'd happened, but decided it was too confusing to try to explain. Flipping through the TV channels, Kyle tried to find something that could give him a momentary escape from the terrifying reality that lie in front of him. But his mind inevitably kept wandering back to the conversation that afternoon. *Who had they talked to? How did they get their hands on his team's recall data? And what were they planning to do with it?*

Kyle found that his thoughts kept reverting back to those two comments Michael had pointed out. *Dosages? Video games? Was this even related to their project? Could it be a reference to something else? Like a hobby?* That person on the other end of the line would seemingly have to have a pretty friendly relationship with their alleged main conspirator, if they went as far as to discuss personal hobbies together.

There was something about that line though. Something that was stuck in the back of Kyle's mind that he couldn't dislodge. *Who did he know that worked on video games as a hobby.....*

Frank! Frank Bernstein! Kyle was sure that Frank had brought up multiple times that he was working on building a video game, even as recently as the lunch they'd had together a few weeks back at the diner in Palo Alto. Now that Kyle was thinking about it, when was the last time he had even seen Frank? He'd been planning to get him more involved with their project since he'd already expressed interest several times, and he certainly had some valuable skills they could make use of. Kyle had unfortunately become too busy to ever get around to developing a plan for him. But even with the tunnel-vision he'd been operating with the past few weeks at the lab, they still should have bumped into each other at least a couple of times. Something strange was going on. This was starting to make too much sense.

Frank has a side project working on a video game. He has access to the lab. And he's also smart enough and skilled enough with technical systems to pull off something like this. But why would he go behind the team's back and try to sabotage our work? Not to mention put his own job at risk, and risk legal prosecution?

Maybe it was too far-fetched to think that he could be behind this. But maybe not. What could Kyle do to know for sure either way? How could he get proof? He could activate the overhead cameras in the lab to run 24/7, in hopes that Frank was sneaking in to access the mainframe when the team wasn't there. But there was just as good of a chance that he had hacked into their server from home. Kyle decided that it might be worth trying follow Frank, just in case he was in fact making off-hour trips to the lab. *Do I even have his home address?* Kyle checked the contact list in his phone. He had Frank's phone number, but not his address. Kyle then remembered that Frank had given him a business card a while back, one that he used for his side consulting gig. That probably had Frank's address on it. Kyle ran into his spare bedroom and began rifling through the drawers of his desk. Inside the narrow top drawer was a scattered pile of business cards. Kyle grabbed the entire pile and quickly began shuffling through them. About halfway through the pile, he found a card that read "Frank Bernstein: Information Systems Analyst / Consultant".

Below the title read an address:

683 Calle Laguna Drive Unit E
Milpitas, CA 95035

At that moment Kyle made the bold decision to drive over to Frank's place and stakeout his apartment. It was obviously a long shot, but Kyle knew he wouldn't be getting much sleep that night anyway, wondering if he had just discovered the culprit behind their information leak. It was now 7:37 PM. Traffic had died down by now, and he could be there within an hour.

Kyle was already shaking in anticipation as he pulled up to the side street near Frank's apartment. The complex was a medium-sized building on a quiet side street, and from Kyle's estimation housed around ten units. Kyle spotted Frank's silver Saab parked in a small lot, and strategically parked his car down a side street out of sight. In the dark Kyle wasn't able to make out the letters on the apartment doors, but from the way the building was set up it appeared the rooms funneled into a front central exit which Kyle could easily keep his eyes on.

Kyle waited patiently for something to happen. He didn't really have a plan in mind if he spotted Frank, and wasn't sure how long he was willing to wait there. Truth be told it was a Thursday night, and odds were Frank would be staying home for the remainder of the evening, probably even going to bed relatively soon. Kyle didn't love his chances, but at this point felt he had no choice but to wait it out as long as he could. As an hour slowly ticked by, Kyle's fatigue started to settle in. He turned on the radio, scanning through the channels to find some loud music in hopes that it would keep him awake. To no avail though, after nearly nodding off several times, Kyle finally succumbed to his need for sleep.

He awoke abruptly to the sound of a turbo engine roar, and as he tried to orient himself and figure out what he was doing sitting in his car parked on a random side street, Kyle checked his side-view mirror and saw what appeared to be a lightly colored hatchback driving quickly down the road. Unable to make out much detail, Kyle immediately checked the parking lot, and under the streetlights he was able to see that Frank's car was now missing. Kyle started up his car and gunned it into a U-turn, flooring the accelerator in an attempt to catch up with the car he had just seen drive by.

He sped through two stop signs, and as he approached a series of cars stopped at a red light, he quickly searched for Frank's vehicle. Sure enough, at the front of the line he made out a silver Saab, the same model as Frank's. As the light turned green, Kyle forced his way into one of the two right turn lanes and made the turn, staying a few cars back as Frank continued straight on the road for several miles. The time was now 10:41 PM, and Kyle wondered where Frank would be heading at this hour on a weekday night. As Frank approached the next major intersection, he continued straight ahead, instead of making the left turn onto the highway on-ramp like most of the other cars. It was now becoming apparent: Frank was driving to the university.

Kyle's heart began to pound in his chest as he continued following Frank towards the UC Santa Clara campus. It appeared as if the stars were aligning just right for Kyle, and he might be able to get to the bottom of this great mystery much sooner than he'd originally anticipated. A few minutes later, Kyle watched as Frank turned his car into the university entrance. He decided to fall back a bit since there was almost no other traffic around, and it would now be much easier for Frank to notice that he was being followed. Kyle pulled over into a nearby lot, put his car in park, and decided he would wait there for ten minutes. This would give Frank enough time to enter the lab and get started on what he was doing, but not enough time to cause any further damage than he already had. Kyle's heart continued to pound, and he could feel beads of sweat running down his sides as he forced himself to try and remain patient. He still was not exactly sure what action he planned to take if he caught Frank red-handed, but he knew that no matter what, he needed to see this night through to its end.

After what seemed like an eternity, Kyle continued driving his car for the remaining four blocks until he approached the main entrance. As Kyle made the turn towards the lab, he was now feeling resolute in his mission.

This was his team's project, and if someone was fucking around with it, he felt righteous in stopping them in their tracks and bringing them to justice. Kyle continued down the alley way towards the rear parking lot, where he saw Frank's Saab parked right near the back of the building. A few rows back, however, he saw what looked to be another car. As Kyle slowly pulled in closer, he couldn't believe what was sitting in front of him: It was Travis' blue Chevy Monte Carlo, unmistakably parked near the back entrance of the lab. Kyle's head spun as he tried to process what this meant. *So this is it?!? This is the answer I've been searching for?!? Travis and Frank have been playing me for a fool! No wonder I haven't heard from either of them in weeks. Has this been going on that whole time?!? Even longer?!?*

Kyle's disbelief quickly turned to rage as he slammed the door of his car. All thoughts of being subtle with his entrance were now cast aside, as he stormed towards the entrance of the building. Marching down the dark entryway, he could see a light at end of the hallway, which must have been coming from the lab corridor.

Kyle threw open the hallway door and sped down the corridor where he could now see the lab, fully illuminated as if it was the middle of the day. Turning the corner into the rear lab entrance, Kyle was shocked to see Travis standing by the recall workstation, organizing several containers on top of a small rollaway cart. Kyle barged past the desks, nearly tripping over himself as he approached Travis.

"WHAT THE HELL ARE YOU DOING IN HERE?!?" Kyle yelled angrily. Travis shot back upon hearing Kyle's scream, and began backing towards the nearby wall. Travis was now mumbling something nervously, and Kyle couldn't make out what he was saying. Kyle could feel the rage building inside of him as he continued to inch towards Travis. Taking in the bizarre scene around him, Kyle saw what appeared to be a collection of amber glass vials, plastic bottles, and a small box full of syringes. He looked back to

Travis, who appeared extremely gaunt, almost sickly.

"What...the hell...is going on here Travis..." Kyle's voice squeaked in an enraged disbelief. "Travis...you better tell me absolutely everything you guys have done here...or I'm going to kick your fucking ass and haul you off to the police."

As Kyle inched closer, he noticed that Travis' eyes were no longer focused on his face, but appeared to be looking slightly behind his head. Kyle turned around quickly, and in a split second he was able to identify Frank, whose eyes were open wide like a madman, pupils fully dilated. The last thing Kyle remembered seeing was a blunt object, looking very much like a hardcover textbook, being swung with surprising speed and power directly towards his face.

CHAPTER 26

It took Kyle a moment to identify the warm substance covering the right side of his face. Slowly attempting to lift his head off the floor, he felt a shooting pain at the back of his eyes, temporarily blinded by the bright fluorescent ceiling lights. Gradually Kyle lifted himself up to a kneeling position, and stared blankly at the small pool of blood that had formed next to him on the ground. Kyle couldn't believe how exhausted he was feeling at the moment, after being so fired up when he had stormed into the lab moments before. He wondered how much time had actually passed since Frank had knocked him out. Frank's eyes…those eyes filled with such rage and desperation. Kyle couldn't get the image out of his head. The blood was still trickling steadily down Kyle's face as he touched his hand to his right forehead. *If I'm still bleeding like this, I must not have been out for that long,* Kyle thought. He checked his watch, and the time now read 11:47 PM. His best estimate was that he'd been knocked out for around 20 minutes. Kyle was tempted to run out of the lab to his car to chase after Travis and Frank, though he knew it would be a futile effort as they were both no doubt long gone by now. Besides, he knew he was in no shape right now to go on a manhunt.

Slowly Kyle rose and steadied himself on his feet. He staggered over to a cabinet where the lab kept some cleaning supplies, and removed a roll of paper towels along with a box of sterile alcohol wipes. He gingerly bent over and mopped up the pool of blood first with the towels, then used a few wipes to remove the remaining traces. Kyle then took a fresh wipe and gently used it to clean the side of his face.

He felt a painful stinging when he reached the area above his right eyebrow, realizing this must have been where he took the brunt of the blow delivered by Frank. Kyle searched the rest of the lab for any evidence of the altercation that had occurred that night. Aside from the bloody garbage bag Kyle was now carrying with him out to his car, there was no sign that anyone had been inside the lab since his team had left earlier that evening. Travis and Frank had done a good job of covering their tracks. They obviously had some experience.

Kyle half-expected to see his tires slashed as he found his car sitting in the parking lot, alone in the quiet darkness of the early morning chill. The road was wide open as Kyle drove through the blackness back to his apartment in San Francisco. Kyle felt he should be taking action in some way to try to find Travis and Frank, though he was having a lot of trouble focusing on anything besides operating his car at the moment. Despite this, he took out his phone and dialed Travis' number, knowing there was very little chance of him picking up. The call went directly to Travis' voicemail, meaning he had wisely turned off his phone after leaving the lab. Kyle debated trying Frank as well, but knew the outcome would be similar.

The fatigue wave again hit Kyle as he rode the elevator up to the 29th floor. Upon entering his apartment, he quickly disrobed and did another crude cleaning job on the cut above his brow, locating a package of old bandages and placing two smaller ones over the cut to keep it semi-covered. Exhausted beyond any point he could remember, Kyle crawled into bed and lay his head on his pillow. Almost now to the point of feeling delusional, Kyle found it strange that his thoughts were now turning back to his childhood. He was thinking about a time when he was a young child, curled up on the couch in the basement of his house, watching his father and brother play cards on the coffee table near the television. He was thinking about how comfortable he felt in that moment. It was not long before Kyle fell deeply asleep.....

Kyle's heart pounded as he shot up out of bed. He checked the clock on his nightstand: 5:13 AM. He had only been asleep for three hours, but was now wide awake as the thoughts of all the actions he needed to take came flooding into his mind at once. Kyle needed to decide how he would go about tracking down Travis and Frank. He needed to figure out how he would inform his team of what had occurred the previous night. They would likely be arriving at the lab in a few short hours. And at some point, he needed to call Jamie and update her on everything that had happened in the last 12 hours. He decided to get the easy part over with, and grabbed his phone off the charger to dial Jamie's number.

"Hey Kyle, didn't expect to get a call from you this early in the morning. How did it go at the lab last night after I left? I hope you guys were able to find the information you needed."

"Hmmm...well, I don't even know where to begin on telling you what we ended up finding out. I'm sorry, I can't remember if you told me you were going into the hospital this morning or not? I'm guessing that you are if I didn't wake you up just now," Kyle apologized.

"I was actually planning to go in at 7:00 to cover a partial shift for a friend, but I know there were a couple other nurses who were interested in picking up the shift a few days ago. If you need me I could try to get a hold of one of them right now to see if they're still available?"

"No it's okay, I don't want to make you do that. I was just calling to let you know I may be hard to get a hold of the next couple hours. Actually probably for the next day or so. Got a lot of stuff to figure out..."

"Kyle, you're making me nervous! That sounds bad. I'll

tell you what, I'm going to get this shift covered and meet up with you to help you out. I'll call you right back." Jamie hung up the phone before Kyle could object. He determined there was no use in arguing, and started getting dressed to get to ready to tackle the day. Jamie called Kyle back about 20 minutes later and informed him she was able to find another nurse to take the shift. Kyle offered to meet her at her apartment, as he would likely be heading south back towards the lab that morning anyway.

On the drive to Jamie's apartment, Kyle tried to sort out how to best approach the team with what had happened last night. The last thing he wanted to do was throw them into a frenzy that would completely distract them from the goals they had set out to accomplish in the short amount of time they had remaining before the conference. And besides, how would they be able to help the current situation anyway? It's not like they would have any clue where Travis and Frank were hiding out.

Kyle called Jamie when he arrived at her complex, and Jamie suggested he come up so he could fill her in on what was going on. Kyle realized that this was actually the first time he had been inside her apartment, and upon entering, he was welcomed by the aroma of freshly brewed coffee.

"Here, I'm sure you need some of this," Jamie said as she handed Kyle a large coffee mug. She leaned in to kiss Kyle on the cheek, and immediately noticed the shoddy workmanship he had done to the cut on his face. "Kyle what happened to your face? You're eyebrow is completely swollen!"

"That's just one of the many twists in the story that I need to fill you in on. I'm fine though, don't worry about it."

"Well those tiny bandages you used to cover up the cut are completely bleeding through. Here let me get some stuff out of the bathroom and clean this up right." As Jamie sat Kyle down and went to work on properly cleaning and taping up his wound, Kyle did his best to bring Jamie up to speed on the events that led to his wild encounter with Travis and Frank.

"Oh my God Kyle! I can't believe he would do that to you! What could he possibly be thinking?"

"I really have no idea. I still feel like I'm in shock from it. I mean once I put the pieces together about Frank, that at least made some logical sense to me. But how Travis got involved in this...I still have no clue..."

"Well, Travis does have kind of an addictive personality. And I know from some of the deeper conversations we've had together that he's going through some tough times emotionally. I know the effect that going into that recall system had on me, and I could definitely see someone having difficulty letting go of that experience. Especially someone who's searching so hard for meaning in his life right now like Travis is."

Kyle had to acknowledge that even he himself had gone into his memory recall session desperately hoping to gain a deeper understanding of how past events had led him to become the person he was today. If he was being honest, it did make some sense that Travis could have become overly attached to this experience. Especially knowing Travis' less than perfect family history. Maybe he really was trying to dig into his past to search for something he felt he needed. Trying to find something that may not even exist for him.

"You might be right. That still doesn't explain Frank though. Or help me locate either one of them. I need to find them to figure out what exactly they've been doing with our system, and what they've shared outside the lab. It's the only way I can be sure we're not walking into a disaster when we go up on stage in a couple weeks at ICCN. How the hell am I going to track them down?"

"Actually, I do have one suggestion. It may come off as a little extreme, but it sounds to me like we don't exactly have time on our side. So the time for half measures is probably over," Jamie said firmly. Kyle was in full agreement.

"My mom works for a law firm over in San Leandro. I know that they sometimes hire private investigators to track down leads for cases they're working on. I could ask her if there's any way she could give us the contact information for one of their guys. From what little I've heard, they can get things done pretty quickly."

"I don't know Jamie...I mean, shit, do we really want to complicate things even more by bringing a P.I. into this mess? Although honestly, I don't know what else we could do to find them in the short amount of time we need to. I guess it's worth a shot, if you're okay with making that call?"

"Of course Kyle. I just want to help in any way possible," Jamie said sincerely. She grabbed her cell phone and took it into the other room, and through the wall Kyle could hear the murmuring of a conversation with what must have been her mother. Finally Jamie emerged from her bedroom.

"Okay, so my mom's willing to help us out. She gave me the names of two local P.I.'s that their firm uses frequently. She said to start with the first name if you want the job done quickly. His rate is $90 an hour, and apparently he can usually get what you're looking for in less than 48 hours."

"That sounds great, let's call him right now and get things moving!" Kyle dialed in the number on his phone and put it on speaker mode so both he and Jamie could listen. After two rings a voice on the other end picked up.

"Hello this is Fabiano Alcheri, how may I be of service?"

"Hi Fabiano, this is--my name is Kyle Drake. I received your information from--the Law Offices of Pinske and Mueller," Kyle said, reading from the notes Jamie had taken down from her mother. "I apologize for calling so early in the morning, but I'm in a bit of a tight situation that I was wondering if you had availability to help out with? I've been informed your rate is $90 hourly and I'm more than happy to pay that."

"Why thank you Mr. Drake. I do in fact have a fair

amount of availability in the next few days, and am always happy to help anyone associated with Pinske and Mueller. Now tell me what seems to be the problem?" With that, Kyle recounted again the events of the prior day, culminating in his assault by Frank in the laboratory. The story sounded even more bizarre the second time he told it, though the voice on the other end of the line was unflinching as Kyle could hear him diligently typing down notes. He asked Kyle quite a few clarifying questions about the last moments before Kyle was knocked out. *What kind of clothes were Travis and Frank wearing? What vehicles had they driven to the lab? Did Kyle know where they had been spending most of their time lately?* Kyle was frustrated that he couldn't provide more detailed information. In truth, he had been the only one to speak during his few short moments in the lab. If only he had shown up a few minutes earlier or a few minutes later, things could have turned out completely differently.

As Fabiano neared the end of his questioning, Kyle was eager to ask him what their course of action should be. "Well as a matter of due course, it would be good to check each of their residences for anything out of the ordinary, or any clues as to where they might have gone. Unless of course you've already taken this step?"

"No, in fact I'm ashamed to admit I haven't yet," Kyle said.

"I wouldn't worry yourself too much about that, it's unlikely we'll find anything of value there this early in the game. But if you have the time, it would still be helpful to me if you could swing by and take a quick look."

"Absolutely, I can do that right now as a matter of fact," Kyle offered. "I'll be certain to give you a call if I find anything. And if you need me to provide any more information on Travis or Frank just let me know."

"Will do, I think I have all I need for now. You should expect a call from me within the next six hours, if not sooner, to give you an update on anything I've found. Thanks again and I will be in touch."

With that Kyle and Jamie hopped into Kyle's car and decided to head over to Travis' house first. It was furthest away from the university, and Kyle knew he would need to work his way back towards the lab at some point in the day.

As they pulled up in front of the surprisingly impressive old Victorian home, Kyle couldn't help but feel regret over this being only the second occasion of his making the trip to Travis' house since Kyle had evicted him from his apartment several months earlier. In a strange way, Kyle was starting to sympathize with Travis' betrayal of his trust. It was now clearer than ever that Travis had been dealing with some deep-seated issues in his life, and there was no denying that Kyle had not made it a high priority to help Travis get what he needed. Even the opportunity he provided Travis to utilize the recall system was primarily driven by Kyle's need for a last minute guinea pig.

Kyle knocked on the front door of the house several times, and waited on the stoop until he finally heard someone inside briskly walking down a flight of stairs. Kyle's heart stopped when the door popped open, but to his disappointment it was not Travis who answered.

"Umm...can I help you guys?" the man answered in an agitated voice, breathing heavily as he spoke.

"Hi there, sorry to bother you," Kyle said. "I'm friends with Travis Trayborn and I haven't been able to get a hold of him for a while. I was wondering if he's home by chance?"

"Travis? No he's not home. I haven't seen him in a while actually. Although I'm not home all that often so maybe he's been in and out. I really don't know."

"Hmmm I see," Kyle said, discerning that Travis and his roommate did not appear to have a fond relationship, and deciding to use this to his advantage. "Well he has something of mine that I let him borrow a while ago and need to get back. Would it be cool if we run in real quick and grab it? I swear it'll only take a minute."

"Ha, yeah that sounds like Travis. Yeah I don't give a shit, come on in man." Travis' roommate slowly plodded back up the staircase as Kyle and Jamie followed behind. Upon reaching the second floor he disappeared into the kitchen while Kyle scanned the area, thinking back to try to remember which bedroom belonged to Travis. The bedroom door was left open a few inches, and Kyle slowly opened it the rest of the way, half-hoping Travis would be passed out drunk in his bed. The odor hit Kyle and Jamie like a brick wall as they entered Travis' bedroom to find half empty cans of beer and half eaten containers of food scattered everywhere. It looked like it had been weeks since Travis had done laundry, with his clothes strewn about the heavily-stained carpet floor. Kyle quickly opened a window to help redirect the stench outside, and in doing so knocked over a stack of screw-top pill containers that were piled up on Travis' dresser. Jamie bent over to pick up one of the bottles, opening the top and immediately recognizing the orange capsule pills as dextroamphetamine, which was sometimes used as a powerful psychostimulant.

"Holy shit Kyle, look at all these pills! I can't believe it...Travis is abusing drugs again! He told me in therapy that he hadn't done anything serious in years. But this is some really bad stuff," Jamie said as she rifled through the extensive collection that Travis had amassed.

Kyle felt sick as he took a seat on Travis' bed and put his head in his hands. Kyle was well aware of Travis previous history with narcotics. In fact he had always felt that it was the forming of their friendship back in Arizona years ago that had gotten him away from those addictions. Though far from being perfect, Travis really had cleaned up his act substantially since he and Kyle had become close friends, to the point where Kyle never really worried about Travis having a serious slip. As Kyle thought back to their encounter in the lab the previous night, and how emaciated Travis had looked, he now could understand what might have driven him to stab Kyle in the back so severely.

Jamie continued to toss Travis' collection into a nearby trash can as Kyle scanned the bedroom for any clues of where Travis could have gone to hideout. Sifting through Travis' disheveled closet, Kyle found very few items that wouldn't be considered garbage to most people, aside from a collection of CD's that looked like it hadn't been used in years, and Travis' modest selection of sports collectibles. It was evident they weren't going to find anything useful, and Kyle was conscious of not wearing out his welcome with Travis' agitated roommate.

A few moments later they emerged from the bedroom. Kyle took with him a random CD enclosed inside a case, held it up to the roommate and said, "Found it, thanks!" as he and Jamie quickly shuffled down the staircase. Jamie popped the trunk of Kyle's car and stuffed the trash bag full of drugs underneath the cover for the spare tire, determined to dispose of it properly when she eventually had the chance.

Kyle and Jamie then began the 45 minute drive from Hayward to Milpitas, where Frank's apartment was located. They endured the drive mostly in silence, each trying to figure out the puzzle of how they could find who they were searching for, and what they might need to do next if they were unsuccessful. As Kyle pulled up to Frank's apartment for the second time in less than 24 hours, he again felt the incredible influx of exhaustion take over his body. He had barely slept the past two days, and had been running on adrenaline nearly this entire time. He forced himself to shake it off, and asked Jamie to stay in the car as he made his way into the outdoor common area of Frank's apartment complex, where he spotted Frank's unit in the corner of the second level. Kyle ascended the staircase and tried to act naturally as he approached the door to Frank's apartment.

He casually attempted to turn the door knob, and was met with immediate resistance. He quickly pulled the handle back and forth a few times, at which point he was fairly certain that both the handle and the deadbolt had been locked by Frank before he'd left. Kyle tried to peer inside the adjacent window, but was unable to distinguish anything through the thick curtains. Disappointed but not at all surprised, Kyle returned to his car and let Jamie know there was nothing of interest to be found without breaking inside.

Kyle laid his head back in his seat, again overcome by exhaustion. With his eyes closed he tried to focus on what his next move should be. He knew it was about time that his team back at the lab would start getting anxious that he hadn't shown up yet. He was still uncertain how he wanted to handle that situation. Kyle began to dream about finding a resolution to this problem in time to solve everything, and allowed himself to continue to dream until he slowly slipped away into unconsciousness.....

Kyle again jarred himself awake, his heart pounding as he looked across the car at Jamie, who had a faint smile on her face.

"It happened again, I can't believe it! How long was I out?" Kyle asked in a minor panic.

"It was probably a little over an hour. I figured I'd let you catch up on sleep a bit. Don't worry about it, you didn't miss anything exciting here. I've seen only one car enter that parking lot, and it was just an older couple bringing in some groceries."

Kyle calmed himself as he sat up straight in his seat. He pulled his phone out of his pocket to make sure he hadn't missed any calls. On the screen he noticed that he had received a text message from Michael about ten minutes earlier. It read: *Hey boss everything okay? You going to be coming in soon?*

Kyle placed the phone back in his pocket, and took a few minutes to contemplate his next move. The clock on his dashboard read 11:25 AM. Kyle knew his team would be on the verge of panic if he waited much longer to communicate back with them. After much deliberation, Kyle resigned himself to the fact that there was little else productive he could do at the moment but head over to the lab, and maybe try to put in some work on revamping their presentation while waiting for the private investigator to give him a status update. Kyle put the car in drive and started on his way down to Santa Clara. He asked Jamie how he should break the news to his team.

"I think you need to be completely honest with them Kyle. They're tangled up in this mess just as much as you are, and they deserve to have all the facts laid out so you guys can work together to decide what to do next. I know they might get mad at you for taking matters into your own hands last night and for keeping them in the dark this morning, but you only did what you thought was the right thing at the time, and no one can really fault you for that. It's going to be okay...we're gonna get through this," Jamie offered, rubbing Kyle's neck as he tried to enjoy some final moments of relaxation before the chaos that would ensue once he broke the news to his team.

Kyle made a left turn past the theater building, and knew he was now only a few minutes away from campus. As he continued to organize in his head how he wanted to let his team in on all that had happened, he felt his phone vibrate in his pocket. Taking it out he saw a call from the number he had dialed that morning for Fabiano. Kyle could feel his heart pounding in his chest as he clumsily attempted to answer the phone while abruptly pulling his car off to the side of the road.

Kyle answered the call eagerly. "Hi Fabiano how are things going?"

"Hello Kyle. Things are moving pretty quickly as a

matter of fact. Do you have a moment to speak now?"

"Yes absolutely," Kyle said as he put his phone on speaker mode and placed it on the center console between himself and Jamie.

"It seems we might have come into a bit of luck on finding Frank Bernstein. I had a friend who works for the Bay Area Toll Authority just alert me that he had a plate match for Frank's vehicle just pass through the Highway 156 West toll station. I was actually already headed down that way to follow up on a lead I uncovered regarding a beach house owned by Frank's extended family. After hearing he was spotted on the 156, I'm fairly confident I know where he could be heading, if you'd like to come down and find out. I'm almost to Castroville already, so I'm sure I have a head start on you. Do you have a pen and paper handy?"

"Yes!" Kyle confirmed, tearing through his center console to quickly find something to write with.

"Alright, address is as follows:

39073 Scenic Road
Carmel-by-the-Sea, CA 93923"

"Okay, got it," Kyle said. "We're in Santa Clara right now, so it'll probably take us...I'd guess an hour and a half to get down there."

"No worries. Unless something out of the ordinary happens when I arrive I'll wait for you to join me. I've taken the step to check out a satellite image of the suspected house, which does not appear to have a garage included. Therefore I'm hoping I can confirm Mr. Bernstein's presence by locating his vehicle nearby. I'll confirm with you once I find out."

"That sounds great Fabiano, thank you so much for the good news, and we will see you shortly," Kyle said as he hung up the phone and peeled out of the gravel road shoulder, sending rocks spraying backwards while making a

U-turn to head towards the southbound highway entrance.

About halfway into the drive to Carmel, Jamie finally broke the silence by asking Kyle a question that again needed to be asked.

"I hate to take your focus off of getting to Frank today, but don't you think you still need to try to talk to your team?"

"Oh God, I completely forgot about that again. I don't think I can handle a lengthy call explaining what I'm doing right now." Kyle handed Jamie his phone, pulling up the earlier text message he had received from Michael. "Can you type this in for me and send it: *Sorry for the delay in getting back with you guys today. It's been an extremely busy morning. No reason to worry, I promise I'll check in with you guys later on today.*"

"Okay...it's sent," Jamie said, handing Kyle back his phone. "Now I'm going to give Travis another try since it's been a couple of hours. Maybe he'll have turned his phone back on by now." Jamie pressed re-dial on Travis' number, but to no avail it went directly to voicemail as it had earlier. They continued down the highway for another couple of miles, when at last Kyle received a text message from Fabiano: *Silver Saab 900 matching plates of Frank Bernstein spotted three blocks away from address. No activity observed at house during initial pass-by. Keeping an eye on the vehicle, call me when you arrive.*

Kyle handed Jamie the phone as he stepped on the accelerator, passing a sign that read 'Carmel-by-the-Sea, 11 miles'. In a matter of a few short minutes, Kyle could potentially be getting the information he so desperately needed.

Kyle and Jamie pulled into the seaside village of Carmel-by-the-Sea, which was quiet on this Friday afternoon in

December. Christmas decorations adorned the quaint shops that lined the streets as Kyle continued driving towards the coast. For a few moments, Kyle allowed himself to think about how nice it would be to take Jamie down here for a quiet weekend getaway. Stay somewhere nice with a view of the ocean. Check out some of the wine tasting rooms, maybe even go antique shopping. In a different world, this could have been a happy trip for them.

Kyle could now see the ocean in the distance as he continued driving west. As instructed he called Fabiano to find his exact coordinates. Fabiano instructed Kyle to find his black BMW sedan near the Carmel River State Park, and park his car directly behind it. Moments later Kyle spotted the Beemer, and pulled in behind. Kyle waited for a signal from Fabiano for what to do next, and moments later the driver's window was rolled down. Kyle saw an arm waving, signaling them to come forward. He gave Jamie an unsure look, and they both exited the car and approached the BMW. "Get in the back seat, please," they heard a voice direct them. Kyle opened the door, and slid into the back seat far enough for Jamie to have a seat next to him. Kyle immediately noticed that the vehicle was impeccably maintained, and though it was an older model, it felt like it was brand new. Jamie shut the car door behind her, at which point the man in the front seat turned around.

"Hello there. Mr. Drake and Ms. Fontana, I presume?"

"That's us," Kyle responded, nervously extending his arm for a handshake.

"Fabiano Alcheri, nice to meet you both," the man said as he gave both Kyle and Jamie a firm shake. "Well it seems we may be in luck today. You may recognize the silver car parked across the street near the stop sign as the vehicle you described to me earlier today." Kyle leaned over in his seat and spotted Frank's Saab parked across the street facing towards them.

"Yes that's definitely the one. So we're still not sure if

he's inside the house?" Kyle inquired.

"Not sure at this point. I haven't checked for activity again since I first arrived here. Though I think now is the time to give it another try."

Kyle felt his resolve strengthen as he imagined confronting Frank and finally putting an end to this saga. He was ready to move forward.

"How should we proceed then?" Kyle asked. "At this point I'm not above trying to break-in if it comes to that. But I suppose we should maybe start by just knocking? Although Frank would recognize Jamie and me. I don't know, maybe Fabiano you can be the one to try and draw him out? Maybe pretend that you're somebody else?"

"Very good, Mr. Drake. That's actually exactly what I am planning to do."

CHAPTER 27

Fabiano wasted no time in getting things underway, exiting the car and walking back towards his trunk as Kyle and Jamie followed behind. Fabiano was shorter than Kyle expected he would be, given his deep voice over the phone and his commanding presence. He seemed ageless, though his evenly dispersed gray hair gave away his age as likely somewhere north of 40. Through his button down shirt and jacket Kyle could see the broad shoulders of a man who likely had plenty of experience handling himself in delicate situations.

"In the past, I've found that the easiest way to get someone who's in hiding to come to the door is to pretend that you have something of theirs," Fabiano informed them as he popped the trunk. "It's preferable if you have an idea for that person's distinctive tastes, and are able to maximize their temptation to see what the item could be. But the majority of the time, just pretending you have a package of theirs that was delivered to the wrong address works just fine."

Inside the trunk was an assortment of various utilitarian items, each neatly organized in a way that seemed to serve some kind of purpose. Fabiano reached into the front corner of the trunk, removing a large white cardboard packaged box. The box was neatly taped closed, and even included a realistic-looking shipping label adhered to its top side.

"Wow that's impressive! Do you have to change the label for the package every time you use it?" Jamie asked Fabiano.

"Only if I anticipate I might have to actually hand the thing over. While I was waiting for you two to arrive I punched in the info I got on Frank's uncle into this portable label printer. All that's inside of the box is a cheap coffee mug and some bubble wrap.

Kyle and Jamie looked at each other, continuing to be impressed by the cunning of the private investigator.

"I also scoped out the front porch of the house earlier like I informed you. There's a covered area above the front door, so it appears that if someone were at home, they would be unable to see the person knocking at their door without coming downstairs and looking through the adjacent window to the right side of the door. This means that if you two wanted to be involved in the action, there's an area to the left of the door where you could be hidden from sight."

Kyle contemplated this opportunity for a moment. "I'd certainly like to approach the house with you if you're comfortable with that. In the event that he's home but we can't get him to open the door, I'd like to at least be able to assess what kind of state he's currently in. You should also remember that this guy could be dangerous. I have him to thank for this gash on my forehead."

"I always take that into consideration, Mr. Drake. And I always try to leave as little of the interaction to chance as possible," Fabiano said, patting his right hip and exposing what looked to be the outline of a handgun. Kyle was momentarily taken aback, but couldn't argue that it made sense for at least one of them to be armed and prepared in the event that things turned violent.

"Do you want to stay back here while we give this a try, or do you want to come up to the house with us?" Kyle asked Jamie. Her response was immediate.

"Hell no I'm not staying here! I'm gonna be right there when we nail this asshole!"

Fabiano looked at Kyle with a sly grin. "That settles that. If you both just follow my lead, this should go off smoothly. Well the clock is ticking, shall we get started?"

The three began the short walk down the quiet coastal street. Kyle's fists clenched as they approached the sidewalk to Frank's beach house. Fabiano stopped them momentarily, and looked up to the second floor windows. The blinds appeared to be completely drawn, and there appeared to be no activity whatsoever inside the house. Fabiano gave them the signal to continue, and slowly they walked up the short sidewalk and ascended the stairs to the front porch as quietly as they could. Kyle took Jamie's hand and stepped over to the left side of the door, standing as close as he could to the wall in order to remain out of sight.

Fabiano stepped towards the right side of the door and inspected for a doorbell. There was none installed, so Fabiano balled his fist and knocked firmly on the door five times. Nothing. He waited about ten seconds, then knocked again on the door another five times. Still nothing. He took a couple of steps back to where he could see the upper level windows, but did not appear to notice any activity. He then called out in a loud but friendly voice: "Hello Mr. Bernstein, are you home? Is this the Bernstein residence?"

Kyle held his breath as he listened closely with his ear pinned to the wall. He could hear the breeze gently blowing in the nearby palm trees, but was unable to make out any noise coming from inside the house.

Seconds later Fabiano continued: "I have a package here for a Gerald Bernstein that was accidentally delivered to my house this morning. I live at 39058 Scenic, down the street a couple houses. Just want to make sure this is the right address before I drop it off?"

Fabiano remained in place towards the back of the porch. Kyle and Jamie stayed as still as possible, crouched and listening for any signs of life. Suddenly Kyle heard what sounded like a squeaking door hinge coming from inside the house. He stood up and continued listening. He could now hear what sounded like footsteps on a hardwood floor. He waved to Fabiano, who stepped back up towards the front of the door. Kyle could now hear the pace of the footsteps growing faster, until suddenly he heard the unmistakable sound of someone quickly descending down a staircase. Next was the sound of the deadbolt being unlocked. Slowly Kyle could see the door being pulled in to expose a small opening, and he heard a faint voice speak. "Hi...you say you have a package for the Bernstein residence? Does it have a first name on it?"

"Why yes it does," Fabiano answered pleasantly. "It says 'Gerald Bernstein' right here at the top. Is that you by chance? I apologize I haven't been over here yet to introduce myself, what a lousy neighbor I make sometimes. My name's Mario Perotta. Like I said I'm your neighbor down the street. Moved in about two months ago now. I'll tell ya this is not the first package I've received in that time that wasn't mine. That damn post office really needs to get their act together."

Fabiano extended his hand towards the crack in the door. Briefly the gap expanded as the person on the other side quickly extended an arm for a brief shake. "Frank Bernstein, nice to meet you," Kyle heard the voice say. He felt his blood pressure immediately skyrocket. *It's on now.*

"Pleasure to meet you Frank. If you don't mind my asking, do you live alone here? I take it you're probably not the 'Gerald' that's addressed on the package."

"Oh no, that's uhh...just my uncle," Frank responded shortly. Kyle could tell the conversation was already close to stalling, and felt the need to take action. He knew the right thing to do was to just let Fabiano do his thing. But it was becoming increasingly difficult to stand mere feet away from someone who had knocked him out less than 24 hours earlier, and to not take action.

"I see. So you're just watching the house while they're out of town I presume? Not a bad deal for either of you. There are few finer places in California than Carmel-by-the-Sea. I'm sure you know that Clint Eastwood was once the mayor of this town, right?" Fabiano said, trying to establish camaraderie with Frank to keep the conversation moving. Kyle was now shaking with anxiety. He felt he couldn't take it any longer. He tried to hold himself back, but without even thinking, Kyle quickly leapt forward and pushed the door in with his full strength. He saw Frank fly backwards onto the hardwood floor as he stumbled forward through the door step, nearly falling on top of him. Frank must have immediately realized who it was, as Kyle saw the look of horror on Frank's face. This fear fueled Kyle even more as he stood up tall to be as intimidating as possible, and slowly began marching towards Frank.

"Surprise, asshole! Bet you didn't expect to see me again this soon!" Kyle boasted, his adrenaline now pumping at full speed. "I think you and me need to have a little talk. Things didn't exactly go as I had planned the last time I saw you."

Frank quickly tried to crawl backwards out of the living room and towards the kitchen, though soon he was backed up against a wall with little room to maneuver. Frank fumbled for words, still completely caught off guard by Kyle's sudden entry. "I...I'm so sorry Kyle. I'm sorry for everything. I never meant for it to go down this way."

"Oh you're sorry?!? For which part exactly? For breaking into my lab and using my team's system without our consent? For putting our entire once-in-a-lifetime breakthrough project in jeopardy? For trying to sabotage us by selling our confidential information to the Basel Institut? For going behind my back and pulling my friend Travis into your plans to destroy me? Please, tell me Frank, which part are you sorry for? I'd really like to know!" Kyle was now fuming, as he noticed Fabiano and Jamie were now standing in the room several feet behind him.

"No...all of it Kyle...that's not what I ever intended to do. I didn't sell your data to B.I. I...I traded it. I needed to...to get closer to her."

Kyle's rage was now mixing with confusion. He was on

the verge of hyperventilation when Jamie stepped forward and pulled his arm gently towards her. "Come on Kyle, let's try to calm this down before it gets even more out of control. We're all going to need to keep level heads to figure this all out." Kyle knew she was right, and forced himself to take a few deep breaths to try and compose himself.

"Alright...sit your ass on the couch here Frank. And then I want you to explain to me what the hell is going on."

Unsure that the threat of violence was really over, Frank reluctantly picked himself up off the floor. Kyle and Jamie took a seat together on an ornate sofa backed up against the fireplace in the living room. Fabiano followed after, taking a seat in a chair closest to the front door. Frank hesitantly followed Kyle's instructions and sat down on the chair across from them.

Kyle again gathered his thoughts. "Okay Frank...start from the beginning, and tell me how we got to last night. I need to know everything."

Frank sat hunched over in the chair with his elbows on his knees, head planted deeply in his hands. His body language was feeble and defeated. He spoke softly when he began.

"I...I have an addiction Kyle. I realize that now. I realized that even before last night. But I've been too weak to do anything about it."

"I can't say I'm surprised to hear you admit that after that stash I saw you and Travis bringing into the lab," Kyle responded. "But what the hell does your drug addiction have to do with you repeatedly breaking into my lab?"

"No, not drug addiction. Kyle...I've become addicted to memory recall."

This admission hit Kyle hard, as the chips started falling into place about everything that had gone down recently. Rapidly, Kyle started to make sense of the crazy events of the past week.

"At first I thought everything was normal. I've always

been drawn to your project and the potential that I felt it could unlock. I was probably one of the few people in the lab that read all of your team's monthly reports, and it killed me when no one showed up to support you after you sent that invite to witness Ryan's pilot run. Sadly I was unable to attend myself, because at that point I was already starting to access the lab behind your backs, and I didn't want to draw any unneeded attention to myself."

Kyle was furious listening to Frank admit this litany of misdeeds, though there was some relief for him in the fact that it appeared Frank was now prepared to tell the truth about everything he'd done. There was still a chance that they could salvage the project in time.

"A month or two back there was a day at the lab when I heard you and your team talking excitedly about something big you guys had just discovered. I listened in and heard that Farida had succeeded in enabling recall. This got me so excited that I couldn't wait around for the data to be published. I had to go into your server and see what your team had really accomplished. And I was blown away by it Kyle, I really was. It wasn't long after that when there was a day your team was working in the lab on a Saturday, and I snuck into the office to observe your full process, unknown to any of you. That was the night when your team left late and.....you stayed around to run an experiment on yourself."

Kyle tried to keep his face from flushing as his fears of his unapproved experiment being exposed were confirmed. He remembered having a weird feeling leaving the office that day, a feeling that he hadn't been alone. Turns out he was correct.

"After this I was able to design a process to where I could run the recall system by myself without being detected. I came in a few times late at night when no one was around to try it out. I started off with innocent stuff, kid's memories just to see how far back I could go. The experience was incredible, even on that earlier version of the system. But then I just kept going deeper, wanting to revisit memories that brought back a happier time in my life. Eventually I found myself stuck in a particular loop that I couldn't get out of. First love, ya know? I kept going back to a summer I spent in Belgium after my college graduation, and a beautiful girl I met there. I thought during that summer that she would be the last girl I'd ever be with. That we could make it so the summer never had to end, and we would never have to go back to our real lives. Young, naïve and foolish. Even all these years later though, I've never been able to forget about her. I've never found anyone else that made me feel even close to the way she did. I just wanted that feeling back... It had been so damn long, and then this miracle machine comes around and offers me the potential ability to relive that summer again? I knew at the time what I was doing was wrong Kyle...but I felt powerless to say no to it. The high that I got going back in time, seeing her again...I couldn't stop myself. I couldn't keep it under control. I wanted more. And that's when I got involved with B.I."

Kyle listened intently, sitting up at the mention of his rival lab. "You said earlier you didn't sell them our information. What exactly were you doing with them then?"

"They offered me money, but I didn't take it. What I wanted was just to enhance the experience even further. I had read some research that B.I. had developed a method for enhancing the sensory perceptions that occurred during dreams and memory recollection. 'Recovered-memory therapy', they called it. It got to a point for me where it wasn't enough to just observe the memories of that summer. I felt I needed to feel, taste, touch them again. I tried a few times to see if you would let me get more involved with the project directly. You always seemed like you were too busy though, and I understand. You had much bigger things to worry about at that time than enabling me to use the recall system. So that's when I made the terrible decision to partner with the enemy. I contacted them, and they offered me the chance to be a test subject for their recovered-memory therapy experiments using psychotropic drugs. And in exchange...I offered them access to your data."

Frank paused, and was now wiping away tears as he spoke. "I can't even begin to express how sorry I am Kyle...to you and your team. I know nothing I can say or do will erase the trauma I've caused you." Frank took a second to compose himself, and continued. "I'm obviously not fit to be working in that lab anymore...so I'm planning to step away from the university and get myself some help. I mean let's be honest...I was never cut out for that environment anyway. But before I leave, I want to make things right with you and your team. I know you guys have the ICCN keynote coming up, and I know I did just about everything in the book to royally fuck that up for you. So I'm going to make you an offer. I'm going to give you the code that I developed while I was using your machine. This code will enable you to calibrate and prepare the recall system in a fraction of the time it's currently taking you. You can run it from any ordinary mobile computer instead of requiring that massive supercomputer you have now in the lab. So this means that if you wanted to perform a live demonstration at ICCN...this should enable you to do so. And B.I. knows nothing about how my code works. So if they did have any intention of using the data I transmitted to try and outdo you at the expo, they'd be in for a big surprise."

Kyle looked intently at Frank's face, and could see that he appeared to be genuine in what he was saying. In performing this mea culpa, he was now giving the team a renewed possibility to achieve what they had initially set out to do. Maybe it wasn't too late. But Kyle knew it would take some convincing to get them to believe that Frank had really reversed course.

"Wow Frank...that's a lot of information for me to process. I must admit it was very big of you to come clean like this. I'm also sorry things worked out the way they did. But I'm also hoping it's not too late to make things right. And if we can use your help to get that accomplished...then I may just have to take you up on that offer."

"Of course. I'll transmit my code to the lab the moment you guys are ready. And if there's anything else I can do to help repair the damage I've done, just let me know." At that moment Frank rose from the chair and approached Kyle. He extended his hand towards Kyle. After deliberating for a moment, Kyle slowly stood up from his seat, and decided to meet Frank's grasp with his own. "I'm so sorry again for what I've done, Kyle. I'm glad we had a chance to have this conversation today. Thank you."

Fabiano held the front door open as Kyle and Jamie exited the beach house and headed down the street towards the cars. By the time they arrived, Kyle realized he probably owed Fabiano an apology for taking matters into his own hands so abruptly.

"Fabiano, I'd like to apologi--"

"No worries, Mr. Drake. I'm not even sure my line of dialogue would have ended up working out the way I intended it to. I admire your determination. Sometimes in life, you just have to go for the throat."

"Well...thank you for saying that...and thank you for all the great work you've done today. We never could have done this without you."

"My pleasure Mr. Drake, happy to see that justice is being served. Shall I continue to try to track down your friend Travis?"

Kyle thought for moment on how he wanted to handle that situation. His current impulse was to head directly to the lab, and finally give his team a long overdue update. But he knew Travis was in trouble, and if he put off dealing with that longer than he already had, things could get even worse than they already were. Just when he was about to tell Fabiano he should stay on the case, Jamie ran up to Kyle with some important news.

"Kyle, I just checked my phone and I got a text message from Travis almost 30 minutes ago! It says: *I know you guys are probably looking for me. I'm done running. I'm at a house in West Oakland near Acorn if you want to come find me. I'm sorry.*"

"Jesus Kyle, that's a really rough part of town. We can't let him stay there. We have to go get him."

"You're correct about that," Kyle heard Fabiano confirm. "Anyplace south of Grand Street in that area of downtown Oakland, you do not want to find yourself near once the sun starts to go down."

Kyle again weighed his options. He decided that he could delay debriefing his team one more time in the interest of making sure his best friend was safe. Kyle thanked Fabiano again, and let him know that he would be in touch if he still required his services after today. Kyle and Jamie jumped in the car and immediately headed east for the 101 Highway towards Oakland. Kyle drove his car well over the speed limit for most of the ride, weaving in and out of the Friday afternoon rush hour traffic that was already starting to form. He had nearly wrecked his car several times by the time he and Jamie finally pulled off the 580 Interstate for downtown Oakland. The sun was already starting to descend, and Kyle could immediately tell they were in a part of town they didn't belong in.

"Alright Jamie, go ahead and give him a call and find out exactly where he's at. He better not fucking flake out on us right now," Kyle said through gritted teeth. Jamie dialed Travis' number, and after the fourth ring went by, Kyle was certain that Travis had gone back to avoiding them. But on the final ring, Kyle finally heard Travis' voice on the other end of the line.

"Hi Jamie, are you here? Is Kyle with you? It's not very

safe here. I'm sorry if I made you put yourself in danger."

Kyle leaned into the phone so Travis could hear him clearly. "Hey Travis, it's me. Yeah no shit it's not very safe here. I'd rather not spend any more time down here than I have to, so can you tell me exactly where you're at and we can come get you?"

"Hi Kyle. I'm sorry man, I know I fucked up. I'm ready to talk now though. I'm sitting outside a house on 15th and Mandela."

"Okay...I don't think that's too far away. We'll be there in a couple minutes." Kyle found their current location using a map on his phone, and quickly located where Travis had told him to meet, only about six blocks away. Kyle tried to maintain as unnoticeable a profile as he possibly could, driving down the biggest main roadway he could find until he finally reached Mandela Parkway. There was no denying they were definitely now in the ghetto area of downtown Oakland, and Kyle held his breath as they slowly continued towards 15th street. Finally they reached the intersection, and Jamie quickly called Travis again. "We're here Travis, where are you? I see a grayish-white house directly across from us, and what looks like an old rundown apartment building to our right on 15th street."

"I'm sitting in an alley behind that gray house. It's okay, you can pull the car back here. No one else is around right now."

"Okay, you should see us pulling up in Kyle's car any minute," Jamie replied.

Kyle located the house Travis was referring to, and carefully maneuvered his car down the narrow alleyway. About halfway down the alley he spotted Travis, sitting on the pavement leaned up against a garage door. Kyle pulled up next to him and killed the engine. Unsure still whether he wanted to show Travis anger or sympathy, and which would be more effective in getting the three of them safely out of their current surroundings, Kyle tried to force himself to make a decision. He had been screwed over by Travis several times in the past, but nothing ever even close to this extent.

Before Kyle could even make up his mind, he looked up to see Jamie running over to Travis and diving to the ground to give him a hug. Kyle followed slowly behind, exiting the car and ambling towards Jamie and Travis. He could immediately see in the way Travis embraced Jamie that Travis was thrilled to see a familiar face. When they finally let go of each other, Travis looked up to see Kyle standing in front of him. For a moment, they just stared at each other blankly, neither of them willing to make the first move. Until Travis finally broke the ice. "Hey Kyle...thank you for coming down here. I wouldn't have asked...but I didn't have anyone else I could call." Kyle said nothing, looking into Travis' eyes and continuing to evaluate if Travis was trying to manipulate him again.

"I know you probably don't trust a word I say at this point, but I truly am sorry for everything I've done to you. I know I really fucked up this time...and I completely understand if you want me out of your life. If I were you, I wouldn't want me around anymore either. I mean how many times can one person fuck up and expect to be forgiven? I know I've already pretty much run the well dry in that regard," Travis said as he leaned back against the garage and lit up a cigarette. "And this...this was a really bad one. I completely betrayed your trust and put your career in jeopardy. Everything you've been working so long to achieve...while I've done nothing but try to fuck up both of our lives. Anyway, like I said, however you want to handle this. Throw my ass in jail, cut me out of your life completely...I won't blame you for any of it."

Kyle looked over to Jamie, who now had tears trickling down her face and she listened to Travis intently. Kyle could feel the last remnants of anger slowly fading away from him. Though in reality, he still wasn't sure how he could continue to involve Travis in his life with all of the dangers he brought with him.

"Travis...I just don't know how things escalated to this point. I mean, look at where we are right now! I don't know what I possibly could have done to you that would justify what you did to me. Now I'm willing to admit that I haven't been a perfect friend to you recently. When I decided it was time for me to take my career more seriously and try to get my life more in balance with it, I probably should have been more straightforward with you. I shouldn't have avoided the topic and ignored you like I did. I admit it wasn't fair to just assume that you wouldn't understand. You're a very loyal friend. Up until last night, I always thought of you as one of the most loyal people I'd ever met." Kyle could see the pain forming in Travis' face as he continued.

"Thinking back now, it does seem like maybe Jamie and I could have handled our situation a little bit better with you too. It wasn't right for us to go around your back like that, to delay telling you the truth until I could find the perfect time to do it. I've been dishonest with you about plenty of things in the past...but that has to be done now. I'm through with doing that anymore. If there's any chance of us staying friends, then no more bullshit. You need to tell me why you did what you did." Travis hung his head to the ground, shuffling his feet as he searched for the right words to explain himself. He took another drag from his cigarette, and attempted to articulate to Kyle and Jamie what exactly had been motivating him lately.

"It's not easy man...it's not easy admitting to yourself that maybe you aren't that special. That maybe you don't deserve to find happiness more than other people do, even if you're convinced that you want it more than they ever could. I feel like I've been sitting around these past couple of years, just kind of waiting to get my turn to take a swing at doing something great with my life. I felt like my chance had to come sooner or later. But the older you get, the more you realize that unless you're one of the lucky few, the only shot you have at achieving your dreams is by busting your ass for them. Once I realized how much time I'd wasted sitting around just waiting for my shot to arrive...it made me such a bitter person. And Kyle, man you were like my one last ray of hope that maybe it wasn't over for me. The fact that you could go out and get wild with me, then still keep it together enough to maintain a prolific career in a respectable field. It helped me believe that maybe I didn't have to grow up so fast after all. Maybe I still could hold on to my dreams, and maybe there was still time for some of them to come true."

"But then when you started to become more distant towards spending time with me...I dunno, I became like...paranoid that you were going to ditch me as a friend and not want to waste your time with me anymore. And then Jamie, you came into the picture and I thought that we really had a connection. Like our lives had shaped us to be similar people. It was stupid of me to get so far ahead of myself, and it's embarrassing to admit now...but in a way I thought that maybe you could fill in the gap that Kyle would be leaving behind if we stopped being friends. Then when I discovered that you two were actually into each other...game over for me."

Jamie wiped her eyes again as she looked back and forth between Kyle and Travis. Kyle was trying to hide his emotion, but inside he felt himself continuing to sympathize with what Travis was saying to him.

Travis took another drag on his cigarette as he looked off into the distant sunset, which was now almost completely settled behind the tall buildings of downtown Oakland. "What's strange for me to think about now is that after that first recall session, I didn't have any idea how obsessed I would become with it. I mean it was an amazing experience, obviously, but all I could really think about was how big of discovery it was for you, and how successful your project was about to become. I was really happy for you...and then that day when we were able to help out Jamie, I was so amped about your technology...that's why it's even more unbearable for me to accept how much Frank and I put the whole thing in danger. It was pretty much a fluke how I even got hooked up with him in the first place. But once he opened the door for me to use the system as much as I needed to...and when he introduced the drug combinations to enhance the recall experience for me even more...I couldn't think rationally about any of it. It became an obsession for me, trying to relive these moments from my past where I actually felt like I accomplished something. It'd been so long for me since I'd had that feeling of success. For my sanity, I felt like I needed to try and find out what secret I might have had back then that allowed me to excel in life. I needed to try to find out how I'd been able to live back then...without this constant fear I have now. But I...I just couldn't find the answers I was looking for. So I became obsessed with the experience itself, going back in time to relive my glory days, one hour at a time. The obsession became so bad that it made me betray the people I care about most." Travis continued to fight back tears as his gaze remained locked on the ground.

"So how did you end up down here, Travis?" Jamie asked. "Kyle and I went over to your house earlier to try to find you...and we found some pretty scary stuff in your bedroom."

"Yeah, I know...I scored that stuff to try and enhance the recall sessions even more. It was really stupid of me, and Frank wouldn't even let me take it into the lab...so I started using it after my sessions, to see if there was any way I could still hold on to the experience after I'd unplugged from the system. It didn't really work, but you know me, that didn't stop me from trying. After I saw you in the lab last night Kyle...I just completely panicked. I drove around all night, not sure where to go, so upset with myself. Eventually I decided to come down here this morning to try to score and escape from the pain I was feeling. I picked up this shit, and I've just been basically staring at it for the past six hours." Travis removed a small plastic bag from his coat pocket, which contained a grainy yellow substance along with several small plastic syringes. Kyle guessed it was some form of heroin.

Travis held the bag up in front of his face, deep in thought as he slowly rotated the package between his fingers. When Kyle had found out which neighborhood Travis was in, he'd half-expected to arrive and find Travis completely loaded, sprawled out inside some nasty drug den with a bunch of other junkies. It was just now kicking in that Travis actually seemed to be lucid, his appearance more normal than when Kyle had seen him inside the lab. Despite how shaken up he clearly was, it seemed he hadn't given in fully to the temptation to escape his problems. At that moment it seemed as if Jamie had a similar line of thinking, as she took a seat next to Travis and took his hand in hers.

"It's not too late for you Travis. You're stronger than you give yourself credit for. I know what it's like to have these self-destructive tendencies. I struggle with them too. You feel tempted to beat yourself up so much for things that, in reality, no one else is judging you for besides you. You and I have both been through enough therapy to know how important it is to be able to get out of your own way." An acknowledging smile briefly crept across Travis' face as he looked into Jamie's eyes, thinking of how she had been able to stand up to her fears and successfully deal with her trauma.

"I see good in you Travis...and I know Kyle still does too. I think it's you who has to forgive yourself. I know first-hand that sometimes you need to face your fears and let yourself grow up...or else life will just pass you by. Believe it or not there's a lot of stuff going on in your world right now to get excited about. It's up to you to decide if you're willing to do what it takes to not get left behind." Kyle was again affected by Jamie's impressive ability to see things for how they really were, and focus on how they could all move forward. He couldn't have said it any better himself: it was exactly what Travis needed to hear. It only took Travis a minute or so to make his decision.

"Ya know...it's scary to me how right you guys both are. I know I've reminded myself time and time again that what I'm doing is self-destructive, and I keep falling into the same cycles. I think sitting here by myself all day, in pretty much the most depressing situation possible...it finally clicked with me internally that I don't want to live like this anymore. Whatever the hell there was about it that used to be appealing to me...I just don't feel it anymore. Call it finally growing up, call it whatever you want to. But I feel like it's finally clicked inside my stupid fucking brain that life is too short to keep making the same mistakes and hurting the people who treat you well. Kyle...what do you think man? Any chance it's not too late to convince you that I really mean it?"

Kyle looked to Jamie, then looked back at Travis. His mind had already been made up.

"What do I think? I think...well I think it's about time we got the band back together." It took a moment for Travis before the meaning sank in. Before he knew it, he was on his feet, lifting Kyle off the ground with the biggest bear hug of his life.

"Careful there scrawny, you're gonna hurt yourself!" Kyle joked as Travis eventually let go. "Well now that the sun is almost completely down, I say it's time we get the hell outta here while there's still a small chance of this day having a happy ending. Sound good?" He threw his arm around Jamie and led her to the front passenger's seat of his car, holding the door open for her. Travis eagerly jumped into the back seat of the car, as Kyle sped off down the alleyway towards the Bay Bridge. It was now finally time for them to rejoin civilization.

CHAPTER 28

Kyle was feeling less than comfortable as he made the third attempt at getting his necktie to sit properly under the collar of his thick broadcloth dress shirt. Fortunately the vacated conference room was equipped with windows to the outside, and Kyle had already cracked several in hopes of letting in some of the cold mountain air to cool him down. He'd been alternating between cycles of extreme nervousness and extreme excitement over what was to commence at the top of the hour, with neither of these emotions helping him maintain the dapper appearance he'd initially achieved. By his count, the team had only been in Zurich for less than 48 hours, and thus far had spent the majority of their time setting up the new recall system to ensure it functioned as well as it did back at the lab in Santa Clara. It was never the team's intention to cut their arrival so close to the beginning of the expo. But once they'd reached the decision to go for the home run and perform a live demonstration, it had taken every available moment of time they'd had to duplicate a system robust enough to travel with them across the Atlantic. Kyle could hardly believe all they'd accomplished when he thought back to the last few days before their departure.

Finally getting his wardrobe to cooperate, Kyle returned to the table in the middle of the conference room where the rest of his team was preparing. "Doesn't this all still seem a little surreal? I really just still can't believe we made it here, after all we had to go through. I guess I should probably snap out of it though, given that we have about...28 minutes before it's showtime," Kyle informed the team.

"Hey don't forget, we've done this process all of three times now on the new system. This thing is practically on rails!" Michael's sarcasm was evident.

"Don't say things like that Michael," Farida chastised. "We've tested everything we can test on this system, multiple times. It's going to work perfectly. I have no doubt about it." Farida's confidence seemed to resonate with the rest of the team. It was comforting to hear their most logic-driven member speak assuredly about their likelihood of success.

"I know, I know, you're right Farida. I'm still just hoping we don't get any crazy curveballs from B.I. thrown into the mix. That would be the last thing we need to deal with today. Though I can't imagine what they could even surprise us with at this point."

Farida confirmed Michael's sentiment. "Exactly. Our system now looks almost nothing like what they were exposed to earlier. Between the brilliance of Frank's coding improvements, and the elegant way in which we were able to integrate them into our existing system...let them try to trip us up! We're now officially the global knowledge leaders in this area of neuroscience. Today's our chance to prove it to the world."

Kyle again felt reassured by Farida's vote of confidence. He was finally starting to get in the zone and get his mind focused on what he wanted to cover in the keynote. He would be covering the majority of the presentation, with each team member stepping in when it became time to introduce their area of expertise into the process. Michael was correct, they had run the full recall process only three times on the new system: twice at the lab in Santa Clara, and once with the system in place in Zurich. Though each experiment had been executed nearly flawlessly, it was still difficult to adjust mentally to operating outside the familiar confines of their laboratory. Kyle made himself push these thoughts to the back of his mind, and continued to force himself to stay focused on the goal ahead. This was the day the entire team had been waiting for, the day where all their blood, sweat and tears would finally pay off. Deep down, Kyle knew this was the day that would give his life the solid footing he'd been struggling to find for so long. He knew he was ready for this moment. He was now hoping the subject of his team's keynote demonstration was feeling as equally prepared.

"Wow, you look great!" Kyle declared as Jamie entered the room from her makeshift dressing area. Kyle realized this was the first time he'd really seen Jamie dressed up so formally, and in her conservative yet surprisingly provocative black dress, he had no doubt in his mind that she would charm the audience.

"Why thank you, Mr. Drake. You don't look too bad yourself. Very professional," Jamie responded with a smile. "I thought I'd be more nervous, but I'm actually just kind of excited to do another recall session! Now that I've been getting to recall happy memories, I don't think I'm ever going to get tired of that thing! How are you feeling?"

"I was definitely pretty nervous before. But I'm feeling ready to go now."

"Great! And how about the rest of the team?" Jamie directed at Ryan, Michael and Farida, who were standing in various spots around the table giving their notes one last review.

"Feeling alright about it. It's just an honor to be given this chance," Ryan responded, putting noticeable effort into trying to avert his eyes from gazing at Jamie's physique.

"Yes honored...truly honored...all that bullshit," Michael joked. "All I know is that I'll be ready for the celebration to start after this whole thing is wrapped up. What do people drink here in Switzerland anyway? Red wine?"

Kyle heard the door to the conference room swing open, and turned around to find Travis entering, wearing his VIP badge that Kyle had managed to swing from the university, since Travis had previously been a volunteer for their study.

"Hey everybody, you guys all ready for your big moment?"

"As ready as we're going to be. How's it looking out there?" Kyle asked Travis.

"It's a fuckin' huge crowd, I'll say that. They seem to be pretty fired up to see you guys, too. The other presenters so far have actually been pretty entertaining, so I think everyone's in a good mood right now. You guys are going to feel like rock stars out there."

"Well that's a good thing, right?" Jamie asked hopefully.

"And I'll tell you another thing, I found those Basel Institut shitheads that tried to fuck up your project. They're all sitting together in a group towards the middle part of the room. In between presenters they've done nothing but fight back and forth with each other. I can't understand what they hell they're saying, but they seem none too pleased about this whole event."

"Probably upset that they're not getting the spotlight this year. Good, serves them right to sit on the bench this time around," Michael said boldly. The thought of B.I. bickering about losing out to this ragtag group of unknowns brought smiles to all of their faces.

"Alright well I think you're up soon, so I'll leave you to it," Travis said, giving Kyle a firm handshake and Jamie a friendly hug. "You guys are writing history today. I wish I had better advice but just...knock 'em dead."

"Thanks man, we will," Kyle concurred.

Moments later a coordinator for the conference stepped into the room, and informed the team that it was now time for them to take their spots backstage in preparation for their introduction. The five of them obliged and followed the coordinator out of the conference room and down a corridor that led to the backstage area. Through the wall to the grand ballroom they could hear the echoing of someone on stage speaking animatedly, which was being followed by waves of applause from the audience. Eventually the team was taken through a doorway that led them onto the backstage platform. They were huddled together in a spot at the side of the stage, where directly in front of them they could now see their recall system, still hidden from the audience behind a drawn curtain.

Kyle pulled Jamie in close to him as she shook with excitement. The introduction was now beginning, and as the curtain was drawn back and their system was revealed to a standing ovation, Jamie leaned into Kyle's ear. "We're on top of the world. And you got us here. I'll never forget this." In that moment, for the first time in Kyle's life, he knew that he was doing exactly what he should be doing.

ABOUT THE AUTHOR

Keith C. Meyer is an accomplished engineer who has worked for the past decade in the biotechnology and high-tech industries. He is originally from the Midwest, and now resides in Southern California. When not learning about new cutting-edge technologies, Keith enjoys anything that gets him outdoors, whether it be training for obstacle races, hiking in the mountains, or just enjoying a craft beer on a patio by the beach.